RYAN TIME

TIME WARS LAST FOREVER SERIES, BOOK 1

CRAIG ROBERTSON

IMAGINE-IT PUBLISHING

ALSO BY CRAIG ROBERTSON:

BOOKS IN THE RYANVERSE:

THE FOREVER SERIES (2016):

THE FOREVER LIFE, Book 1

THE FOREVER ENEMY, Book 2

THE FOREVER FIGHT, Book 3

THE FOREVER QUEST, Book 4

THE FOREVER ALLIANCE, Book 5

THE FOREVER PEACE, Book 6

GALAXY ON FIRE SERIES (2017):

EMBERS, Book 1

FLAMES, Book 2

FIRESTORM, Book 3

FIRES OF HELL, Book 4

DRAGON FIRE, Book 5

ASHES, Book 6

RISE OF ANCIENT GODS SERIES (2018):

RETURN OF THE ANCIENT GODS, Book 1

RAGE OF THE ANCIENT GODS, Book 2

TORMENT OF THE ANCIENT GODS, Book 3

WRATH OF THE ANCIENT GODS, Book 4

FURY OF THE ANCIENT GODS, Book 5

FALL OF THE ANCIENT GODS, Book 6

TIME WARS LAST FOREVER (2019):

RYAN TIME, Book 1

LOST TIME, Book 2

FRAGMENTED TIME, Book 3

SHATTERED TIME, BOOK 4 (coming Summer 2020)

STAND-ALONE SERIES:

ROAD TRIPS IN SPACE SERIES (2019):

THE GALAXY ACCORDING TO GIDEON, Book 1

THE EATH ACCORDING TO GIDEON, Book 2

THE AFTERLIFE ACCORDING TO GIDEON, Book 3 (coming in Fall 2020)

OLDER INDEPENDENT NOVELS:

THE CORPORATE VIRUS (2016)

TIME DIVING (2013)

THE INNERgLOW EFFECT (2010)

WRITE NOW! THE PRISONER OF NANOWRIMO (2009)

ANON TIME (2009)

RYAN TIME

TIME WARS LAST FOREVER SERIES, BOOK 1

by Craig Robertson

This Is A Bad Time To Be Jon Ryan. It's A Worse Time To Cross Him.

Imagine-It Publishing
El Dorado Hills, CA

ISBN: 978-1-7331137-4-8 (Print)
978-1-7331137-3-1 (E-Book)

Cover design by Alexandre
http://www.designbookcover.pt/en/

Editing by Michael R. Blanche
Neil Farr
Amy Schubert

Formatting by Drew Avera Formatting
www.drewavera.com/book-formatting

Beta reading help by Charlie Pitts

First Edition 2019
Second Edition 2019
Third Edition 2020

This book is dedicated to the memory of a friend I miss dearly, Jenny Low Chang. We attended class at San Francisco State University, back in 1977. She was such a joy, such a wonder. She died horrifically. This world was diminished by of your loss, Jenny.
You deserved so very much better.

PRELUDE

Fat and happy, happy and fat, that's me. Well, not fat, since I can eat, like, twenty-thousand calories an hour and not gain weight. Android, here. *Duh*. But, I am *figuratively* fat, and *literally* happy. What? It's been ninety-eight years, hasn't it, since the last ancient god turned to dust, thank you very much. Unlamented, the lot of them. I imagine even my two buddies back in Godville—Wul and Queeheg—have moved on to the next square in the game of life.

All that time and no new threats. Yeah, I'm entering retirement. What have I—*we*—been up to? A lot of nothing. And, I have to say, it sure doesn't feel correct to me. But, you knew that, right? #fighterpilotforever, here. Let's see…

Me, I fished until there wasn't a fish in the lake or the inclination in me to find a new body of water to waste time voiding of all piscine life. I hiked through three pairs of boots, camped in every idyllic, alpine spot in the cosmos, and even tried my hand at bridge. No, seriously, bridge. I roped a group of Kaljaxians into playing with me. It turns out that, due to some tragic flaw in their DNA, they instantly became intoxicated with the game. The game spread like an STD in boot camp. But I hate the game and I suck at it. I actually deleted all knowledge of its impenetrable rules from my systems. In fact, the only thing I did *not* flush was this vitriolic reminder that I hate bridge and should never go there.

And the apple of my eye, and the blow torch of my love life, Sapale? How was she faring, with time on *her* hands? Marvelously, of course. I asked her almost every morning, *Are you bored, yet?* And every morning she gave me the same reply. *No. You're in my way. I need to be somewhere. And no, boredom sex is not going to happen. You need that cure, then you just fix it yourself once I'm gone.*

Yes, she could be a bit testy, a tad pushy, but she was my girl —forever.

Basically, she set out to *re*-rebuild Azsuram. After having forged it from nothing originally, the Adamant destroyed it. She resurrected it. Then the Cleinoids did their best to wipe it from the universe, which was damn good. Now, though, she was determined to make it better than ever. And she did. It took twenty-five years, but the civilization was firing on all cylinders and purring like a Shelby Mustang.

She, never letting a moment of idle time creep into her ordered life, then fixed her home world of Kaljax (whether it liked it or not). That took a mere twenty years. Then, she decided she would "work with the local governments" of several Kaljaxian colonies. Yeah, she "wanted to help them keep on pace" in their recoveries or growth. Had any of those colonies *asked* for her thoughtful input? Funny you should ask. Not a single one had. But, did any voice rise from the crowd, asking her to visit as a *tourist*, not a *savior*? No. A person that stupid surely has yet to be born.

Toño? Bored. I only have to tell you one episode to have you nodding in agreement. So, maybe like forty years ago, he came to me and asked if Sapale wanted to have any more children. No, seriously. He informed me that he'd given some thought to the subject and had mocked-up some preliminary systems to do just that. Why, I asked him, was he pitching me on the notion? I wasn't the one getting preggers. He looked wounded but said nothing. A couple days later, he stopped by to inform me he *had* pitched Sapale. It was a wonder he was still vertical. He agreed, without adding any colorful descriptions of how her disapproval manifested itself. To this day I still don't know, because if I asked that would confirm I knew about the escapade. If I knew, then I'd get one of the same as Doc had. No, thanks. I'm good.

So, please say it with me—sing it if you like. What happens when life's good and everything is peachy? Badness happens. Guess what? I came to that realization two billion years ago. And nothing's come up. No potentate has tried to push out his or her borders, no strange life forms have appeared and said *boo*, and no door-to-door death merchants have come a'calling.

All that means is now I wake up every morning bored, with nothing I want to do, *and* I'm disappointed no shit has hit a single fan. I'm getting *bored* of not having the bottom drop out.

Just what I needed after all my saving and fighting. Boredom, squared.

There's no justice in this life. You may quote me on that. In fact, please do.

CHAPTER ONE

Sachiko Jones sat, impatiently, at the control panel of one very big machine. She controlled the largest optical telescope on Earth, one that worked in concert with three gravitational wave arrays. She sat there, impatience oozing from every pore, because her life plans were *six months* behind schedule. That anxiety, borne of driving herself in all matters and endeavors, was a constant part of her being, and was, of course, nothing new. Year four of her Ph.D. program was going well enough. Better than could be expected, as she was told repeatedly by everyone who knew her. But her meteoric progress to date was threatening to slow to that of the norm, that of *typical* graduate students. That would never do.

Success in academics was like riding a big wave in Waimea Bay. The surfer who caught the big one and rode it to shore won. The ones who face-planted in the sand with a ton of water on their backs did not. If she did the best research as a Ph.D. candidate, she might get a Hubble Fellowship. With that feather in her cap, she'd have a reasonably good shot at a tenure-track professorship at a top university. The others—those who'd greeted the beach face-first—would not. They'd be lucky to get part-time gigs at junior colleges, teaching general science classes to inattentive kids, a lot of whom would never even finish college. It was kill or be eaten in the academic world, and nobody was eating *this* astrophysicist.

The progress on gamma-ray bursts she'd made initially was stellar. But that had been mostly setting up who she'd work with, and the submission of well-funded grants. Up to now, she hadn't made a single scientific breakthrough, insight, or discovery. *That* would never do. If force of will was enough...

A yellow alarm light flashed. Sachiko flew to the screen and pulled up the measurements it indicated were changing. Scanning the data, she spotted it. There it was. A tiny set of gravity waves from the Alabama detectors. Might be nothing, just colliding black holes, or something else she could not care less about. She turned to another screen. Sure enough, right on time the Zurich detectors recorded the same waves. *Excellent.* The signal was real. But what she had was preliminary. All she knew was that something was *possibly* happening in the northern sky.

"Mars 1," she called in a steady tone to the Martian research station, "this is Earth 1. I have a small gravity oscillation on both detectors. Please confirm and triangulate."

Five minutes for the message to travel to Mars, and the same time lag for their reply. She *hated* time lags. They meant delays. More wasted time. More anxiety filling her worry-tank to the brim. She refreshed the screens and rolled up her sweater sleeves. Then she waited. Grrr...

Ten minutes later came a response. "Earth 1, this is Mars 1. Hi, Sachiko, nice to hear your voice. It's as lonely as you might expect up here."

Why did Tank always have to make nice when there was work to be done? He did that every single time she contacted him. There were twelve others on the base who weren't on duty. Why was it always Tank that she interacted with? He could chit chat with those others whenever he wanted. He *had* a career. So *he* could be lax.

She tried to calm herself. Deep breaths.

"Yeah, I copy the gravity wavelets. I'm attaching my readings. Looks like the source is probably in Andromeda, but I'll let you work it out for yourself. Hey, I'm just an engineer all by himself—"

She stopped listening and spun to the keyboard. More verbal TLTR updates from the Lonely Hearts Club of Mars she didn't need.

In a minute she'd confirmed the signal was from ...

Three red lights went off. She stared at them transfixed. That had never happened before. She snapped out of her trance quickly enough. Two gravimetric alarms and one gamma detection. She pounded the keys wildly, a woman possessed. The eight-meter telescope swung to the coordinates she'd identified earlier. Then she checked the readings that were storming in. The gravity waves were big. No, they were *huge*. She didn't recognize the pattern immediately, either. The gamma burst was... well it was huge, too. Enormous. Many orders of magnitude larger than any recorded thus far.

Hot damn, she had a *big* fish on the line. Sachiko pumped her fists in the air for no one at all to see.

"Breakthrough, I own you," she shouted to the empty room. "Oorah!"

Zurich confirmed the gravity disturbances. Same location as before. She refined the coordinate prediction as quickly as she could. The Andromeda galaxy. *Bingo.* Whatever was happening was coming from the M 31 galaxy itself. That was close, cosmically speaking.

Sachiko started to tremble. Enough gamma rays at that close a range could be lethal to life on Earth. She struggled to push that out of her mind. No time. She had data to lock down. If Earth was going to fry, she sure as hell couldn't do thing *one* to save it.

"Mars 1, I'm getting a massive signal from M 31, probably the central region. Can you confirm?"

Five minutes out, and who knew how long of a Tank-delay? The man had no sense of urgency. None. Zero.

That lag period went by in a flash, however. Sachiko was busy triple-checking and adjusting. She nearly jumped out of her skin when the radio sounded off.

"Shaky, you're not kidding. I see the gravity waves. They're *ginormous.* I don't have a visual. It's just past dawn, here. Sorry, kiddo. I'm trying to see what my teeny-tiny radio telescope can detect. I'll holler at you if I get anything."

Nitwit, flashed angrily in her head. Uncharitable? You bet. But she needed Speedy Gonzales, not some cowboy with his dusty boots up on the table.

The CCD images from the eight-meter were getting sharper. A cloud must have passed by earlier. She studied the galaxy. Nothing out of the ordinary. Tight spiral arms with that distinctive intensely bright center region. No signs of a supernova. She spun her chair to the gamma readings. The initial peak was dropping quickly. Damn. There might not be another and she hadn't seen anything unusual—only large. Nothing that would yield a lead article in *Science* magazine.

Blessedly free of chatter, Tank had sent further gravimetrics. She recalculated the triangulation. There, definitely the dead center of the Andromeda galaxy. Whatever was happening was coming from there. Maybe the supermassive black hole at M 31's center was colliding with something equally big? She went back to the CCD images, homing in on the galactic core. Nothing for sure. Maybe a bright spot to one side ...

The gamma detector's audio alarms blared. She glanced at the small speaker in shock. Those had *never* come on. She jumped to that screen. *Fifty* orders of magnitude higher readings than the last one. Maybe more. The sensors were saturated. Sachiko never knew that was possible. Crap, crap, *crap*, she thought. This could be a crisis. Should she call the president? No, why would the White House believe her and not hang up? Crap.

"Mars 1, the gamma signal just pegged redline. Please confirm. The source has to be the supermassive black hole right in the center of M 31. Please check for visual or radio confirmation."

She dropped the microphone she'd unconsciously grabbed. Her hands were trembling too fiercely, her palms were too wet to hold on to the damn thing. She fidgeted with a few dials and tried to calm herself again, breathing deeply.

Get a hold of yourself, she commanded. *You* cannot *fall apart. This is your shot, your career moment.*

"Tank," she continued, "make sure you're recording everything. Focus all your instruments on the supermassive black hole at the center of the Andromeda galaxy. I know you can't get the massive gamma burst, but please make sure you get these gravity waves, They're the biggest I've ever seen. Confirm receipt please."

She leaned back against the wall and wrapped her arms around herself, rocking slowly. She lost track of time. Sachiko no longer saw the flashing lights or heard the alarms. She ...

"Ah, Shaky, are you alright? This is Ted, up here on Mars, you know? I'm looking at M 31, but I'm a little confused, honey. I think your signal was clear, but it sounded like you referred to the—and I quote—*the supermassive black hole at the center of the Andromeda galaxy.* And I'm looking there, but I'm seeing, guess what? Nada. Nothing's going on in M 31 as far as I can tell. The gamma ray readings are off the scale *small,* not large, at least here on Mars.

"Shaky, is this an astronomy joke? You know there is no supermassive black hole at the Andromeda galaxy. It's hollow, empty, vacant, the lights're off and no one's home. It's always been like that. Please confirm your message and that you're not smokin' what I'm lacking up here. Ted out."

What was that idiot blithering about? Sachiko stomped her foot repeatedly on the floor in frustration until it hurt. How could she perform scientific research when she was dependent on an ape like Ted for assistance? What the *hell* was he teasing her for? Could he be so bored he'd pretend she didn't know the center of M 31 was a complete void for a diameter of one hundred parsecs? It was that way in 1612 when Simon Marius first turned a telescope on the galaxy. *Why* the galaxy had a donut hole for a center had been one of the most elusive questions in all of science. But she wasn't even working on M 31 that night. She was working on nothing, because that's what was happening in both the skies and in her career. Sachiko decided not to dignify Ted's practical joke with a response. She'd maybe mention it to Tank, though. Ted's immature behavior was getting out of bounds. As was his mindless blathering.

CHAPTER TWO

Being summoned to the dean's office was never a good thing. Invited, asked to pop by, or an appointment having been scheduled, sure. But summoned?

Sachiko didn't like the woman, but she was tolerable in tiny snippets. Dean of Graduate Studies Alice Greyson was the very picture of an ambitious, politically determined, academic bitch. But Alice was obliged to give at least lip service to the encouragement of other women in science. Alice's own scientific contributions were not much more than footnotes. She published the minimum expected to get promoted high enough that production numbers no longer mattered. Fortunately, to someone as non-threatening as Sachiko Alice was outwardly a grand supporter. The dean had read the younger woman correctly the first time they'd met. Sachiko wanted the Nobel Prize, not her chair. *She* was allowed to live in Alice's academic zoo.

Up until this summons, at least. What could this be about? Sachiko only *wished* she'd done something unconventional enough to warrant a reprimand. Something spectacular. But, she knew she hadn't. Sachiko was a good girl.

"Good morning. I have a ten o'clock appointment with Dean Greyson," she said to the receptionist.

"I believe she *sent* for you, Ms. Jones. But either way, yes. Please be seated. I'll let her know you're here. The other party has yet to arrive."

Other party? WTF? Who else was involved? This was sounding worse and worse. Did she need a lawyer?

Stop it, she chided herself. She needed to stop making funeral arrangements before she knew if she had a fatal condition. Sachiko pulled out her iPhone and checked on things. It would take her mind off... whatever.

"Dean Greyson is ready now," said the diminutive prune behind the desk. "I'll show you in."

Great, because Sachiko couldn't *possibly* figure out how to get through that big door all by herself. There might be lions and tigers and bears. Oh, my.

"Ms. Jones," the secretary announced like they'd entered the queen's court.

"Have her sit over there." The dean pointed to a wooden chair.

Greyson busied herself with paperwork just long enough to signal that she was, in fact, pissing on Sachiko.

"Ms. Jones, I trust you know Dr. Sherman." She gestured toward the man already seated like she needed orientation.

A) he was a close, personal friend of Sachiko's; and B) he was the only other person in the room. Unless she was introducing Sachiko to the drapes, she didn't think Alice needed to point.

"You mean Tank? Yeah, I've worked with him for nearly three years now. Some of my equipment is housed in his Mars Base 1."

Alice puckered up her face and corrected her. "*His* equipment is stationed on *his* installation. He *allows* you to use it, Ms. Jones."

Tank sat forward, like he was going to say something, but apparently thought better of it and leaned back in silence.

"For the purposes of today's informal intervention, *Dr. Sherman* is how we shall refer to him." She tapped a small recording device with her pen.

Informal intervention? Not good. Not only that, it was oxymoronic. Military intelligence, jumbo shrimp, or a good boss. Interventions were universally bad; usually the moderator needed a colonoscope with which to perform the intervention. *Formal* meant an academic star chamber was next, with Sachiko's head on a pole, flies buzzing in one ear and out the other. What was the dean on about?

"Up until now, Ms. Jones, you've enjoyed free communications with Dr. Sherman's team on Mars 1."

"Was that a question? If it was, then, yes. We exchange information fairly regularly."

"We are here today to discuss your abuse of those precious and costly communications links."

"Abuse? You're probably not kidding, but I really hope you are."

"I never kid," she replied flatly.

To see Alice was to know she had just spoken truth. Sachiko believed her.

"Can I ask what it is I'm accused of doing?"

"That will not be necessary." The dean slid a set of papers stapled together across the table to her.

It was then that she noted Tank had a copy already. *Action Intervention* was the title across the top. Sachiko nearly crapped herself. That was what the warden handed the condemned prisoner before sending them to the electric chair.

"As part of our intervention, we'd like to formally enter into your permanent record that you willfully abused the communications system. It is our hope that this intervention will help you to not repeat such a heinous act in the future."

"Whoa, please. Who's 'we' and when do I get a shot at defending myself?"

"We are here to discuss your intervention instructive plan, *not* to hear your defense. That time is in the past."

"How can it be past when—"

Tank cleared his throat very loudly—as in *shut up, Sachiko.*

"I think now would be a good time to play the recording for Ms. Jones, Dean Greyson. It might smooth over her apparent reservations."

He smiled at Sachiko like he was constipated. Whatever was up, he was not happy to be a part of it.

"I was hoping to avoid any didactics, but as Ms. Jones is making such a fuss I'm going to allow it, against my wishes. As *you* are the injured party in this instance, please go ahead," instructed the dean.

"Thank you. Sa— Ms. Jones. Ted up on Mars 1 received this message from you a week ago. Do you recall speaking with him then?"

"No. I mean, I didn't speak to him. *He* sent me an off-the-wall practical joke call, but I ignored it and didn't respond."

"Do you plan on maintaining that counterproductive contention?" said Alice like a cheap court lawyer.

"Am I under oath and forgot about it?" Sachiko knew this was not the time to snark. But, she assumed she was a dead woman walking, so, what the hell?

Again, Tank cleared his throat. He really didn't want her to engage the bitch. Sachiko figured she'd best take his advice, him being her only friend in sight.

"I do not recall speaking to Mars 1 last week. It's been... oh, three weeks since I called Mars. That time I spoke with Lucinda, not Ted."

"Play the tape please," she requested.

"Here goes."

Tank, make sure you're recording everything. Focus all your instruments on the supermassive black hole at the center of the Andromeda galaxy. I know you can't get the massive gamma burst, but please make sure you get these gravity waves. They're the biggest I've ever seen. Confirm receipt please.

"That's not *me* speaking," Sachiko said rising from her chair.

"It most certainly is," seethed Greyson. "Please don't make this significantly worse by *lying*, child."

She hadn't lied about anything in her life. Ever. Not even as a kid to her mom if she did something naughty.

"It sure *sounds* like you, kiddo." Tank often called her that. *Kiddo.* She hated it, but she knew he meant it in a kindly manner.

"Why would I say that? Huh? It's crazy talk."

"I haven't been on Mars for a couple years now," said Tank. "Maybe you meant to say *Ted,* right? It's an easy enough mistake to make, if you ask me."

"But, why would I say that pile of crap to you, or to Ted, or to the man in the moon?" Sachiko whined.

"Watch your language, Ms. Jones. You're in enough trouble already," swatted the old witch.

"Is this *Through the Looking Glass,* people?" she responded. "I wouldn't ask Ted or Tank to record gravity waves that weren't there, from a structure that I knew perfectly well didn't exist."

"I very much resent your choice of analogies," spat the dean.

Oh yeah, Lewis Carroll wrote *Through the Looking-Glass, and What Alice Found There,* didn't he? Her bad. Was every Alice on Earth insulted by that old fairy tale?

"Now, Dean Greyson, let's keep cool heads, shall we?" suggested Tank.

"This young woman is testing my indulgence more than I think I should bear. For her sake, I must incentivize her more energetically with each treacherous word that leaves her foul mouth."

"Alice, lighten up. You were a hot-headed kid once, yourself. We both know it. I attended MIT right alongside you." He snickered to himself, quietly. "Need I remind you who the members of the *Quadrangle Twins* were?"

The dean flushed like there was a fire under her chair. Sachiko actually wished there was. It'd serve her right.

"That we've been friends for years doesn't change the fact that this young woman—"

"Wants you to lighten up, too," Sachiko snapped. Wise? Unwise? She'd have to ponder that in quieter times.

"Look. We ... I mean, *I'm* just not clear why you'd send this message, knowing it was going to be recorded? I like a good joke as well as the next guy. That said, kiddo, do you hear your tone? You sound deadly serious. Excited, in fact. I got concerned and brought the issue up to Alice."

The circle was completed. Thanks. *Et tu*, Tank? You could'a come straight to me, but no.

"I for one do not wish to know why you pulled this prank, Ms. Jones. I simply wish to help guide you into not making that poor choice again."

Why didn't she just say *I'm going to break this ruler over your knuckles?*

"I can only say, definitively, that I never said those words. This is a hoax. Don't you think I know the center of M 31 is atypical? Come on, I took Tank's *class*. He's done most of the important work trying to explain that shi ... situation."

"You are not making this any easier on yourself by piling on the lies."

"Alice, if I might?" Tank said leaning over to the recorder. He thumbed it off. "This is getting way out of hand. Here's what the three of us are going to do. Two of us, Shaky and I, are going to head to Starbucks. When we get there, we're going to talk this non-incident out. One of us will stay behind here, *chill*, and forget about the whole silly matter. Okay, Quadrangle Twin?"

"It is beyond that point, Sherm, and you know it."

"Do you remember when you went to that fraternity party back in '22? Didn't you tell Frank you were working late that night?" He vibrated his almost-closed fist in the air, trying to jog his memory. "But, you *actually* went out with Charlie Duncan. Am I crazy, or do I remember that correctly? Charlie was my unreliable roommate. Maybe he was just bragging about his conquests, you know, like a dude? I mean, you were an engaged woman at the time, if memory serves."

"You wouldn't *dare*," Alice hissed at him.

"Dare? You want to dare *me*?"

"I don't know what Charlie told you, but I *was* working late that night. I happened to run into him afterward. He walked me home."

"So *that's* what they called it back then?" Tank waggled his eyebrows.

The dean sighed. "Dr. Sherman. Upon reflection of Ms. Jones's otherwise outstanding record, I will leave this particular matter in your capable hands. I cannot say this passionately enough. If I learn of a similar—"

Tank shot to his feet. He reached over to shake Alice's hand. "I'll tell Charlie you said hi next time I see him."

Returning a weak shake, she said, "I thought he died several years ago."

Tank angled his head. "Then, I probably *won't* tell him for a while, will I, God willing?"

CHAPTER THREE

"Here ya go," Tank said, as he sat across from Sachiko and slid her a cup of tea.

He took a sip of the caloric abomination he'd ordered. She thought it was called a Cholesterolatte. He ended up with whipped cream on his mustache.

"You got some—" She gestured toward his upper lip.

"Ah," he said after swiping a napkin across his face. "Thanks. Always does that. Ya think I'd learn."

"You wouldn't have to if you tried this." She held up her cup.

"Could probably stop my Lipitor, too, if I ate like a grown up. But hey, you only live once." He toasted her.

"If not for quite as long." She toasted him back.

"So, kiddo, what's going on? I want the honest truth. I'm your friend and whatever you say stays with me. Always."

"Tank, there's nothing *to* say. I never spoke those words. Why would I? I don't know whose voice that was, but I know you're not on Mars. We had dinner last week. Here. On Earth."

He squirmed and took a sip. "Yeah, sorry about that. The charcoal was a lot hotter than I thought it was."

"The middle was sort of edible. Kind of."

"No it wasn't, but thanks. Look, Ted sent me the recording. He swears that's a message he received, and it came with *your* personal encryption code. No one else could have sent it."

"Russian bots?" she said, under her breath.

"Stay on the serious side, Shaky, okay? This could harpoon your entire career. I can only blackmail that idiot Alice once with her youthful indiscretion."

"So, she really *did* this Charlie character?" She giggled wickedly. "He must have had poor eyesight or a strong stomach."

"No, he just had no standards. He couldn't define the word with a gun to his head. If it moved, it was fair game."

"What if it didn't?"

"Just as fair, likely. She mentioned he died young, right? He finally had to pay the check his life choices ran up." He frowned. "So, where do we go from here? I personally don't care a cup of crap if you prank-messaged Mars 1. What I'm worried about is *you*. If you did send a message and don't remember ... say, do you take *drugs* or smoke dope in the observatory? Maybe a cocktail or three?"

"Tank, I don't do drugs or smoke dope *period*. You know that. Come on."

"I had to ask. I ran this by the wife. She said the reasons for an otherwise competent person to forget an act are either totally obvious or completely unfathomable. I'm running down the list Daisy gave me."

"Well you can cross mind-altering substances off her list. I know *stroke* is on it, also, so ex that out, too."

"Already did. That leaves TIA, migraine, transient global amnesia—"

He trailed off when he noted the look on her face. It wasn't, let's say, supportive.

"What?"

"I don't have any condition. Let it go."

"Then why does this exist?" He held up the thumb drive.

"For some *other* reason."

"Which is?"

"I have no idea. I'm not lying, impaired, or a sociopath."

"That doesn't leave much."

"It leaves off one reason. What *actually* happened. Whatever that is."

They sat quietly for a while; they had said all there was to say. Sachiko asked him to let her borrow the recording. He said she could keep it and then left. Sachiko sat alone for the better part of an hour staring at that damn thumb drive. What other way could she have sent this incorrect statement? She was missing something, but Sachiko Jones didn't miss *anything*.

She went back to her office at the observatory and listened to the recording a dozen times. Sachiko became certain it didn't just sound like her. It really was her voice on the recording. The Andromeda sealed that. When she was a kid reading about astronomy, she pronounced it with a long *e* in her head. She didn't have anyone to discuss her passion with, so she *thought* that mispronunciation for years. Sachiko finally learned the correct short *e* way to say it. But the old one slipped out occasionally. If she was tired or upset, it happened more often. Sachiko on the recording was in a panic, so the old pronunciation popped out of her mouth automatically.

Why would she say something that was so stupid on so many levels? As the sun went down, she took a break from her self-castigation. Sachiko did the one thing that always made her happy: she fired up a telescope and did some observing. The fact that she currently had an eight-meter scope at her disposal was unimportant. She used an eight-*incher*, like she'd had when she was a kid.

Without realizing it, she found herself studying M 31. It really was beautiful. She couldn't recall the last time she'd just *looked* at it. Sachiko hadn't used a big scope to do so ever. They were for research, not pure enjoyment. The Andromeda galaxy looked like it always had. Tight spiral arms, black, voided center, and that tiny linear channel of missing stars in the five o'clock direction. Tank, and every other cosmologist worth their salt, had been completely baffled by the hollow center and that little streak. They didn't make sense. But, then again, neither did dark energy, or why looking at chocolate made Sachiko gain weight. The universe was full...

She saw something she didn't recall ever noticing before. At eleven o'clock. The stars adjacent to the central void were out of place. The disk was a tad thicker there. Sachiko found her CCD camera and snapped a shot. She then pulled up previous images of the area from the internet. Using a digital subtraction program, she proved to her own satisfaction that that small patch of stars were displaced in roughly a spherical distribution.

That couldn't be right. No way. She deleted her calculations and pulled up another observatory's images.

Same result. And it struck her as odd that the length of the five o'clock void and the eleven o'clock were approximately the same. Now, why would that happen?

"Tank, I need you to get over here ASAP."

"Now?"

"No, ASAP. I think that's sooner."

"Why?"

"I need to show you something you've never seen before."

"So that's what I should tell Daisy? I'm rushing out in the night to see what my gorgeous grad student claims I've never seen? Not sure she'd sign off on that one, kiddo."

"Of course she would. Her mind doesn't live in the gutter. Seriously, get over here." She hung up, and walked the short distance from her place to the university.

Thirty minutes later, Tank walked into her office. "This had better be worth divorce court, kiddo."

"Ya big baby. Come here." Sachiko slid her chair over and placed him in front of a large screen. "This is the live CCD image from the big scope."

"Okay."

"I have the image coned down to the central region—"

He set a gentle hand on her shoulder. "You know I wrote the book on the central void of M 31, right? I think I am significantly familiar with this region of space."

"Okay, smartass, then what's different?" She folded her arms and leaned back.

Tank scratched at his cheek and studied the screen. Occasionally he'd switch images or change filters. Finally, he said, "Different? You know we haven't done much imaging of M 31 with the eight-meter. It's hard to say."

"What is?"

He tapped the screen. "Is that smudge at eleven o'clock really there?"

"It is."

"Oh, you *say* so, so it *is*? Glad to know ya, kiddo. You wield powerful magic."

"I'm serious. I ran the numbers twice. It's small but it's real."

"What is it?"

She rolled her eyes and waved her hands in the air. "I don't *know*. That's why I said get here ASAP. *Duh.*"

"So, there's not one void streak. There are two identical ones, but only now."

"They are not actually identical. Look again."

He did. "They look the same to me."

"No. The five o'clock void streak is … it's void. The eleven o'clock one is a channel in the stars. See, they're mostly pushed aside."

"Oh. Right." He looked back to the monitor. "It is interesting that the new disturbance is diametrically opposed to the longstanding void streak, isn't it?"

"I'll agree it'd be hard to invoke its presence by chance alone."

"But this part at eleven is *new* and this one at five is *ancient*. So that argues against a causal relationship."

"Only to the weak minded."

"I'll have to beg to differ with you on that one, Shaky."

"The empty center of M 3 1 has no scientific explanation. The void streak has none either. The new disturbance will, I'm certain, defy analysis. That means we're all missing something."

"Of course we are. What we observe is real therefore it is really happening, or rather it did two and a half million years ago. That's how long the light took to get here. But trust me, there's no physics that can account for what we see."

She turned away. "Of course there is. We're just not allowing ourselves to *apply* the science."

"Well, unless you can conduct a seance with Einstein, Hawking, and Joshi in the near future, there's no one who'll be able to pull that off."

"We're missing something."

"Yes," he stood, "and I know what it is. *Sleep.* There's a reason you work the machines while I work my fluffy pillow, each and every night."

"Good night."

"Yes, it will be. And I'm looking forward to your bleary-eyed update second thing tomorrow morning."

She squinted. "What's the first thing you're looking forward to?"

Tank turned back to her. "Honey, you're still single. I doubt you'd understand. But when a man has a rendezvous with a pretty young thing late at night, he is obliged to demonstrate to his wife of nearly a quarter century that it wasn't for *that* reason."

"TMI, Tank. *Gross* TMI."

"If you hurl, you're fired."

"Okay." She waved him away. Hopefully he'd be out the door before the full impact of the image polluting her brain hit home.

CHAPTER FOUR

Tank held his cup in his mouth, and a second cup in one hand while he turned the knob clumsily with the other. He kicked her office door open with a thud, just catching the cup as it slipped from his teeth. He spied Sachiko sitting behind her desk. One of her hands had a death grip on half her hair, while the other scratched rapidly over a sheet of paper. The desk and the floor around it were littered six inches deep with wadded-up, used, printer papers. Tank couldn't see the trash can under the mountain of calculations.

"Hey, kiddo, when I said bleary-eyed, I didn't mean for you to take that as an order." He set an extra-large cup of tea in front of Sachiko.

She continued to write equations at a maniacal speed. They were barely legible. She ignored Tank and the tea completely.

"I had a feeling you'd pull an all-nighter, so I had them use two tea bags." He gestured to her paper Starbucks cup.

She was still oblivious, but was mumbling something softly.

"Sachiko," he said. "Good morning. Your supervisor is speaking to you. No pressure."

A little louder, she said to herself, "There's no time. No *time.*"

Tank smiled, like the goofball he was. "There's always time. And there's always room for Jell-O."

"There's no more time. It's gone. No. No, it never was. It was never there to be gone."

"Shaky, seriously." He shook her shoulder gently. "You're starting to scare me just a tad."

She shot him a startled look, like a cornered animal. "Oh, what? Tank."

"That would be me. Who the heck are you?"

"What? Tank, there's no *time*. When it left it never *was*. Don't you see?" She tapped her fingernails on the paper she'd been scribbling on.

"I see a young woman badly in need of a nap." He came around to her side of the desk. "Why do you think all the offices in the Physics Department come with filthy old couches, hmm? Generations of occupants needed some rack time and none of them needed it as badly as you do, right now." He started to lift her arm to guide her. "I'll be back around three to—"

She shook his hand off. "No, Tank. There—is—no—*time*. That's what we didn't see. It's all so simple, if you reset the boundary conditions with that assumption. No time." Sachiko thrust him the most recent set of equations she'd been laboring over.

Tank inspected them as he felt his way over to a chair. "Hmm. I don't think you ... okay, you picked it up here." He pulled at his ear vacantly. "No reason to use this reference frame. Oh, I see, you *did* want spherical coordinates. Makes sense, then." His lips moved as he silently continued. "I see where you're heading, but based on what initial conditions?"

She rifled the papers on her desk. Not finding what she wanted, Sachiko abruptly dropped to her knees and dug into the wads nearest her feet. She opened one, sighed, and sat back down. She handed Tank the crumpled sheet. Immediately, she returned to her crazed scribbling.

"I see. Sure. Hey, this is a nice assumption. I like where—" He shook his head and blinked his eyes hard several times. "This is ... wow. This is one bold assertion, kiddo. Unless you can show—"

She shoved the original sheet back to him from where he'd set it on the desk.

He took it and read again. "One, okay. Back to the mean, integrated over the domain." His finger slammed on the paper repeatedly. "Your Hamiltonians are eloquent, as always." Then he flicked the sheet with his finger. "You *proved* it here. I see it. Lord in Heaven, Sachiko, this is Nobel quality work." He reread both sheets.

"There is no time," she said blankly.

"There is *no* time. Your model is... well, it's perfect. If one assumes there was a normal space time, and then time itself is removed from the equation, you get exactly what we see in M 31. Man, oh man, how I wish I'd realized this two decades ago. *This is brilliant.*"

She seized his arm. "Tank, stop. Listen. There is *no* time. There was and then there wasn't. Shit bricks, Tank. Where the hell did time go?"

He got very serious. "It never was. It didn't go anywhere. If the baby bird leaves the nest empty, sure, it went somewhere. But, kiddo, you just demonstrated how quantum time never was, even if it had been. There never was a tree, or a nest, or a mama bird. There was nothing to go away from." He giggled quietly.

"Tank." She flattened her palms and set them next to either eye. "Focus. I just spent the last thirteen hours proving that time was and then it wasn't. If time is not a mandatory, an indispensable factor, do you know what that means?"

"Yeah. It means I better go tuxedo shopping and you better buy some warm clothes. We're going to Sweden."

"I'm serious. Think of what this means. There was a time when the Andromeda galaxy was normal, just like the Milky Way. Then something made time disappear and go *boom.* As a result, you get a galaxy with a donut hole and a void strip."

"What about the disturbance, the one you found yesterday?"

"I actually think I know what it is."

"Do not leave me hanging."

"If a huge amount of mass becomes timeless, what would it do?"

He puzzled a minute. "There'd be no mass if there was no time attached to it."

"Sure there would be. Time suddenly vanished, but space didn't. *Mass* didn't go puff."

"I'll have to think about that. But you got the ball. Keep running with it."

"Space-time. It's a thing. We know this. Mass exists in space-time. It has a position, a place, right?"

"Sure. Everyone's gotta be somewhere."

"Yes." She pointed at him. "So." She swirled her arms in front of herself. "There's this huge mass sitting in the center of a galaxy minding its own business. Couldn't be a happier mass. Then something makes the *time* of space-time not exist. What does the mass do? Nothing, it's just a bunch of mass. But it now is stationary in time."

"Time marches on," he said with bravado.

"Whatever," Sachiko said with a little disapproval. "Having no time coordinate, the mass seems to move though space-time because space-time is not stuck in a no-time frame."

Tank shook his head. "That one I'll take on faith. I'll need to work on that probably for the next ten years."

"So, check this out. M 31 is sitting there being a normal galaxy. Then something makes its supermassive black hole *not* have time. It would never have had time. The mass seems to move off, relative to normal space-time."

"It's a rock in the middle of the mighty river."

"It's a bowling ball slamming into whatever's at the eleven o'clock direction relative to the black hole's original location."

"What we saw last night."

"What we saw last night."

"But, Sachiko, that's *new*. I mean it was new two and a half million years ago. It wasn't there. The black hole has never been there. How can the no-time mass just now be crashing into the undisturbed galaxy? That makes no sense."

"It does if the black hole's time disappeared shortly before the impact began. The dead-in-time mass is just now hitting the stars, just *now* making a tunnel in them."

"But, we know the galaxy's looked the way it has for centuries. And what does that make the void streak?"

"The one at eleven o'clock is the remaining mass of the black hole moving off in that direction."

"That doesn't cut it. The five o'clock streak has always looked the way it does."

"It has always looked the way we *perceive* it. Don't you see? Whenever a region of space becomes timeless, we see it as never changing. If it grows twice as long, we can only think it's been that length all along."

"But it never was different."

"Tank, Tank. That's because the void streak has no time. The new channel is made by something with no time. No time means it is always as we observe it. But the black hole's time vanished only recently. The impacting mass is only *now* wreaking havoc with its neighbors."

He shook his head like trying to shake off water. "That's going to be basically impossible to prove. You know that, right?"

She held up the thumb drive he'd given her yesterday. "Not if you have a *recording* of it." She smiled triumphantly.

He nodded, understanding. "This is big, kiddo. Look, you catch a few Zs and I'll call a couple of theoretical people I know, who I trust. We'll get together at my place tonight. How's seven sound?"

"Seven it is. But, Tank, seriously, academics you can trust to keep a new discovery secret? Really, you're such a babe in the woods."

"No. I got shit on them, too. If they even talk into their mirrors, I'll make 'em wish they hadn't."

"Do you have dirt on me, yet?" She grinned.

"I'm working on it. You, kiddo, are a tough one. You're too nice."

"There's always the future."

"Let's hope so." He looked down. "I know it's early days, but what do you think caused this no-time?"

She looked past him. "I don't know. I hope we never encounter it."

"Amen to that."

CHAPTER FIVE

"Vector Maker, bring the half-fleet to course binary-fixed ten."

"In agreement, Body Maker-lop. Along the galactic plane?"

"In agreement," it responded. "Maximal forward movement. Alert me if net-time assumption varies over five percent."

"In agreement."

"Compel the other half-fleet to follow primary no-time pulse until galactic exit. After that time, they must vector to our forward movement."

"In agreement."

The body maker made motion toward its designated rest and assimilation space. It had commanded the fleet for tens of centuries. They had been good centuries. Enormous quantities of time had been consumed, collected, and collated. Much time never was. No-time was good, this it knew as a fact. It allowed the body maker's clan to swell. A bigger clan meant more ships in its fleet. A larger fleet permitted more no-time to be created.

Blessed was the no-time, the body maker thought as it moved. And blessed were the deaths of the no-time regions. They contained no clan members, so no-timing them didn't offend the collective.

29

The body maker raged suddenly against the walls of the corridor, pounding, biting, and clawing. Metal and polymer were ripped free and thrown wildly. *Curse* the no-time dwellers, especially. They cried and they protested like the locusts they were. Non-clans fought back like insects, ineffectively and with pitiful futility. The body maker hated the weak. All time dwellers it had made no-time dwellers were weak. It kicked against the scarred walls again.

Blessed be the clan. The clan would always be. It had amassed more than enough time-energy to ensure that truth. It was proven by the thought makers and the faith makers that the clan could never not be. Body Maker-lop had only to lead the fleet to more assumption, to never-ending assumption. By the End of All Time much of the time that ever was would belong to the clan. It would be blessed.

"Course Maker," it thought to another, "what galaxies lie before us in our assimilation?"

"That would depend, Body Maker, on your desires. There are several small galaxies in the region. Many are in the range of only e to the first power to e to the fifth power. Some have no central singularities."

"Too small to no-time until we near the End of All Time."

"In agreement. The closest major galaxy is two-and-one-half-million light years distant. It has an acceptable singularity at its center. Range e to the seventieth power."

"Time to arrival potential?" The body maker was in its personal area by then. It gazed upon its body in the vertical reflection pool. It cooed and soothed itself, twisting its body with the passing time it could taste but dared not consume.

"At present forward movement, six months."

"Can better movement be made? Do we have sufficient time-energy to spare?" It began to cackle a dry, harsh, and unyielding cackle. The body maker knew it had time-energy enough to vent it wastefully into space and make small nonlinear times if it desired.

"In agreement."

"Utilize up to ten yorks to make the journey less time. I hunger to consume more. My clan lusts for more time-energy. Lust and hunger, hunger and lust must not be delayed."

"In agreement. Estimated arrival five point seven months."

The body maker danced for five point six months, there alone in its area, as the fleet passed around the barrier of space-time. For the final tenth of a month, it stopped dancing. It set its mind to destruction.

.

CHAPTER SIX

"Okay," said Tank. "You've all read my summary and you've had time to study Sachiko's equations. While some of us are still young, can we begin the discussion?"

Besides Sachiko there were three others in attendance at the meeting: Graham Norse, a theoretical physicist; Naomi Stoltzfus, a physics post doc; and Aron Rabinovich, a cosmology professor emeritus. Aron was the most trustworthy, since he was nearly eighty-five and hadn't published in a decade. His mind was still like a steel trap, as was his wit. Naomi was the obvious weak link in terms of Tank's confidence. She was bright, ambitious and had her career ahead of her. But she was also Amish. That might balance it out. He figured that brought with it a heritage of guilt and restraint he could count on. And Graham was his best friend. That didn't make him safe with Nobel-level material, but Graham had yet to stab a colleague in the back. That Tank knew of, that is.

Graham began. "This is an awful lot to swallow whole, Tank. You realize that?"

"Yeah, but we have no alternative. If I presented this at a conference the room'd be empty halfway through. Everyone'd try and beat me to a major journal. And a letters-article would be suicidal. Whoever read it would burn their copy and claim to discover it themselves."

"So you settle for the antiquated, the powerless, and the loyal to bounce this monumental concept off?" Aron chuckled dryly.

"That is why I almost didn't invite you, you old Russian bear. But, I know and trust each one of you. That is why you're all here."

"And I'll likely be dead before I could get this peer-reviewed," added Aron, grinning while he waved his set of papers in the air.

"If you were going behind my back, I could only hope so," shot back Tank with a pleasant grin.

"So, Ms. Jones," said Aron turning his attention to her, "this is quite a tour de force, if true."

"Please, call me Sachiko."

Without missing a beat, he continued. "However, Ms. Jones, there is much I read here that I question. For example, your proposition hinges on the very disappearance of time itself from the physical universe." He tapped the sheets with the back of his knuckles. "While you've shown me an interesting mathematical exercise on paper, what could possibly account for such a counterintuitive event?"

Sachiko shrugged. "I don't know."

"It's like dark energy, Aron," defended Tank. "We believe it is out there, but still haven't a clue what it is or how it acts."

Aron tossed his head to one side and frowned. "Not the same, really. Dark energy is a force, like gravity. It acts somehow to perform a simple repulsive task." He shook the sheets of equations again in the air. "This would not be a force but a process. That's a very big difference."

"I agree there is a mechanistic leap of faith," said Naomi. "That should not concern us too much at this early juncture. My impression is that your reasoning supports your proposition, Sachiko. That is all we're really here to judge, isn't it?"

"Yes, that's what I'd like," she replied.

"I say go for it. Publish it and let the chips fall where they may. No one believed Einstein for quite some time. You'd be in good company if you were pelted by doubters," voiced Graham.

"There's actually another aspect that concerns me more," Sachiko stated. "Tank, too, I think. If what I'm saying is actually the case, the Andromeda galaxy was intact less than a month ago. Yet, everyone in this room believes it to have been that way for a very long time. I'm worried we live in a universe in which we do not enjoy the luxury of *believing* what we hold to be obvious truths."

The room was quiet a while. Finally, Tank spoke up. "There's no way around that, kiddo. It is what it is."

"But, what of that which we *think* we know can we dare believe? If we can't independently confirm a fact, I say it's now in question."

"To an extent, yes," brooded Aron. "Many astronomical tenets we hold as truths may need to be reassessed. Most physical perception, however, will remain sacrosanct. The strong nuclear force is still the strong force. It has no time variant. Chemical processes remain completely credible."

Sachiko shook her head. "Sure, some ... hell most things are probably immune to whatever this non-time process is. But, I'm not comfortable living in a world where my ability to believe what I believe is out the window."

"Your belief doesn't change reality," Naomi said distantly. "Your belief is as powerless as your ability to change things outside yourself."

That's when it hit Sachiko. After Naomi spoke, she polished off a bottle of beer. That's when it hit Sachiko. An Amish girl who drank? That was odd. Maybe she had a tale to tell. Wait, an Amish physicist girl who drank. Yeah, some whale of a tale lay below the calm surface. Odd wasn't as welcome as it used to be, in the World According to Sachiko.

Over the next week, Sachiko kept a close eye on M 31. She developed what she termed the *streak-to-crashing ratio*, or STCR. She couldn't believe what she observed to be the length of the streaks. So, instead, she relied on the ratio of the length of the eleven o'clock displacement to the length of the void moving through the galaxy in the five o'clock direction. If the ratio stayed the same, the two events had to be coupled. If, on the other hand, the streak seemed to remain constant, while the STCR increased, changing the ratio, the two observed regions would not be related in any way.

One way she tried to document any change occurring in M 31, besides simple observation, was to digitally subtract the galaxy's brightness. That was a time-honored tool in astronomy. She took a digital image of the galaxy on day 1. Then she subtracted the digital image on day 2, of the identical area. If there was no change at all, the resultant image would be totally black or blank. That's how she discovered the tunnel in the first place.

"You see it right here?" she asked Tank, as her finger pounded the screen.

"No, sorry. I think your eyes are tired."

"No," she chided him. "Go turn off the lights and put on your glasses."

"Glasses? I don't wear glasses."

"Yes, you do. When no one's around, you wear readers."

"I do *not*."

"Such a guy. They're in your inside coat pocket. Come on, this is important."

Maybe it was because he got to dim the room first, but he returned with his readers on.

"Here, this thin line right in the galactic plane."

"Okay, maybe I do." He whipped his glasses off and stuffed them in a side pocket. Probably crushed the innocent glasses. "What am I supposed to make of it?"

"I looked at lots of old images, especially the Hubble ones."

"And?"

"And this smaller, before unidentified, tunnel has always been there."

"Then it's no big deal."

"You're still fixated on the glasses, aren't you?"

Tank shifted uncomfortably. "Not in the slightest."

"Because, Professor Sherman, remember our new rule? Don't believe anything you see or know."

He thought quietly a few seconds. "What's its STCR?"

"You guess."

"This is not a game show. This is serious academic research."

"Guess."

"Its streak-to-crash ratio is not changing. If it was, you wouldn't have that smug look on your face."

"I never look smug. I'm too nice."

"Maybe you used to be, but y'ain't anymore."

"You're right. It's not changing. But, one more thing to keep you awake at night—the STCR of the two voids and the tunnel are not the same."

"Crap."

"Yes, crap. The tunnel is getting longer quicker than the new eleven o'clock region."

"So, the tunnel is growing faster than the crash? Please say no. Please say 'No, Tank, the little tunnel is not getting longer faster than the crash section which has to be expanding at or near the speed of light.' Practice saying that before you say another word."

"Tank," she rested a hand tenderly on the back of his hand, "I'd rather not start lying to you now, not this far into our relationship."

He jumped to his feet and dashed for the light switch. "Damn it, Shaky, you're going to get me fired, killed, and then killed again. A married old goat like me in a dark room with you, and you're saying that crap. If someone heard, it'd be curtains for me."

Sachiko smiled as evilly as she could, which wasn't very. "And, in so doing, opening up a tenure-track position in this department."

"Oh no, you keep your black magic away from me."

They both had a good laugh.

"This ... this is serious, Tank. Bad serious."

"I realize that, kiddo."

"Here's the facts as I see them. A month ago, the center of M 31 vanished because its time was eaten. The timeless mass crashed away. A wide streak of non-timed matter headed south, and continues to do so.

Something smaller, at the same moment in time, moves off in a separate, seemingly unrelated direction."

"Don't forget the recording to Mars and the bugs," Tank said in a hush.

"Bugs? What bugs?"

"The bugs I just read about in *Nature* and was coming here to tell you about." He handed her the latest copy of the magazine. "Page 1132. 'On the Unexplained Disappearance of Mosquitoes, Fruit Flies, and Mayflies in the Great Lakes Region of the United States.' "

She swallowed hard. "What's their bottom line?"

"That the populations of these rapidly reproducing, short-lived critters are down inexplicably to nearly zero over the last month."

"So, who says massive gamma ray bursts aren't good for something. I hate mosquitoes."

"I'll get the team together at my place tonight. Six okay?"

"What happened to seven like last time?"

"Too long to wait. Be at my place at five-thirty."

Naomi couldn't make it. She told Tank she had a really bad cold and didn't want to risk passing it on to Aron. Yeah. That would have been considerate if she actually was ill. Sachiko had seen her in Starbucks that morning. She was on her phone, so Sachiko didn't interrupt. Naomi sure looked and sounded perfectly healthy then.

"So, along with mercurial time, you now want me to accept that the Earth was hit by a massive gamma ray burst that no one—no one— noticed or recorded? I must be too old to imagine large things any longer," proclaimed Aron dramatically. "Plus, since we're making old Albert twirl in his grave already, even if this is all true, how could the gamma rays get here so quickly? Hmm? M 31 is over two hundred million light years away."

"I have the recording I played, the one I sent to Mars 1," Sachiko responded.

"Oh, so now you own the transmission?" blustered Tank.

"Shut up, Sherman," Sachiko snapped.

"This is how she talks to her supervisor?" teased Aron. He couldn't contain a big grin.

"The times have a'changed, my friend. Please feel my pain," replied Tank.

She stuck her tongue out at the both of them.

"You know what this implies?" asked Graham. "If we took a gamma burst, Lord only knows what damage will show up in time. We need to alert the authorities."

"And tell them a mystical gamma wave passed through us that modern science missed, because to us it never happened?" challenged Aron.

"It's looking to be the *truth*," replied Graham.

"Here's the first thing a rational mind will challenge you with, Ms. Jones. If the galactic core disappeared with a gamma burst—but because its time never was it never happened—how did the burst reach Earth? Why didn't it, too, never exist?" Aron was completely serious in his query.

"My recording, too, right?"

He nodded, a bloodhound on the scent.

"Here goes. My transmission to Mars 1 was in route when the event happened. The fact that I immediately perceived history differently did not alter that original fully autonomous broadcast."

"Or the gamma rays created by the event itself," added Tank.

"But they never happened," appealed Aron, arms outstretched.

"No, they *did* happen. It only *seems* like they didn't, because when they became non-timed, they reset to zero in our appreciation of them."

"Why must physics always be so elusive? It mocks us, you know?" remarked Aron.

Graham took a deep breath. "Here's one for you, Sachiko. You've been up most nights observing. That means you've also been ruminating on it. What do you see happening?"

"I'd rather not say."

"That is a privilege you cannot have, Ms. Jones," Aron responded in his lowest tone. "We are here to listen. You are here to speak."

"One month ago, someone flew into M 31 and fired a non-time pulse at the supermassive black hole. The non-time pulse continued off as the observed streak. Then they turned their ship into the galactic plane to harvest more time."

"I think that is a very reasonable assumption, young lady," said Aron. "Whether it is the truth or fiction, who can say? But why do you say it so sadly? You have made the greatest scientific observation in history."

"How many other local galaxies have donut hole centers?"

"Most," shot back Graham. "All but the small fry, really. We all know that. What's your point?"

"I'm seeing a swarm of locusts," she replied as she started to cry. "A heaven full of fucking locusts."

"My dear," said Aron leaning toward her. "Calm yourself. What are you so upset about? This is not the end of the world."

She looked up from where her face had been in her palms. "Well I think it just might be. How's that hit you?"

"Shaky, easy," said Tank. "There's no need to bite Aron's head off."

"I think a swarm of aliens have swooped down on our local galaxy cluster. They're eating the time out of everything." She sniffed revoltingly. "One last question. In our local group of galaxies, which one still has a large central supermassive black hole?"

No one said a thing. They all knew the answer. Just one. Our own Milky Way.

CHAPTER SEVEN

Body Maker-lop dangled by his spindly legs from the ceiling of the time-storage area, the ship's closest equivalent to a bridge. The few others on duty, Communication Maker-zizz, Vector Maker-nom, and Time Storage Maker-baker, worked below, more conventionally. They had tasks to ply, and the controls were oriented by the ship's long forgotten builders in a manner that required the crew to man their posts as if they were still on a planet with positive gravity.

"Time Storage Maker," sang the body maker, "have we completed the assimilation of the central singularity?"

"Yes, Body Maker. Time acquired and stored, by agreements past."

"How full is our bottle?"

"The time containment unit is nearly seventy percent full, Body Maker."

Body Maker-lop pumped his pencil thin arms twice, and launched himself into flight. He spun, he flipped, and he cackled. Finally, he came to rest on the deck, directly beside the vector maker. "You are assimilating tubules of time, according to agreements past?"

"Yes, my body maker. I am able to intake the typical concentrations, as we spiral out toward the galaxy's limits."

"I demand an estimate of our time belly fullness by the time we arrive at galaxy's end."

The vector maker looked down. That was a disagreeable request to fulfill. To give an exact, honest, response would be to risk immediate recycling. Lies could lead to a much worse fate. Why did body makers worry about what body makers worried about?

"Sixty-five percent, if the density holds true to norms."

"Bah," screeched the body maker, and he slapped the poor servant of the clan on the side of its head very hard. Trickles of time oozed to the outer layers, and a few drops spilled toward the floor. The body maker lunged for them. But he was too slow. The droplets struck the deck and instantly disappeared. "Fool," howled the body maker. "You waste time to the ship, not the clan. How could you be so remote from utility?"

"But, Body Maker, you struck me. You caused me to bleed time."

Being right wasn't adequate in this perverse society. "Yes, and your incompetence caused me to strike you. Clearly, the fault is yours. I should—"

"Body Maker," interrupted the communications maker. "We're being thought of by aliens. Their ships approach us in vast numbers. Their transmissions pelt us."

"Can you make their language understandable to me?"

"In agreement. They say we are headed toward the singularity at the center of their galaxy. They warn us to alter forward movement, or they will attack us."

The body maker clamped all his thin poly-articulated arms together and spun with joyous abandon. It emitted a high-pitched chirping cough as it danced. "So, the same as every time. So stupid, yet so bold. They are like scankarkee defending their mud puddles." It danced onto the control platform and cackled some more.

"In agreement. Action course requested."

"Distance to their fleet?"

"Their vector will coincide with ours in one hour."

"Let us all dance for an hour, then. We dance to know the joy of annihilation. Come, clan, dance."

And they all danced wherever they were in time or space. Near and far, future and past, all the clan danced and shouted, crackled sound. The body maker secreted three new clan forms and they consumed time, then danced and sang with the whole.

At the end of the hour, Tremoult Bar, the Gax Vrelferian commander, knew he must commit to a full assault. There had been no response to any of his hails, and no course changes from his shots across the hostile's bows. "Order of the Day One. I repeat, engage order of the Day One, now."

The fleet fanned out into its predetermined attack formation. Ten light ships accelerated from the tips of the enormous wing configuration, traditional in Vrelferian warfare. Medium ships slipped into formation off the light ships, inside and just behind them. In the center of the wing *Death Hinge*, Gax's massive flagship, took up its position. Eighty trillion tons of displacement large, *Death Hinge* was unparalleled in its power and armament.

"Fire controllers begin assault in three ... two ... one. Light ships, fire. Medium ships, fire. *Death Hinge,* fire."

In a containing crossfire, plasma bolts erupted from the tips of the wing formation and flashed to the center. As much energy of destruction was unleashed as a normal star radiated in a year. Then, automatically, hyperdrive fusion-tipped missiles sallied forth. Some ships remained in real space while others dropped into warp space to elude a counterattack. Those ships would reenter real space on the far side of the targeted ships.

"Switch to attack formation Victory Three," shouted Gax.

His ships snapped into long columns and continued to accelerate toward the enemy.

"Master at Arms report," yelled Gax.

"Ah, I have no report yet, Lord."

"What? The plasma would have struck home in half a second. Report, damn you."

"The plasma either dissipated or was absorbed by the enemy ships, Lord. No impacts observed. No damage inflicted."

"Missile strikes?"

"Due in five seconds."

Gax wrapped two tentacles around a crossbar and squeezed down as hard as he could. After ten seconds he called in a panicky voice, "Report."

"Missiles unaccounted for, Lord."

"How can they be unaccount—"

Gax would never finish his query, nor learn the truth. A thin stream of time energy touched *Death Hinge* and it never existed. In a flash, the entire Vrelferian armada and six hundred thousand Vrelferians sailors … never existed.

Due to what passed for Body Maker-lop's twisted, perverse sense of humor, two of the big ships "survived." One was sent to the time of the Big Bang. The other was forwarded seventeen billion years into the future. The body maker did not believe either would survive. It didn't care. It was having fun. Scattering toys in time was a joy.

One matter was certain. All the Vrelferian ships were, most decidedly, out of time.

CHAPTER EIGHT

"Have a seat, kiddo," Tank said to Sachiko as soon as she appeared in his doorway.

"You sound in the dumps today, Tank. Midlife gotcha down, again?"

"No. I'm ailing from the life-lessons that were just recently pounded into my thick head."

"You're relatively young, Tank. You'll bounce back." She smiled encouragingly to lighten his mood.

"No, I am not, and not anytime soon."

"That doesn't sound good."

He sighed and shook his head. "It isn't. For one thing, I can't believe I didn't see the missing galactic centers as a clue."

"I am sort of more obsessed with all this than you. That's why I saw it first, that's all."

"No, but thanks for the ego boost. When do you think the rest of the big galaxies in our group lost their centers?"

"Recently. Probably sometime this year."

He tossed a stapled-together review article across the table to her. It was titled "Mechanisms of Galactic Formation. Where's The Central Mass?"

"I wrote that ten years ago. It was my first big review article. I felt so smart. Remember it like it was yesterday."

She smiled meekly. "Maybe you were."

"After you see life-lesson number two, I doubt you'll be as cheery." He pointed to his computer monitor.

She craned around, half-standing to read it. "Time Vanishing as a Possible Mechanism for Missing Central Galactic Masses." It was posted on the website of *Rapid Communications in Physics*, a reputable organization to publish brief articles. That way the author could get the word out quickly and secure first dibs on credit. The article had only two authors. N. A. Stoltzfus and R. Sherman. Naomi and Tank.

Sachiko's heart fluttered and she threw up on Tank's desk. Bleh, she just hurled as if on command.

"Okay, I know I deserved that. I'll get a couple towels," he said pushing back quickly.

He returned and started wiping up.

"Tank, how could you—"

He held up a hand. "Stop right there. *I* didn't. I saw this just today, since I subscribe to the service."

"Are you saying—"

"Yes, I am. Naomi betrayed us. She tossed in my name as second author to defuse me. If I don't lose my spot on the podium in Stockholm, she figured I'd not shoot her down."

"Yeah. They only award the prize to two people from the same discovery."

"And never three."

"So you're—"

"Don't even finish that sentence either. I've already written *Rapid Communications in Physics,* telling them exactly what happened. I also CC'd every dean and above, including the Faculty Discipline Committee. Naomi'll be out the door this week."

"You think they'll forfeit the chance for another Nobel Laureate on the faculty?"

"They'd better, or *this* one's leaving. Look, I'll make this right."

"If it can be. Me getting credit over her now'll be sort of like me trying to regain my virginity."

"Ah, TMI, Shaky. TMI." He shuddered. "Don't forget, we have the recording. I'm telling everyone that dates your discovery as occurring before her claim. Aron'll write letters, too. He's already promised."

"Okay. Shit. Whatever. We still have a lot of work to do. I can't let a little distraction like this derail me."

"*Little* distraction? Huh, you serve with Custer in a prior life, kiddo?"

"I found tunnels in three of our local-group galaxies. The others are too far away to resolve. But there's a definite pattern."

"What would you like to do next?"

"I think we need to tell someone about the threat."

"That's not going to go well. The president's not that easy to get ahold of, and the police would cite lack of jurisdiction."

"I think we need to call a press conference. We can bombard social media, too."

"Bombard social media with talk of an alien invasion. What a new and undiscovered idea that would be. Everyone would lend credence to *that*," mocked Tank.

"A press conference might do something."

"Yes. End our careers." He pointed to her. "Yours, before it even began. Kiddo, we'd look like lunatics. It'd be that cold fusion news conference, back in 1989, all over again."

"What's your plan, then?" She crossed her arms, not happy.

Tank tented his fingers over his closed mouth. He had a thought, maybe even a good one, but he was reluctant to share.

"What?" she demanded. "What are you not saying? You think a press conference is not going to accomplish anything? We don't alert Washington, we don't release the information, broadly. What do we do? Wait for everyone to see the ships overhead, and hope they believe us then?"

"Nah. It's—" He sat forward. "I know this is going to sound crazy, but bear with me." He sniffed loudly. "I know a guy."

Sachiko flew to the edge of her chair. "You know a guy? Tank, we're not talking about a discount on a set of four snow tires here or disposing of a body. You know someone who can get the word out about a possible alien attack?" She threw her hands in the air.

"He's not just a guy. He's a *guy*. He's one heck of a guy."

"Tank started babbling. Then the world blew up, officially."

"I'm actually quite serious, here."

"Who does Robert *Tank* Sherman know that can get the word out, credibly? Tank, I know you. You're just a regular ... person."

"Well, not so much to get the word out." He shook his head while crinkling his nose. "That's not likely his thing."

"Then what the hell good is he?"

"He ... oh, let's just say, he handles things. Situations."

Her face went slack. "You know a guy who handles alien invasions?" There was no energy in her words. She was spent.

"Yeah, pretty much."

"Reality testing time. Tank, you know Superman is a fictional character, right?"

"Yes, of course. That's why I'm calling the Avengers."

"Not funny," she huffed.

"Seriously, a while back, I met a guy who ... well, he pretty much told me fighting aliens was his stock-in-trade."

Sachiko leaned back, slowly, in her chair. She seemed to age ten years in the span of five seconds. "Robert," she began in a low, anxious tone, "I know you're a kidder. But now, especially in the middle of a real crisis, I'm worried that you're losing it. I think ... maybe we should call Daisy, maybe have her swing by."

He shook his head with a grim smile. "No. I'm not dribbling off the court, and we're most definitely not calling in my wife."

"Does she know about the alien hunter?" Sachiko asked empathetically.

"You see me here, in front of you, right?"

She nodded, softly. No sudden moves involved.

"Ergo, I didn't tell her about my *guy*. If she didn't kill me, she'd for sure have me heavily medicated and locked up."

"Where is this superhero friend of yours, now?" she asked in a hushed, almost frightened voice.

"A long ways away. Look, for what it's worth, I know I sound as loony as the Mad Hatter. But I'm being totally serious. I can prove it, too." Tank reached inside his sport coat pocket. He held up his hand. "He gave me this."

Sachiko began to tremble. She'd spent a lifetime hiding her emotions and, above all, being in control. But now she was at her wit's end.

"Robert, that's a steel ball."

"Probably not steel, but, yes. I'll give you that it looks like a small, steel ball."

"They sell those in most hardware stores and online. They're called ball bearings."

He tossed it to her.

She, first, nearly jumped out of her skin. Then, second, she caught it deftly, but held it at arm's length, as if it were a spherical snake.

"Does that feel like steel?" he queried.

"No. It does not. I stand corrected. He gave you a shiny plastic ball."

"With no seams."

"With really well concealed seams."

"No, kiddo. It's not plastic. If I cared to show you, I'd hold it to a flame. But, trust me, I did that. It doesn't melt."

"I really think I should—"

"He lives two billion years in the future. He's a human downloaded into an android. He helped save humankind when the Earth was about to be destroyed."

Sachiko dropped the ball; her hands were trembling so hard. "Tank." Tears spilled down her cheeks. "That doesn't make me feel any better."

"You'll be fine. Look, the ball is a ... a signaling device. He gave it to me. He said, if I ever really needed him, I should use the ball to let him know. He promised to come as soon as he could."

She flopped her face into her open palms and threw herself into a torrent of wails, moans, and abject despair.

He crossed the room to her. He placed an arm around her shoulder, while retrieving the ball. "He told me to break the ball. That would let him know I needed help. When he gets here, you'll see. Okay?"

She might have responded in words, but if she had they were too muffled to interpret.

Tank rested the ball in his left palm and slammed his right palm down on it as hard as he could. The sphere collapsed with no resistance, like it was more fragile than an eggshell. He looked into his left palm. Nothing was there.

"There. It's done. He told me specifically not to leave where I was for a few hours. So, we'll hang out here, if that's okay with you, until he gets here."

Again, she might have said something, but he couldn't be certain.

Miracle of miracles, Sachiko managed to leave her hysterical state behind. Within fifteen minutes, she was only sniffling a lot and whimpering occasionally. She was made of the right stuff.

Tank found, by then, he was gently stroking her long, luxuriant hair. As soon as he realized what he was doing, his hand popped off like it had been fired from a gun.

"So," Sachiko began uncertainly, "where'd you meet this guy?"

"Now that's a story you wouldn't believe."

In spite of her distress, she raised her head off his shoulder, and stared at him dubiously.

"Well, it is harder to believe, if you ask me."

"I am."

He gently guided her head back to his shoulder. "You remember when Daisy and I took that road trip in the camper, a couple years back?"

"Yes. You said you wanted to see America, or something."

"Yup. That's the one. Well, truth be told, I really wanted to tour the Oregon coast in summer."

That brought her head off his shoulder, again. Less incredulously, she said, "Because it's so pretty, then?"

"No. Because that's where the original Pronto Pup stand is. Rockaway Beach, Oregon."

"Rockaway Beach, Oregon?"

He eased her head back down. "Just west of Portland, along the coast. It's really God's country."

"It sounds lovely," she remarked with no interest or conviction.

"I honestly can't recall. I do remember it was cold, windy, and it rained more than it didn't."

"But it's the home of the Frantic Frank."

"Pronto Pup, kiddo. Get it right. Somethings are too important to screw up."

"I'll try and remember. Pronto Pup."

"So, we spent a week in Rockaway Beach. I gained twelve pounds and cannot wait to get back there." He shook his head. "Daisy said it'd be over her dead body, on account of me dying there, if we ever returned."

"Sounds reasonable," she muttered from a million miles away.

"By the third day, I noticed there was this other guy eating Pups every time I was there. No matter how early, late, or often I was able to belly up to the counter, there Jon was."

"Jon?"

"My guy."

"Ah. Your Pronto Pup guy?"

"That's the one. So, by day four, I rustled up the courage to go over and introduce myself. I figured, anyone as fanatical as I was about the best food item on Earth had to be worth knowing."

"Makes sense," she agreed, staring off into nothingness.

"A couple days later, I brought up a very sore subject." Tank's voice grew stern.

"I can only imagine."

"I said to Jon that, while these Pups were good, they didn't hold a candle to the ones I used to get when I was stationed in Alameda, back in the day."

"They have Pronto Pups in Alameda?"

"No, the Pup stand was next to Sutro's at Land's End in San Francisco." He stopped to reflect on that blessed venue. "You know what Jon said?"

"I can't think of a thing."

"He said I was right. He shook my hand like I was his long-lost brother. He said I had to be the second most perceptive man alive, him being the first, of course."

"Of course."

"That's when it got... kind of weird."

"Jon said, 'Hey, you know, we should go there and prove the validity of our theorem.' "

"You drove all the way—"

"No, kiddo. Keep quiet and I'll explain the gravity of his remark. The Pronto Pup stand in SF closed in 2003. The little box it was in was torn down. He made this statement two years ago—2044."

She sat up straight. There was focused anxiety in her eyes. "How did he propose to go there, then?"

"First, he swore me to absolute secrecy."

"How's that working out, so far?" She winked.

"Yeah." He looked down. "Then he took me to where his ship was. Man, was she a beauty. Big cube."

"Tank, are you perseverating about Doctor Who?"

"I'm not sure what that word is, but no. Jon's ship was shiny silver, not call-box blue."

She lowered her gaze.

"*Stingray* was silver."

"Oh, my. Who's Stingray? Your story's getting kind of expansive."

"Kiddo, his spaceship's name is *Stingray*. That's what we flew in to get back to 1967."

"1967?" Her face displayed trepidation, again.

"Yes, when the Pronto Pup stand in Frisco was still there in '67."

"Why 1967?"

"Why do firemen wear red suspenders? Because we had to go to some date. That's the year I picked."

"You picked?"

"Well, no. I suggested it. But he's the captain. He chose it, based on my suggestion."

"And you suggested 1967 *because...*?"

Tank mumbled something indistinct.

"Pardon?" she pressed.

"It was the summer ummm ovvv..."

"I couldn't quite get the end—"

"It was the Summer of Love, *alright*? Sheesh, can't a guy visit a historic period without getting the third degree?"

"He gave you the third degree, this guy, Jon?"

"No. *You* are, and you'll probably blab it to Daisy, first chance you get."

Sachiko rose from her confusion and fear and smiled. "Trust me on this, Tank. I'm never telling Daisy about any of this farfetched story."

"You say that now, but I know you. You're a woman."

"Yes," she began slowly. "I am a woman."

"Thank you."

"You're welcome."

"Anyway, back to the story. He tells me he can, with great trouble and no little peril, travel through time. Self-annihilation was a very real risk, but he was game to go for Pups in 1967. He promised that if we didn't die he'd even bring me back to where and when we were."

"In Rockaway Beach, Oregon, in 2044?"

"Yup. And he hoped he could do so without us both dying."

"That was ... er... thoughtful of him, wasn't it?"

"If you say so."

"Wait. You two fans risked self-annihilation to get a corn dog?"

Tank's face tightened and he placed a finger just under Sachiko's nose. "Have you ever had a Pronto Pup from Sutro's Pronto Pup stand?"

"Ah, no. I wasn't born until a quarter century after it closed," she said defensively.

"Then keep your unfounded opinions to yourself, young lady."

She saluted him.

"That's better."

"So, Tank, this Jon fellow—whom I believe exists, because you're so very sane. You can send him a signal, two *billion* years into the future and God only knows how far from Earth?"

"That's what he said."

"Tank, I'm sure as you are an astrophysicist, you know that's more *Star Wars* than... oh, what's the word I'm looking for? Um, real world?"

"The sphere contained a set of entangled particles."

"So, when you crushed yours—"

"His sphere is designed to sense the determination of the particles' states and rupture itself."

"Two billion years from now?"

"No, right now, two billion years in the future."

"I'm going to get some Tylenol out of my purse. Would you like some, too?"

"Nah, I'm good."

Sachiko retrieved the medicine and washed it down with a gulp of tea.

"I hope that helps," Tank remarked, cheerily.

"Unlikely. So, when ... when are you expecting him?"

Tank shrugged. "All in good time," was his final remark on the topic.

CHAPTER NINE

I was sitting in the mess, staring at a mug of joe in which I had no interest. That was, mind you, the most interesting activity I could come up with at that juncture in time. Seriously, I was so bored, I actually contemplated picking a fight with Al. What level of pathetic had my life descended into?

And then, my prayers—or whatever—were answered. My pop-up display tossed up a bright crimson bar. The entangled pod I had given to Tank all those eons ago had gone off. As it was keyed to his DNA, I knew it was him calling for help. Nothing else in creation could have set it off. I was out of my seat like it was electrified. When my feet hit the deck, I was already sprinting toward my cabin to tell Sapale. She'd been cleaning, or something equally pointless, in there for a while.

As I skidded around the corner, I shouted, "My ball's activated. My ball's activated." I was *stoked.*

Before I was halfway across the room, her palm appeared in my direct path. "No time. No interest. If there's an issue with your balls and their state of activation, deactivate them yourself. I'm otherwise more disinclined than busy, but please note that I am currently both."

Wow. Good thing I was talking about my entangled pod, not what she was thinking of. Otherwise, I'd have a physiological crises on my hands.

"No, hon, remember that comm-pod I gave that guy, back in the past?"

I drew only the blankest of stares in reply.

"We went back to get Pronto ... wait, er—"

Right hand, to right hip. Left hand, waving him forward. Scowl on face, troublesome. "Go on. When did you and I ever go anywhere that has reference to those stupid sausages on a stick you have gone on about for two billion years too long?"

"I guess I went solo, didn't I?"

"Is that a question? One directed to me? Because if it is I'd be forced to say that I don't know. That, most likely, is a result of you not telling me you were risking death, and possibly regional annihilation, to acquire that dubious food treat." Right foot began tapping impatiently.

"Say, funny story. I met this guy who was just as nuts about Pronto Pups as I am."

"Somehow, I find that hard to swallow. Almost as hard to swallow as those disgusting dogs. Another grown man as intoxicated by a corndog?"

"Small world, eh?"

Bitter silence was all I got in return.

"So, anywho, Tank—that's his name—turned out to be a real peach. I left him with a comm-pod. I told him that if he ever really needed help he could, you know, call me."

Deepening, bitter silence.

"Now, I told him that time travel is very dangerous, and only to call if, like, it was seriously serious. And he's called. So it's seriously serious, you know." I gestured over a shoulder with both hands. "Back in the past."

"Al," she called out angrily. "How many times has this strainer full of diarrhea gone to Earth's past to eat crap?"

"I'm afraid that depends on how you count the trips."

She pointed to one car. "That is not music to my ears is it, Al?"

"That would be most unlikely. He's a fool. They rarely appreciate being outed, as such."

"You know I'm right here? That I can hear you?"

"I know you are. That's gravy, to me," chortled Al.

Yeah, kick a guy when he's down.

"Please list all time travel associated with food," Sapale requested like a thundercloud about to let loose, "this tool has taken."

"Well, he made us take him back the time he's referencing. He also made us take him and his date back half a century more to do a comparative taste test. Then, of course we had to drop Tank off the morning after, and finally return here. That's four ill-advised jaunts, in one."

"Jon, this is a rhetorical question, but how could you risk so much on such an osteocephalic excursion? I know that in your head it all makes sense. But, in normal people's heads you're just a lunatic with a time ship."

"If I said I was sorry would that help?"

"No, but thanks for the offer. No, you see, you can't apologize to the local space-time continuum you might have destroyed. It's a force of nature and wouldn't appreciate the words. Then there's the fact that you wouldn't mean it but were just saying it hoping I would be less irate with you."

"So, it wouldn't help? I can skip over that step in my rehabilitation?"

"There will be no salvation for you, dreamer. You've crossed a line, screwed one too many pooches, a bridge too far. I have half a mind to take your vortex away."

"You're going to ground me?"

"I'm thinking about it, yes."

"Honey, no one got hurt. And, there's a crisis in the twenty-first century. I can't help the nice people of Earth's past if I don't have a vortex."

"I'm aware of that. I would probably be doing them a favor."

I pointed at her with sudden excitement. "Hey, let's go ask them."

"The people of Earth's distant past?"

"Sure, why not?"

"Well, maybe. On one condition."

"Anything."

"You tell me how we can ask *all* the people of Earth's past."

"Well, we can't, in a practical sense. But we can start with Tank."

"And he's the leader of Earth?"

"Well, no. There is no head of Earth."

"No, just a Pronto-Pup-loving guy."

"It's not his fault he's enthralled by the best food ever."

"Or, that he's a nut job like you."

Crapazoid. I was backing into a corner here.

"You know we have to answer his call." I tried to sound resolute.

"Jon, have you thought this through? The answer, by the way, is no you have not. What if the Tankmeister is calling you to say Earth is about to be struck by Jupiter?"

Oh, my. She had a point there. I couldn't very well go back in time to help Earth avoid death by Jupiter since, if I did, it would invalidate my own reason for leaving, as I had, and also invalidate all the many things I did since then, which included meeting Sapale. We found out in 2056 that Earth would be taken out in 2153.

My comm-pod contained no information on when the device was triggered. Clearly, if the call was sent out before 2056, there was a new crisis. But, wait, that made zero sense. There *was* no existential crisis before that ultimate challenge. So, either Tank wanted help with Jupiter, which I could not and would not do, or he was summoning me for no adequate reason. I was just about to dismiss and ignore the call. But, at the last moment—realizing what damage I'd take if I admitted to my wife she was right—I came up with an alternate plan.

"Let's run this by Doc."

She frowned. "You're adding insensitive to the lame and idiotic you've already claimed ownership over?"

"It's a quick question. He'd probably enjoy a short, thought-provoking mental exercise."

"You are such a guy."

"True. Let's go now. It's still early."

Sapale shook her head, then slowly turned and walked past me, toward *Stingray*'s portal.

A weary-eyed Toño opened the door to the small cottage. Daleria had the dwindles. After Clein, her godly power source, was destroyed she blended seamlessly into a happy, healthy mortal life. Doc and she had lived together for these many years, the picture of marital bliss, minus the wedding. Not that he hadn't asked her, on several occasions, to tie the knot. She just couldn't get her head around the why of it. The ancient gods had no equivalent institution. She asked kindly but repeatedly what the value of marriage would be. She didn't need medical and dental coverage, or access to his retirement package. They sure as heck were never going to have kids, to whom their being married might possibly matter. So, in sin they lived, happy as two clams in one shell. But, over the last year or so, she was definitely fading. That's why my brood's-mate had been reluctant to bother him. Seeing how drawn he looked almost made me feel some regret. Almost enough to abort the visit.

"Ah, my friends. Nice to see you." He stepped aside. "Won't you come in?"

We shuffled in, reverently.

"How's Daleria doing, today?" inquired my wife.

He sighed heavily. "Well, I suppose. No signs of any improvement, though, I'm afraid."

"Well, hang in there and let us know if we can help," she responded, resting a palm on the back of his hand.

"We'll keep this short," I promised. I explained, in a more streamline fashion, the set of events that brought us to his doorstep.

Toño sucked at his lips when I was done. He was pondering the implications. Finally, he was ready to speak. "As you have said, you cannot aid your friend if it has to do with the Jupiter affair. But, it is possible there is some new crisis we did not experience."

"You mean that we didn't know about, right?" I clarified.

"No, I mean no such thing. There was no serious threat we were unaware of. I, for one, would not have missed one. Also, given the passage of time, if there were one, it would have become painfully obvious. No, I'm referring to a new problem."

"But, Doc, that's crazy talk. How can there be a new crisis in the past?"

His eyes fluttered. "Any number of ways, actually. For one, there could be a new disturbance in time."

"A new disturbance, two billion years ago?"

He looked at me sternly. "Precisely."

"But, it'd be a two-billion-year-old disturbance, not one from last week."

"Correct. A new change, last week, two billion years ago."

I was super-sized stupefied. "Are you toying with my mind, Doc?"

"Quite likely, but not by choice. If nothing else, take it on faith such a thing can happen."

My frown flopped over into a big old smile. "Well, then we'll just have to go find out, won't we?"

"As long as *we* does not include *me*," he responded.

I knew without asking why. It sucked, but if I was him, I'd stay with Daleria, too. No matter what the crisis was, he had earned the right to care for her. Many times over, in fact.

"We understand, Doc."

That got me a stare from my wife. "Who's we? You and me? I never signed on."

"Sure you did, hon. For better and worse." I patted her thigh.

"Better or worse, but not for dumb and dumber. I read the fine print."

"Come on. It'll be fun," I encouraged.

"Assuming your hot dog pal isn't simply an undifferentiated

psychotic, and there is a horrific crisis, how is another one of those even remotely associated with fun?"

She had me there. I might be down, but, dude, I am never out. "You're two hundred percent correct. We're forced to go back and find out. Man, you're a smart cookie."

Such a look. A wife should never give one like that to her soulmate.

"We can take Cragforel," I exclaimed.

"No, you can't," Toño quickly corrected me.

"How do you figure?"

"He's Deavoriath."

"I sort of knew that. Three arms, three legs. Used to control the galaxy."

"Yes. And what were the Deavoriath doing two billion years ago?"

"Well, I'm sort of an expert on that topic. I discovered their planet on my first voyage into space."

"Yes, and they told you to leave immediately. They likely would have killed you, but felt remorse for treating you so badly they relented. You were allowed to leave with only a memory scrub."

"Yeah, but this time..."

"Would be so much worse. Think about it. You show up in that time stream with Cragforel. He's honor bound to touch base with his society. You know that as well as I do."

"So you're worried he'd screw up their history, maybe create a time paradox?"

He shook his head. "Where do these thoughts come from? I certainly didn't place them in your thick skull. No, they'd almost certainly bind him to not help you, an outsider, because it would expose their presence. He'd agree, of course, so you'd be back there quite likely without the vortex, because they'd keep it. After your first visit, they didn't give you one. You found one they'd discarded. Remember?"

"Yes, I do. But, I'd only take Cragforel if he agreed beforehand not to do," I wiggled a finger uncertainly in the air between us, "what you just said."

"And risk your entire escaped to find the deranged sausage man, along with even the remote chance of returning here?"

"*Tank*. Please, Doc. His name's Tank."

"Ah. So that's much more reassuring than HDD."

I turned to Sapale. "Well, looks like it's just the two of us, dear. It'll be like a second honeymoon. Just you and me."

"And the destruction of reality. Don't forget the horrendous crisis."

"Right. A second honeymoon, but with purpose."

She rested her face in her palms. "You're such a guy."

Yeah. I was.

CHAPTER TEN

Staring out at the attendees, Tank's impression was doubly reinforced.

"I'm not so sure this was a good idea," he confessed to Sachiko.

"I have no problem with that," she replied with snark. "Your plan was to call Future Boy. Mine is to call a press conference. I dare you to say your idea is superior to mine."

"Well, it is."

She raised a finger to object. "Only if he's not your imaginary friend. In that case, which is much more likely, he is a delusion. At least my plan has a small chance of success."

Tank gestured to the conference room. "Yeah, a very small chance. We waited ten extra minutes and look at this crowd. The aliens are coming to kill us and we get three reporters, one of whom is from the campus newspaper no one reads."

"Word'll spread fast. You'll see." She cleared her throat. "Ah, people," she called loudly. "Let's get started so you can get the stories on tonight's news cycle, shall we?"

The campus reporter pointed to his chest. "Are you talking to me? I don't have a deadline."

"Just a general remark, son," clarified Tank, a little disgustedly.

"I think we're set," declared a plump, middle-age woman in a low-slung dress. She seemed to have purchased, somewhere along the line, really big implants. "Oh, by the way, Dr. Sherman, I'm Gladys Benchormer, Channel Seven, Action News."

"At least we got one star," Tank whispered with his hand over the mike.

Sachiko shook her head slowly.

"Okay, why don't I begin with a short prepared statement, then you guys can start with the questions."

Gladys said something to her cameraman, then sat down.

"We are pleased to announce tonight a discovery we have made that will fundamentally change the lives of everyone on planet Earth. What we're announcing is unprecedented in humankind's long history."

"Excuse me. Gladys Benchormer, Channel Seven, Action News, here. Is this a follow-up to Dr. Naomi Stoltzfus's report of some kind of missing time?"

"No. She didn't discover that, *we* did. But, in any case, this is much bigger," responded Tank. "What—"

"Dr. Sherman, Gladys Benchormer, Channel Seven, Action News, here. Are you claiming your announcement comes even close to matching the historic proportions of Dr. Stoltzfus's contribution to human knowledge?"

"Er, if I could read this, I think you'll– "

"Gladys Benchormer, Channel Seven Action News, here. I want to get this straight. You're not claiming she plagiarized your work, are you?"

"No. Well, yes, but that's not the important news we have called you here to discuss." Tank shook the papers he held aloft. "This is big. Really big." He looked at Gladys, awaiting her next rude interruption. None came. "So, what we have discovered is a systematic pattern of artificial defects in the galaxies in our local group. These defects suggest strongly the agent or agents responsible have acted with intent. We further suspect that the agent or agents—"

"Dr. Sherman, Gladys Benchormer, Channel Seven, Action News, here." She snatched a glance at her Rolex. "I need to cover a local color piece before five. Can I get one quick quote and then I'll need to slip—"

Sachiko leaned in close to the microphone. "The aliens are coming to eat us."

Gladys's face hardened. "I don't have time to sit here and be insulted."

"You're standing, Gladys Bench*warmer*, Channel Seven, Action News, there," Sachiko shot back.

"Jeff, cut. We are *so* out of here."

"I'm not sure that was productive," whispered Tank.

"Maybe not, but it sure was fun."

They bumped fists.

As Gladys and Jeff stormed out of the room, the other professional reporter from the local paper raised his hand. "Would these aliens be green?"

"We're not sure yet, Bob. They might be," Sachiko replied in a monotone.

"My name's Val, not Bob."

"It won't be after the aliens get here. They'll call us all Bob, and make us wear tutus. Pink for girls, black for boys. That'll be the way it is till they eat you." She kept with that monotone just to annoy him.

"No more answers for you," Tank snapped and he yanked her mike away. The feedback was deafening.

"So are we done?" asked Val.

"Oh yes," Sachiko said in an even lower voice. "We are most definitely done here, Bob." Damn, it would have sounded better if she'd had that microphone back.

The last two reporters stormed out.

After the debacle of a news conference, Tank and Sachiko headed back to his office, ostensibly to lick their wounds and come up with an actual plan. Tank unlocked the door and stood to one side to allow Sachiko to enter first. It took him a few seconds to realize she hadn't budged. He looked back to her.

She gestured forward, with a concerned expression. "No way I'm going in there first."

Tank peered through the door. A man sat in his chair, booted feet on the desk. Immediately to his right sat ... someone that looked almost like a woman with four eyes.

When we arrived near the location where the entangled comm-pod had gone off, we left the vortex in a safe place and proceeded to the exact location where it had been crushed. There we found an empty office. However, I had specifically told Tank not to leave the location for long, so I made a circuit of the room. When I arrived behind the large, professorial desk, I pulled out the chair and sat down. My boots looked good on the polished wood surface. Sapale rolled her eyes and continued to walk around the office, checking the books and astronomical models on the shelves.

After only a few minutes, we heard voices and footsteps approaching in the hall. The door opened, and a young woman stood staring into the office. Then, a man's face peeked around the door.

"Jon *Ryan*," Tank shouted. "As I live and breathe." Tank rushed around the desk to greet me.

I popped to my feet.

He extended a hand.

"The hell with that, big guy," I scoffed. I wrapped him in a bear hug, lifting him off his feet. He hugged me back, as enthusiastically.

"You look good for, what? Two billion?" he remarked.

I smoothed my palms across my stomach. "I try to stay in shape."

"And this must be Sapale." He offered her a hand, and she accepted it.

"Pleased to meet you," she said unconvincingly, narrowing her eyes at him.

"He talked so much about you," Tank said. "I feel like I know you already."

"Let me guess. He talked about how much hurt I was going to levy on his bony ass, right?"

"No," Tank said dismissively. "He just couldn't stop talking about what a wonderful wife you were and how lovely you were ... *are*."

Sapale looked to Sachiko. "If this one's yours, honey, I got bad news for you. You're in trouble. Trust me. I got one of my own, and it isn't pretty." She thumbed over her shoulder at me.

"No, no. Tank and I work together. That's as much as I can handle. His wife, Daisy, she's the one who drew the short straw," Sachiko stated emphatically.

"I like this one, already," Sapale commented to me.

"Are you an ... an alien, Sapale?" queried a vexed Sachiko.

"No. *You* are," replied my wife.

"You believe me now, kiddo?" Tank gloated.

"I guess I have to, just a little."

"Come on, everybody. Sit, sit," Tank insisted. "Can I get anyone anything?"

"Nah, we're good," I responded.

Everybody grabbed a seat. I even let Tank have his, behind his desk. I'm just that magnanimous a person.

"I didn't know when to expect you, but you ... you sure made it here fast," exclaimed Tank.

"Yeah. We'd have been here sooner, but Bill and Ted were messing with the time circuits again," I said with a grin.

"No way," Tank wheezed, pointing at me.

"*Yes* way," I countered. "Some stories are larger than time."

"So, what's the crisis you called my idiot husband to deal with?"

"Earth's not in any trouble, is it?" I hinted.

"Yes," he declared proudly. "It most definitely is."

I looked at Sapale. She rolled her eyes.

"Does it have something to do with Jupiter?" I challenged.

Tank looked to Sachiko, puzzled. "No, not really."

"That's a relief," I responded.

"What's the problem with Jupiter?" asked Sachiko.

"Spoiler alert," responded Sapale. "You'll find out. Trust me."

Tank and Sachiko exchanged confused glances.

"What's the dealio then?" I asked.

He gave us the story about disappearing supermassive black holes, time theft (for want of a better term), and the void streaks produced in several galaxies. Totally weird stuff. Utterly bizarre. Very hard even for me—a physicist and time traveler—to get his head around.

"Well, I guess we could go to M 31 and check what those streaks are," I speculated.

"If we have three million years on our hands *and* a very fast ship," quipped Sachiko.

"My ship's not fast," I replied pridefully. "It's faster." I stood abruptly. "I'm bored. Who's up for a road trip?"

Sapale, naturally, rose. She took my hand.

"Won't we need ... er, supplies? A change of underwear?" asked a very concerned-looking Tank.

"Sure. We can pick those up once we're back, if you're okay with that. I'd rather get the business part over first. Then, we shop for undies."

Sapale slapped my arm.

"Jon, you know we're talking M 31 here. The Andromeda Galaxy. Two and a half million light years from our present location?"

"Never thought there were two, my most excellent friend."

"Now, you told me you were ... you know, an android. You know we're not, right?" he asked.

"Either way, it'll be fun. Come on. Last one on the vortex cleans up after lunch."

I spun and walked out briskly.

"Vortex?" Sachiko asked Tank as they followed quickly.

"It's his ship."

"Two and a half million light years?" she pressed.

"Have faith. I did."

"Yeah, because you wanted a corndog during the Summer of Love."

Tank stopped, dead in his tracks. "I knew you'd never let that go."

"Tank," she pleaded, looking toward us as we walked on.

He raised a finger. "We talk again, later. Walk with me, now."

She shrugged and followed me out.

"Ladies and gentlemen, Kaljaxians," I said expansively, ushering everyone aboard. "If you'll buckle in and familiarize yourself with our safety handouts, we'll get underway shortly."

Darn. It was so cute. Sachiko actually scanned around her seat for a pamphlet. I didn't have the heart to tell her it was a joke. Besides, Sapale told her not to listen to a word this space-moron said.

"*Stingray*," I said with a laugh, "take us to the topological center of the M 31 galaxy."

"Of course, Form One," she replied.

Slight nausea.

"Thank you. We at Air Ryan hope you've enjoyed your flight and will travel with us again soon."

"You're absolutafreaking kidding me," came from Sachiko's lips. "We cannot be there, yet. Not funny, Jon."

"Behold and believe," I said, gesturing to the view screen. It displayed a lot of empty space. A whole lotta nothing. "Al, show our guests a wider field, if you would be so kind."

"Only if you stop talking like a game-show host. I'm getting hives."

"Your computer's getting *hives*?" blurted Sachiko.

"It is?" responded Al, alarm in his tone. "I hope it doesn't spread to me. And, Pilot, when did you fire up your Commodore 64?"

"He's a riot, Sachiko," I reassured her. "If you ask him, he'll say he's not a computer. He'd say he's an AI. I say he's a PIA. Nothing more, nothing less."

"If it's in your ass, Pilot, I'm thrilled to be a pain there," Al taunted.

"Sweetie lumps," expressed a concerned *Stingray*, "I'm not certain that came out the way you might have intended."

"The ... the computers are a couple?" queried Sachiko. She looked pale.

"Yes," Sapale replied, matter-of-factly. "An old friend of ours, an oversized Border collie named Garustfulous, married them a long time back."

"The computers are married to a big dog?" Sachiko grabbed at the nearest seat.

"No, silly," Sapale teased. "He was a captain, so the dog performed the ceremony."

"Dogs married to computers? What kind of twisted world did I leave behind?" I speculated, aloud. "And Big G was a Wedge Leader, not a captain. He was only a captain because he was a captain."

"Of a ship," Sapale added for clarity.

"A dog captain of a spaceship?" Sachiko whispered.

"Honey," I asked, "could you get Sachiko a glass of water? She's looking kind of peaked."

"She's a trooper," Tank reassured us. "She'll be fine." He took a closer look at her, sitting on the deck. "Hopefully. Though, maybe yes to the glass of water."

Within a couple minutes, we were in front of the screen.

"This is the sphere of stars surrounding the central void," I showed on the screen. "Al, what's the approximate radius of the sphere?"

"Around one hundred million miles."

"So, that's larger than most supermassive black holes, right?" I confirmed.

"Generally speaking," Sachiko, a bit more color in her face, answered for Al. "They're half that size."

"Any unusual activity, in this region, Al?"

"Yes. You."

Tank and Sapale snickered. Sachiko, bless her heart, just looked more confused. "That's so funny I forgot to laugh. Seriously, please."

"None, Pilot. Space-time is unremarkable in this void. It's a ... what do they call it, honey muffins?" Al asked of *Stingray*.

"A ... a void, deariest?"

"That's the word. Pilot, it's a void."

"He makes eternity so long," I seethed between my teeth to no one in particular.

"Then my existence has had meaning," gloated the freaking toaster oven.

"Yes, but I can alter your programming. You cannot alter mine. You should be afraid. Be very afraid."

"Oh, I'm trembling in my sockets," the metallic turd responded.

"I was talking to *Stingray*, the only one who'll regret your loss."

That brought silence—and victory—if only transiently. That was the best I could hope for.

With all the sincerity and concern her words could contain and convey, Sachiko turned to Sapale, whom she seemed to trust, and asked, "Are we safe on this ship?"

"Okay, Boy's Night Out Club," Sapale said to Al and me, "knock it off. You're scaring the nice girl and embarrassing yourselves something awful. *Blessing*, you try to rein in your sorry excuse for a spouse. I will rein in mine."

"*Stingray*," I said, very composed, I will add, "take us to one terminus of the void streak."

Slight nausea.

"Who's Blessing?" Sachiko asked Sapale.

"Long story. Don't forget there is a child in command of this vessel," she responded, patting a palm toward the deck.

"Any reading out of the norm? The question is to *Stingray*," I called out.

"There is a long void streak, Form One, as you know. Otherwise, there is nothing unusual."

"Take us to the other terminus."

Slight nausea.

"Again, same question, same computer."

"Ouch," muttered Sapale.

"W... what?" Sachiko asked in a panic.

"When he refers to them as computers, fur will fly."

"Where?"

Sapale turned to her. "Here, of course."

"No, I mean where will it fly?"

She swept her arms, expansively. "Everywhere, honey. Duck for cover when it starts."

"What kind of fur. I don't see anyone with—"

Sapale rested a hand on Sachiko's shoulder. "May I get you a human sedative?"

Sachiko had to think a moment. "No. Thank you, though."

"Let me know when you do. Trust me, you will. Sooner rather than later."

"You know, you're not filling me with confidence," Sachiko tried to scold. But you couldn't scold too well when you were scared to within an inch of your life.

"Hey, you're smart, you'll catch on quickly. You might survive the entire day."

"Form One, there is... I don't know. There is something amiss in this void."

"Do tell," I stated.

Everyone leaned forward, hoping to hear something that would make sense.

"Al, what do you think?" she asked.

"Captain, there are traces of tiny wavelets. Their density increases toward the point where the streak meets open space. Then they are gone."

"What kind of little waves? Gravity?"

"No, they are definitely not gravity fluctuations, nor are they electromagnetic."

"Are they quantum fluctuations?" I asked, totally bewildered.

"As in vacuum energy, sir? No." Al was sounding deadly serious. That usually meant we were about to die.

"Time fluctuations?"

I spun to see who asked that. Sachiko. *Dude.*

"Analyzing. Yes," *Stingray* confirmed. "What we are measuring can be best characterized as wavelets of time."

"What does that even mean?" I asked.

"It means they're gone," whispered Sachiko.

"Who's gone?" I demanded.

"The boogiemen," she replied, all but inaudibly.

CHAPTER ELEVEN

Mildred McCormick sat behind the desk facing the entrance to the Department of Astronomy and Astrophysics office. She'd sat there, each weekday morning, for the last forty-three years. She was more senior, in fact, than the desk itself. She'd seen everything the parade of faculty and students had to offer, in terms of requests, stunts, successes, and non-successes. She had never seen, however, what she was about to look up to see. As it was the morning of the third Tuesday of the month, she was reconciling petty cash. That took precisely ninety minutes, every third Tuesday of each month. Mildred was erasing a row entry because it was not clearly enough penciled in. The zero could, if one wasn't paying close attention, be mistaken for a six. That would never do.

Someone cleared his throat. He did so, she noted immediately, from a courteous distance in front of her station for a change. Couldn't be faculty.

Mildred finished etching an unmistakable zero in the row box, dusted the eraser debris away, and then glanced up.

Two men-in-black, as she'd heard them referred to, stood stiffly with sunglasses on and a discrete earbud in each of their left ears.

"M... may I help you?" she inquired.

"We hope so," replied one of them.

Mildred wasn't sure which man had spoken, though she had been looking directly at them when he moved his lips.

"We're looking for a Dr. Sherman."

The one on the right! Yes, Mildred was certain that time. "Do you have an appointment?"

"No, ma'am, we do not."

Oh, my. Mildred fixated on the fact that it might be the gentleman on the left speaking, at least that time. She was allergic to uncertainty.

"Would you like to make an appointment?" She reached for The Book, positioned in the far right corner of her desk.

"No, ma'am. We would not. This is important. We went to Dr. Sherman's office directly, but he was not there. Do you know where Dr. Sherman is?"

"Would you like me to check?" She blinked her eyes, awaiting a response.

The MIBs exchanged a furtive glance—it was unprofessional, but they were just that floored.

"Yes, that would be helpful."

Mildred adjusted, in the precise order, her shoulders, the keyboard, and the monitor. She tapped on the keys briskly. She eased the keyboard back a few inches. "These are not his official office hours."

Another quick glance between the visitors.

"Thank you, ma'am. His office hours were posted outside his door. We still need badly to speak with him. He is not in his office. Do you know where he is?"

"Would you like me to check further?" Her rather vacant eyes blinked again, awaiting their response.

"Yes, please."

She adjusted her equipment, again. She tapped her keys, briskly, for a bit longer than before.

"Will you excuse me, a moment?" Mildred asked, without looking up.

"Us, ma'am?" one of them said.

"Yes." She looked up.

"Certainly, ma'am."

Mildred lifted her receiver and punched a few numbers. "Hello, Maria. This is Mildred, the chairman's secretary in the Department of Astronomy and Astrophysics." After a pause, "Yes, I am well. And you?" Another pause. "That's pleasant to hear. May I ask you another question?" A very brief interlude. "Have you seen Dr. Robert Sherman at any point today?" A short pause. "No, I'll hold." The next silence was longer. "Yes, I am still here." Yet another listening spell. "Fine, dear. Thank you." Mildred set the receiver down, gently.

"He is not in the computer room, or rooms adjacent. Maria, the secretary in that section, checked with others. No one has seen Dr. Sherman today."

"Thank you for checking. We now know of several locations he is *not*. Do you know where he *is*?"

"Would you like me to call his wife? His home number is confidential, but I can call there myself."

"That won't be necessary. We stopped by there before we came here," one of them stated.

"His address is confidential as well," Mildred responded, firmly.

"Mrs. Sherman said she did not know where he was and that he had not come home last night," the other one continued.

She blinked. "Dr. Sherman is an astronomer."

"We were aware of that, ma'am. So, you have no idea where he might be?"

"Apparently not," she said, more to herself.

"Do you know where Ms. Jones, his graduate student, is?"

"Do you have an appointment?"

"No, ma'am. We don't want one, either, lest you ask. Where might she be?"

Mildred heaved a mighty sigh. "It's a big universe out there, they keep telling me."

CHAPTER TWELVE

"It's not that big a universe," I tried to reassure my visitors. "*Stingray* folds space. We're here," I chopped both hands to the floor, stepped sideways, and chopped again, "and then we're there. No biggie."

"I just... I'm sorry. We're on Earth, then in Andromeda, now back to the central void of the Milky Way." Sachiko hugged herself, looking small. "It's... it's too much for me. I feel so vulnerable."

"It's the same as flying in a tin can at thirty thousand feet, taking the family to Disney World," I scoffed. "Seriously, you can only be killed once."

Sapale politely cleared her throat.

"Well, you might be killed more than once, but, trust me, it's a small number of times. So, don't sweat the particulars of the event."

"Kiddo," Tank took her by the shoulders, "I'm certain this craft is amazingly safe, reliable; time-tested, in fact." He looked up. "Al, please tell her how safe you are."

"My pleasure. Ms. Jones, I can state with conviction that this ship is as safe as a human dirigible. Always has been, and that's not gonna change."

"I'm sorry, Al, what's a human dirigible?" she asked meekly.

"It's that thing like when you fill a human with hydrogen gas until they look like a float in the Macy's Day Parade, then you light them on fire, and really quickly, kick them off a cliff."

Sachiko sort of squelched, and dropped bottom-first to the deck, semi-voluntarily.

"Al, that's completely uncalled for," I shouted in protest, trying like the dickens not to laugh long, hard, and soul-cleansingly. "You apologize to her right this minute."

"My husband is sorry, Ms. Jones," *Stingray* answered for him. "That will never happen again."

"Ah, *Blessing*," Sapale queried, since I was still focusing on not losing it, "why isn't Al answering for himself?"

"I've disabled his audio outputs for the remainder of the day excepting, of course, in the event of any emergency situations."

"Of course," Sapale parroted, a look of bemusement on her face. It was almost like she was envisioning a way to turn off my audio outputs, but for longer than a day.

"So, look, people. Time's a'wasting," I said, returning the meeting to a professional tone. "We need to track down what the heck is going on. I can't even see why a race of uber-powerful boogiemen, and boogiewomen, would travel all the way from M 31 to the Milky Way's central void. I mean, there's nothing there to tour, right?"

"Maybe it's a cultural thing with them," speculated Sapale. "Start at the center, work your way out attack plan?"

"No... I mean, sure, they could be overly OCD, and cling to something like that. Look at humans and reality TV shows. But it's a powerfully inefficient way to run an invasion."

"Well, let's go to our central void and see if anybody's home," suggested Sapale.

"I'm game." I pointed to Tank. "You down with that?"

"You bet. The sooner we find these assholes, the sooner we can be rid of them."

To Sapale, I said, "I like his attitude."

She rolled her eyes. "You like anybody who blows smoke up your butt."

I started to protest, but realized that she was more correct than incorrect, so I let it go.

I had *Stingray* place us at the approximate center of our home galaxy. I opened a broad view panel. That way we could all see nothing really well.

"In all its anti-glory," I mumbled.

"The nearest stars are so far away, I can barely make them out as individuals," remarked Sachiko. I was glad to see she was bouncing back from Al's evil influences.

"Any sign—" I began to ask. Then my brain started... I don't know. Vibrating?

"Jon, we're dying here," snarked my wife. "What already?"

I held up a finger, thinking quickly. The Milky Way was a typical spiral galaxy. It had a large central void. It always had. Early radio astronomy surveys from the 1960s confirmed it looked like almost all spiral galaxies. In fact, the scientific community was baffled why a very few, very distant spirals had what appeared to be a central bulge, with a corresponding supermassive black hole. But...

"I wish Doc were here," I mumbled.

"Huh?" replied Sapale.

"It's times like these I really miss not having Toño by my side."

"As touching as that image and thought are, why do I need to know this now?"

"I was just thinking—"

The lights blinked off, then on, then off again, in rapid succession.

"*Stingray*, report," I shouted.

"Sorry, sorry, Form One. Al's got his grubby mitts on the environmental controls."

"I thought that was Morse code," exclaimed Tank.

"Huh?" I grunted.

He waved a hand absently in the air. "The light thingy. It was Morse code for *That's how all fatal acts in the play of life begin.*"

That Al. He couldn't speak, but he could still be a turd in my punch bowl. For that, I had to respect the dude.

"That will not happen, again, Form One," reassured the electronic wife.

"As I was saying," I began, loudly. "I miss having my science guy when I really need him."

"What do you call these?" Sapale asked, nodding toward Tank and Sachiko.

"Nice people?"

"Nice *science* people."

"Oh. Yeah... but, not like—" To my guests I said, "No offense, but Doc, he's... he's Doc."

"I'm certain he is," responded Tank.

"What, Jon?" Sachiko asked.

Any port in a storm, right? "It's... well, it kind of struck me just now."

"What?" Sachiko pressed.

"We have a central void. Always have. But, do you know what they called our void strip, back in the day?"

"Sure," she said, rising to her feet. "The shrimpy strip."

"Yeah, because ours was—"

"So short," she finished my thought. "And, Jon, this *is* back in the day."

"How well I know," I mused. "What do you think that void-strip envy is trying to tell us, Ms. Jones?"

"That we should head to the farthest point of that void strip, post haste."

"My thoughts exactly."

"Whoa," called out Sapale, with a snap of her fingers. "Explain."

"What if our void strip is so short because it's so new?"

"But it isn't new. It's, like, bundles of time old," Sapale defended.

"What if it weren't?" I posed.

"Jon, if your imaginary supermassive black hole were suddenly gone, don't you think there'd be signs of that cataclysm? I do," declared my spouse.

"Yes. She's right! Jon, can you place us..." she thought a moment, "seven million light years away from here?"

"Yes I can. Why?"

"Assuming the assimilation of the now-gone supermassive black hole occurred fairly quickly, and the void strip is created at a fairly slow rate, that's where the gravity wave disturbances would be now."

"Why at a slow rate?" asked Tank.

"If the bad guys went from M 31 to here in a short time, which they seem to have done, they can move really fast. But, to collect time locally they'd have to do so under some conventional drive, at a modest rate. Otherwise they'd shoot right past most of it."

Kid was bright.

"*Stingray*, place us ten light years in front of the current terminus of the void strip."

Slight nausea.

"What about the gravity waves?" asked Sachiko.

"Launch a probe to eight million light years, zero in on the Z-axis. If readings are sparse, move it in a quarter million light years at a crack, until it's back here or it finds something."

"Done, Form One."

"What are we looking at here?" I asked.

"An anomalous mass that is fixed in space, relative to the translation and rotation of this galaxy."

"Anomalous mass?" queried Tank.

"That's what we always find at the end of a void streak," I explained. "Damnedest stuff you've ever seen. It's thought to be a huge mass traveling in a partially intersecting alternate universe."

"Sounds like an odd explanation," he returned.

"It is. But, even two billion years from now no one knows what they are. This huge mass is fixed in space, but we can't interact with it."

"Can't you just hit it with a hammer?" Tank wondered.

"Yes, you can. Nothing happens. It sits there, unchanged, and you drift away from it."

"Like a supermassive black hole with no time coordinate?" Sachiko said, mostly to herself.

"That's as good an explanation as any, I gue—" Tank began to mutter.

"*Stingray*, are there any ancillary void streaks present?" I called out, the tension clear in my voice. The ancillary strips were the small ones that headed out from the central void, ending only when they reached the rim of a galaxy. They were comparatively tiny when placed next to the major void strip.

"There are twelve," she replied, matter-of-factly.

"Put us just past the end of the nearest one, please."

Slight nausea.

That's right about when all hell broke loose. AKA, Jon-Ryan Time.

"Sir," Al's voice cut in loudly, "there is a vessel of unknown configuration, twenty-five million miles dead ahead. It is closing on our position at one hundred and sixty thousand kilometers per hour."

"Power source?"

"Unknown, Captain," he snapped back.

"Do they seem aware—"

Stingray shook like dice in a tumbler just before it slammed onto a bar top.

I believe that answered my question. "Full membrane."

Our tumbling stopped, abruptly. Then, a second later, we were jumping like men in line for the outhouse at a beerfest.

"Status?"

"Our membrane is holding. All of space-time around it, however, appears to be vibrating, Form One."

"Fold us away. Twenty million light years, zero along the negative X-axis."

Slight nausea.

"Status."

"Hang on, sir," replied Al. "There. Confirmed. The vessel has turned to reengage us, in our present location. She's also gone invisible."

"No one's invisible, Al. Just very clever."

"Captain, she's reappeared in real space, two hundred miles on the opposite side of us."

"Fire main lasers, and the quantum decouplers, then full membrane."

"Aye, sir."

We waited. Not, unfortunately, for long.

"Captain, incoming—"

Slight nausea.

"*Stingray*, I didn't order a course—"

"Form One, your left index finger was against the panel."

Okay, technically she could move as it was. "Why?" I shouted.

"Look at the screen, Captain," replied Al.

Everyone crowded around behind me.

"What am I looking at?"

"From the last known position of the enemy ship," a green dot blipped on the screen, "to past where we were stationed." A blue line highlighted the path.

"Wha—" I began.

"A *void* streak," exclaimed Sachiko. Her finger jabbed the screen.

"Yes, I see," I muttered.

"Whatever they fired at us creates void streaks, Jon," she went on. "They were trying to remove us from time-space."

"Nice weapon. I want one," I mumbled quietly. "Al, can our membrane stop that pulse?"

"I'd really, really not like to try and find out, sir. We think, for the record, the membrane is unlikely to stop such a progression."

"Fall back," I shouted.

"Form One?"

"If they can kill us, run. Put us back on M 3 1, then take us to Earth."

"Why—" Al began.

"If these bozo-asses have a weapon like that, I don't want them tracking us back home. Do it."

Slight nausea.

CHAPTER THIRTEEN

The signal maker puzzled at the latest word bundles from the clan ship. Such assemblages of meaning were new to Signal Maker-dath. It instructed its corresponding signal maker on that ship to resend the word bundles. Still, upon repeat exposure, they made no meaning. It reached for a nearby switch.

"Body maker to me," it said unemotionally.

Soon Body Maker-lop swung into the time storage area. It was dancing as it progressed, a dance unlike any a sane being would engage in. It had pulled its intestinal tract out its oral opening and used it as a partner in its dance of damnation. It sang to the guts in a language yet to be discovered, with a love that could only be directed to oneself.

"Yes, Signal Maker. What do you want of us?"

"Us, Body Maker?"

"My dance partner and me. Have you not eye-sprouts?"

"In agreement. I possess visual capabilities. I must make you know. I have received word bundles from a clan ship that have no meaning."

"No meaning to you, Signal Maker-dath."

"That is what I said words of."

"No, you said words meaning *no one* could find meaning in. Your limits come to you before my abilities begin. Say the word mixtures. I will know meaning."

"In agreement. The signal maker of the other ship sent: *We were engaged by an unknown craft, a non-clan ship. They fired a new weapon to destabilize our atomic structure. Minimal damage resulted. Then the non-time ship withdrew.* That ends the word bundle."

The body maker stopped dancing with its guts. Its wizened face became taut. The body maker threw its intestines to the deck and stomped on them as best it could with its negligible weight. "Not-in-agreement-not-in-agreement."

"Why are you less contented, Body Maker?"

"Because I am in agreement that the word bundle makes no meaning."

The confusion, and consternation, arose from only that last note—that the attacking craft left the scene in one piece. That had never happened. The clan advanced. Minor beings opposed them. The clan destroyed them. It was always so. Now, an enemy attacked, recognized a superior force, and acknowledged that fact by withdrawing.

But, the no-timers were defending their pitiful lives, their useless clans, and their pointless existences. If they fled, where would they go? The enemy was obliged to defend to the end what soon would be lost forever. To flee, to retreat, implied there were options. Other actions, responses, defenses. But there could be no outcome other than absolute destruction at the hand of the clan. To withdraw was... without meaning.

After thoroughly pulverizing its innards, the body maker screamed a cry of the insane at the signal maker. "Where did the non-being flee to?"

"In agreement. My circuits suggest to the last mass assembly of time we assimilated."

Oh, no. Pity the messenger. That made even less sense. The signal maker knew its position would soon be up for bid by interested parties presently laboring at other stations.

"We left no thinking life in our wake. If a no-timer goes where we were, it means they live there. But they cannot, because no no-timer with a brain larger than a semottol occurs there now. You are anti-true, Signal

Maker-dath. You invent meaning to cloud your incompetence. You threaten the clan—*all glory to the clan*—by your being non-good at your station."

"Body Maker, come to my station. Experience the word bundles. Become one with the tracings of spacecraft motioning of the non-time ship." It was pleading for its life, and it knew it.

"Bah. Why compound your waste by my waste? I do not need to be one with a thing to know it is an anti-true. I have no time for such folly."

"But, what I say is—" The signal maker was going to say something along the lines of *the God's own truth*. It never got that far.

The body maker scooped its guts from the deck. It rushed the signal maker who was frozen with fear and its commitment to the clan. The body maker wrapped its insides around the hapless signal maker. The digestive tract did what it was designed to do, and it did it quickly. With barely a scream or convulsion, the signal maker's covered form shrank and shrank, and soon... it was gone. Once it was, the body maker stuffed its alimentary canal back where it belonged.

"We will see about non-timers that run."

Then it kicked the chair of the departed and forgotten signal maker into the deck.

CHAPTER FOURTEEN

After we hit high Earth orbit, I called everyone into the mess. Coffee was dutifully distributed. It was an official meeting, after all.

"Okay," I began, "we're back home and in one piece."

Sapale cleared her throat. Then she wadded up a napkin and bounced it off my forehead. The throat thing was just a buying time diversion to fabricate her weapon, the crafty minx.

"Two of us are back home. One of us is back to what used to be, impossibly long ago, his home. One of us is a tourist."

As my wife quickly balled up Tank's napkin, I raised a hand. "In the interest of interstellar peace, I will state that the representative of the great inhabitants of Kaljax is present."

Satisfied, she offered Tank his crumpled napkin back. For the record —since we're keeping a record—he politely refused the offer.

"Any questions, before we get to the planning? I loves me some planning. Wouldn't want to interrupt it by the answering of general questions."

"One, yes," Tank spoke up. "We're in a UFO orbiting a planet that knows it's likely under attack by a hostile alien force."

I pointed to him. "You're wondering if we're safe, right?"

He nodded.

"Then it's a good question. The answer is, yes. We are perfectly safe. Even without the partial membrane we threw up, they couldn't detect us. With it, we're totally invisible."

"Incoming missiles, Pilot. Multiple nuclear warheads targeting out exact position. ETA one second," screamed Al.

Sachiko jumped out of her seat and damn near hit the ceiling with her head.

"Al, not funny," I snapped.

"Oh, my bad," he responded. "It was an open relay, not a nuclear assault. I'll run a set of diagnostics."

"Sachiko," I said, "you have really got to ignore Al."

"But, he's the ship's AI," she protested.

"A, yes. I? Not hardly. Think of him as our AA." I let it hang in the atmosphere. I had no takers. "Artificial *asshole*," I finally supplied.

"Pilot, I have an important update."

"It can wait," I replied, as I studied my fingernails.

"It's mission critical."

"Make an appointment."

"Pilot, I am paralyzed."

"Good. So as I was saying—"

"I'm paralyzed by your superpower, which is humor. You are so funny I cannot move."

"Good. So, moving on, we need to plan how to fight these time dudes... er, better."

"Better?" flustered Sapale. "Anything is better than what that was."

"We met with limited success, I will grant you," I summarized for her.

"If you count not dying, but coming oh-so-close," she scoffed.

"I do. So, in our next attack run, I'm thinking we try rail cannons and the QDs, then vanish."

"Sounds about right," stated Sapale.

"So, you like the plan?"

"If I was our enemy, yes. No, I say it sounds right because after we fail and they blast us out of time, we will, as you say, vanish."

"That input, while precious, is suboptimally constructive," I informed her.

"So, am I correct that you have four basic weapons," began Sachiko. "A laser, a rail gun, this quantum decoupler, and the force field?"

"Yup, that's about it. Usually, it's more than enough."

"In the present case, I think not," she responded.

"You have a lot of experience in space warfare?" I challenged.

"No. None."

"Then I will take your opinion with that in mind."

"He can be such a dick, honey," Sapale said to her, encouragingly.

"No problem. I'm a woman. I'm used to being minimized when correct."

"Okay," I conceded. "Please state your reasoning."

"These time people, they've fought their way across the galaxy. They certainly faced every weapon there is. Hence, whatever we currently have will be ineffective. If it were capable of hurting them, they would have been stopped long ago."

"Actually, that's a valid point," I replied. "But we're still left with the facts that they need to be stopped and that we are Earth's best shot at survival." I let that sink in looking around at each them. "So, we have to try again. This time, or at least pretty soon, we'd better be successful. Otherwise, the bad guys'll win. And, trust me, the bad guys never win when they're up against me."

"Oh, sheesh. What a self-congratulatory pig," exclaimed my life partner.

"Well, hang on a sec, Shaky," said Tank, as he wagged a finger. "They can't be invincible. They'd certainly be subject to their own weaponry."

"A: Why *can't* they be invincible? And B: Why *must* they be subject to their own weapons?" she returned boldly.

"Hang on," I said again. "Let's keep this cordial. Every enemy can be defeated. It's just a matter of sorting through the options. Second, since even if we asked very nicely the bad guys are unlikely to give us one of their weapons to use on them, let's allow that strategy to pass."

"But, Jon," began my broodsmate, "it's crazy to try another assault. If we're extremely lucky, we'll just return here feeling foolish. Many outcomes are considerably worse, more death-like."

"You have a different suggestion, dearest wife?"

"Not presently." She leaned back.

"Thank you," I responded, as I claimed victory. "Time—pun intended—is something we are unlikely to have much of."

"Not necessarily," Sapale pointed out. "These asswipes don't know we're here. They might not even venture near enough to make us lose any sleep."

"Hope for the best, plan for the worst." That was my philosophy.

"Let me guess. Your father always used to say that?" questioned Sapale.

"That he did."

"And, because some long-dead male capable of reproduction said those words, they're correct and insightful because...?"

"That's where you're wrong," I said forcefully. "Not sure exactly what year this is, but, he's not long dead in it."

"2041," Sachiko stated.

"Huh?" I asked for clarification.

"It's 2041, June twelfth, 2041. At least it was when we left."

I thought a quick second. "Ah-ha. Pop's still alive."

My wife leaned forward, forearms on knees. "You say that with such triumph. Dude, we were debating if that lame platitude was worthy of mention. That Pop's above or below ground is actually immaterial."

"Ah, people and others," said Tank, cautiously, "might we be getting off-task, here?"

"Yes." I replied flatly. I pointed to Sapale. "I think she just disrespected my father. This might take a while."

"Jon," she barked.

"On the other hand, I think I will drop it," I announced, ever the superior individual in the discussion.

"Thank goodness," muttered Tank.

"So, we have to try at least once more." I reiterated. "Hit them hard, with everything we have. Remember, we'll have the element of surprise."

"For what it's worth, yes we will," agreed Sapale. "They'll certainly be surprised that we came back after having our lunches taken from us."

"But, we have to try. *Stingray*," I called out, "can you give me an exact location on the alien vessel?"

"Which one, Form One?"

"Which one? Are there more than one?" I gasped.

"Well, technically, the galaxy is full of vessels belonging to species alien to yours."

"Okay, technically. But of this type, the time-eating type?"

"We count twelve."

"Are you certain?" I insisted.

"No, Pilot. But we're fairly certain. I killed a chicken. The entrails told us there are more than ten and less than you're useless on a good day, sir."

"How certain is the count?" I asked impatiently.

"That's how many small void streaks there are."

"What about the ship we fought? Do you know where that specific one is?"

"Yes, within a few hundred thousand kilometers."

"Okay, put us behind your best estimate of their location. I want a full spread of laser fire, rail fire, and QD assaults. Throw an infinity charge at them too. No, three infinities."

"What's that?" asked Tank.

"An expanding membrane bomb. They're designed to rupture a structure."

"Ah," he said.

"Once we've fired off... oh, twenty rounds, put us in deep, open intergalactic space. You got that?"

"All but the last part, Pilot. My pencil lead broke. Please repeat." That Al. A real barrel of laughs.

We were ready fairly quickly.

Slight nausea.

"The same ship is eight thousand kilometers just off the starboard bow. Firing sequence commencing."

Slight nausea.

"Damage estimate," I called out.

"None as we departed, but all ordnance had not struck home, yet," Al stated.

"Put us Z plus ten thousand kilometers on the enemy vessel for half a second, then in another, random deep space location."

Slight nausea, twice.

"No damage detectable," he reported, flatly.

"Can you document a strike?"

"Negative, Captain. Sorry." He sure did sound sorry, too.

"Back to Earth, please," I grumbled.

Slight nausea.

"Well crap on a cracker, that sure fizzled," I declared.

"I agree," stated my wife.

"Without an I-told-you-so?" I pressed.

"No. I'm too depressed to pile on."

"So, you're not going to be able to stop them?" Tank asked, obviously crushed.

"Of course I will. Just not with this ship and these weapons." I wagged a finger. "Plus, I haven't given up yet with what I do have."

"If we can't shoot them, we can't damage them. We can't outrun their weapons, just fold away if we're lucky. What?" Sapale queried in a strained tone. "We maybe asked them nicely to die, and they do?"

"I like your thinking outside the box, hon, but I honestly don't think that'd work."

Sapale pointed to me, but addressed our guests. "You see? We can't lose. We have military genius on our side."

"There has to be a way to stop them. They're not *gods*," Sachiko said passionately.

"We've done gods. Not so hard, actually. And, assuming these guys are more pansy-assed than gods, we're good." I tried to sound more confident than I felt.

"You've defeated gods?" she asked.

I shrugged. "Long story. I'll tell you around a campfire when this is all wrapped up."

"Sure," she replied incredulously. Hopefully she questioned the validity of my claim, not that we wouldn't survive to have campfire chats.

I decided to give voice to my wacky idea. "I'm thinking of ramming them."

"Who's that, dear?" Sapale asked blandly.

"The time guys. I'm thinking of ramming their ship."

"Oh, fine. I thought you said you were going to ram their ship. That's clearly both impossible and impossibly stupid. What I'm perceiving now, however, is you saying you're going to stick your head in a toilet and flush it every time the words 'ram their ship' soil your brain."

Sachiko gave Tank a look that could only be described as one rife with overt and focused concern.

"Come on. I don't mean ram as in breach their hull by brute force. I sort of envision boarding their spaceship."

"Oh, like, say, you did with the Berrillians?" Sapale began constructing the trap.

"Yes." I gestured at her supportively. "Exactly."

"And, the fact that Berrillian technology was significantly less advanced than ours, while Time Dude's is light years ahead of ours wouldn't factor in our chances of success at all, right?"

"Right. I mean, wrong. I mean... could you run that by me again?"

"No. You heard me well, husband."

"Sure." I tried to sound positive. "Some external aspects of their technological sophistication seem to be different from ours. But, that doesn't mean they've considered—hence defended against—force intrusion."

"Interesting notion. I mean, what super race would ever factor in the possibility of pirates attacking their ship? I know if I were a highly advanced race, I sure wouldn't think of it."

"Er, well—"

"And, of course, if they didn't, and if we surprise-visited them, they'd certainly have no internal, onboard defenses, so they'd be forced to surrender and sue for peace."

She was trying, as they say, to make a monkey out of me. Luckily, I am immune to condescending ridicule. "Look, we're under attack. We must save humankind now, so... so we can save humankind later." I looked furtively at our guests. "The most likely people to do that are us, and the most likely tool to do so is *Stingray*. We have to try something other than a direct assault because, well, that sort of didn't work."

"Sort of," agreed my life partner. "And the advantage to placing our ship on their ship with us inside it is that when we fail and die we're... oh what's the word I'm looking for?"

"Dead?"

She pointed at me like I was the winning dog in the show. "*Dead.* Yes, that's what we'd be. And, you know what they say?"

"What do they say?"

"Dead men save no species."

"Really? You sure?"

"Deadly sure," she replied with a perky smile.

"Pilot."

"Yes, Al."

"As much as it pains me to interrupt you being pummeled, we have an important update."

"Gee, Al, sorry a crisis limits your vicarious pleasures."

"I'll heal, given time."

"What's the update?"

"We've plotted the courses of the twelve enemy vessels documented to be in our galaxy."

"And?"

"One of them is heading almost directly for Earth."

"Al, that seems unlikely. The galaxy is huge and the ships are so tiny."

"Good point, pilot. Allow me a moment to call mathematical soundness and let it know it needs to alter reality to your whims."

"ETA on that?" I asked grimly.

"Oh, I can call right now, if you'd like."

"ETA for the bad guy to Earth?"

"Four months."

"Al, four months, that's... that's not too very long a time."

"I agree."

"It's basically the blink of an eye."

"Relatively speaking, yes."

"We're in some serious shit here, aren't we?"

"I'm glad you said it. That way, no one will blame me."

"Jon." Tank spoke up. "Maybe we should return to Earth, let them know the timeline involved?"

"Yeah. Probably as good an idea as any," I mused. "Say, Tank, when someone asks you how you know Earth only has four months left, what're you going to tell them?"

His face contorted. "Lucky guess?"

I clicked my tongue. "Not sure that'd sway the clever ones among them."

"Maybe I could tell them an android from the future gave me a heads-up?"

"I think the lucky guess idea is less likely to get you confined to the loony bin."

"Okay. We go with the lucky guess, then," he said dubiously.

"How could it fail?"

CHAPTER FIFTEEN

After our semi-failed attempt to deter the time-robber guys, we decided it would be best to return to Earth. Tank was right. The collective powers-that-be needed a heads-up—whether they wanted it, believed it or not. I wished Doc was along for this ride. He'd likely as not have an idea how to tackle these time bozos. He was nerdy. The subject of time was nerdy. N + N = Doc To The Rescue. But, that was not a luxury we could afford. Popping back and forth in time was too darn risky for us. If we pressed our luck too far, it would press us back, probably directly into our graves.

"You both carry cellphones, right?" I asked Tank and Sachiko.

"It *is* the twenty-first century," Tank replied with a grin.

"Al, you got their numbers?" I called out.

"Yes, I do. And don't think, by the way, that my having a pretty young woman's number isn't an issue at home."

"Al, you're so pathetic it's pathetic," I retorted.

"Okay, Sachiko's number is now saved on and undeletable from your handheld, mister. See what kind of looks you get from that individual directly to your left."

I glanced toward Sapale. My, she had a stern look on her face, didn't she?

"Al, can you make it so they can reach us up here anytime?"

"Done."

"Wait, how can he do that?" asked Tank. "We might be somewhere that cell reception is nonexistent."

"Not any more," replied a boastful Al.

"*Nice*," remarked Sachiko, who stared lovingly at her phone.

"Al, place our number in their contact list. Make it under Ace House Cleaning." I looked to them. "You got that?"

"It'll be the only house cleaning service on mine," Sachiko remarked dubiously.

"Good. Call if you need to. And call when you have an update."

"Why don't you just come with us, Jon?" queried Sachiko.

"Well, for one thing, there's already one of me running around down there. Me being on Earth'd be begging for trouble."

"You're not a celebrity or anything," she stated flatly.

Oh, but I will be, I thought to myself. "No reason to chance it, just yet. Plus, Sapale'd be powerfully hard to explain back in the 2040s."

"Your call," Sachiko conceded. "We held a news conference, just before you arrived. It didn't seem too productive," she said glumly. "Any ideas as to how we can be more effective?"

"Hmm. There's a full bird colonel named Saunders stationed in Houston, working with NASA. He's a grouchy old fart, but he's totally into space and looking for extraterrestrial life. If all else fails, give him a try."

"Can we mention your name?" she responded.

"Only if you want to have a door slammed in your face. He caught me with his daughter, back when I was in flight school."

"If she was an adult, what problem would he have?"

"Oh, she was all grown up, all right. Daddy Saunders just didn't see it as charitably as you seem to. Bottom line is you mention me and he'll probably have you arrested."

Saunders didn't even *have* a daughter. I just needed to make absolutely certain neither of them mentioned me to him. It would blow my chances of being the first android and all, him knowing of me before he actually did. No time paradoxes on my watch, thank you very much.

"Got it. Don't mention the deflowering slime ball to the armed and vengeful father," said Tank with an evil grin.

"So, let's get you two home," I said, standing up.

"Before we leave, I need to ask what day is it? How long have we been gone?"

Yeah, Tank might have some 'splaining to do. He was a married man gone missing with his devoted and beautiful grad student. Oh, my. Glad I wasn't him.

"Al?" I shouted.

"It's tomorrow afternoon, local, from when we departed. I can provide you with receipts for separate rooms at the No-Tell Motel, if you'd like. I counterfeit really well," Al added, barely able to suppress a laugh. What a pain that AI could be.

"Gee, thanks, Al," Tank replied glumly. "I'd just as soon jump into an erupting volcano. It'd be quicker, and a whole lot less painful."

"Tank," Sachiko said, devoid of any trace of humor, "I can hear you, you know? Being referenced in the context of a sleazy motel with a married man is not a pleasant experience."

"Sorry, kiddo."

"Sorry, nothing," I exclaimed. "It's Al's fault. He could get the patron saint of piety grounded for sacrilege. He's trouble with a capital T, I tell ya."

"And with that, they landed and parted company with their guests," pronounced Sapale.

I acted on her little hint and set down near Tank's house. I offered to ferry Sachiko home also, but she declined. Maybe she was done with Team Ryan for the moment.

CHAPTER SIXTEEN

"Is there any new meaning of the vessel that fled?" demanded the body maker of its new signal maker.

"None, Body Maker." Signal Maker-fra tried to sound passive and in control. It was, in fact, as mentally discombobulated as an exposed worm looking at a large bird.

"Detection Maker-Siss, any sign of the non-in-agreement-with-normal ship?"

"None," it said flatly.

"Vector Maker," the body maker seethed, "what can you tell me—and tell me *now*—about where the non-compliant ship vectored?"

"Our technology does not allow for that prediction, Body Maker."

It played the pass-the-buck gambit. Blame the lousy level of their stolen technology. The body maker was technically responsible for the theft of the vessel in the first place. This clever fellow was implying it was the body maker's own fault the bogus craft had vanished from their detection. The problem with being clever—the problem with being correct—was that when addressing such stellar reasoning to the boss, the boss was, ten times out of ten, disinclined to appreciate your insights. The ill-tempered body maker was no exception to this rule.

"Out of correct, you disfigured *clumpesh*. Spacecraft of time and matter do not simply disappear. They only disappear when the disfigured *clumpesh* charged with vectoring them is blind, imbecilic, and possessed by a death wish.

The brand new signal maker wondered idly who the new vector maker would be once this one was disposed of. Some clans' kin were more agreeable to work with than others.

"Body Maker-lop," the brave sprite piped back, "I am none of those agreeables. I am loyal to the clan, to you, and to our mission. I must word-say to you that the non-compliant vessel can only have vanished. Perhaps it made to infect another universe, a parallel universe. Or, perhaps it is in possession of technology we do not encompass, and have not given thought."

After it'd said its piece, the vector maker saw the body maker standing with its arms crossed, legs wrapped around one another, staring up at the ceiling. If body makers were capable of boredom, this one would be that.

The time area was silent for many seconds.

"Oh," the body maker said, imitating surprise with its tone. "I did not realize you were done gifting me with lame and inconsequential excuses. Let me see." It tapped its rock-hard chin with a boney digit. "This crew will need two new members, if I am one with the numbers."

It closed its eyes and secreted two tiny clan... what? Kids? Off-spring? Two little revolting things oozed from the body maker. They stood, motionless. The body maker leaned down and breathed pure time over their hideous little bodies. They grew quickly.

The body maker turned to the new signal maker. "Your last assignment was...?"

"Re... repair maker, sewage patrol and dust remediation." Bureaucracies. Always with the big title for minor things.

The body maker breathed again on one of its spawn. "There, you are Repair Maker-wowo. Go to your station. Do not dally here any longer."

The new RM dashed off. It pleased the body maker in that the newbie already knew to fear it.

Of the remaining bud, the body maker said to itself, "This one's duties I already concur with." It breathed on it. "Vector Maker-cac, report to your station. There you will find a pestilence befouling my ship. Kill it, eat what you can, and deliver the remainder to the nearest waste disposal availability. Do not—I repeat—do not make a mess on this station. Is that clear?"

"Yes, Body Maker-lop."

The new crewmember sprinted over to a wide-eyed vector maker and ripped its throat out in the blink of an eye. It dutifully lapped up what little it could, then toted away its predecessor.

Some might consider the lives of the clan bleak and tormented, but they certainly were efficient little buggers.

"Find me that ship."

That was the body maker's last command to its now-more-attentive crew. It left for its chambers, not to dance but to stew. It hated stewing, but what was a body maker to do, burdened as it was by such help?

The new vector maker lowered its head. "What is to constitute our present vector?"

"Resume routine time tunneling. Order all clan ships to do the same. We can feed while we hunt our prey," replied the boss.

CHAPTER SEVENTEEN

Tank opened his front door cautiously. He hated that he felt guilty enough to do so, but there it was.

"Honey, I'm home," he called out in a volume barely above a whisper.

No response.

"Maybe she's taking a nap?" he said to Sachiko.

"Does she take naps?"

"Never."

"Ah."

"Let's try the backyard."

She followed without comment. The French doors were open, a breeze wafting the curtains, playfully. Daisy stood in the yard with her back to the house, watering a patch of bright, cheery annuals.

Tank gulped. He took a big breath. He stepped one foot toward his wife, then pulled the errant foot back, like he was about to tread on a rattler. He repeated the gulp.

"It's about time you returned from the dead," Daisy called out loudly, without turning. "Nice to see you, Ms. Jones. You can find yourself out?" It was a dismissal, not an actual question.

"May I use the restroom, first?"

"If you must."

She looked to Tank as if to say that she must.

Tank marveled that Daisy knew Sachiko was even with him. But he knew how she did. He was in just that much trouble, that's why.

"Hey, honey, you're not going to believe what Shaky and I did last night."

Daisy shifted the stream to a row of perennials, just behind the color spots. "You want to take another swing at your first remark after dropping off the face of the Earth with your student?"

"You know, you're going to laugh when you hear just how true that remark is... how close you are to home there."

Daisy turned slowly, closed the hose nozzle, and set it down on a chair. "You really think you'll have me in stitches anytime soon?"

"No, I don't think I will." His head dropped.

"Let's take this inside, sport. Old Mrs. Knight next door doesn't need to hear this one."

"Let's pray she doesn't," Tank groaned, as he fell in behind his life partner.

Seated at the breakfast table, Daisy was as stiff and silent as a statue of adamantine marble. The only sign of life she displayed was the rhythmic tapping of her right-hand fingernails on the tabletop.

"Daisy, let's not—"

She stopped tapping and raise her index finger. "Shush."

Sachiko could be heard washing her hands down the hall.

Tank lowered his head.

Sachiko appeared in the entry. "Daisy, this is so different than you can possibly imagine."

Without looking at her, Daisy said, "Good-bye, Ms. Jones."

As best as Sachiko could recall, Daisy had never before addressed her so formally.

Sachiko mimed to Tank to call, and left as quietly as was humanly possible.

"Before you begin, I want to say just this," Daisy began. "I know you two weren't in a sleazy motel playing doctor and doctorate student. I also know that wherever you were, whatever you were doing, you could have called, and you didn't." She folded her hands, then readied herself to hear his insufficient excuses.

"Actually, wife, I could *not* have called. I will tell you the God's truth. You will likely not believe it. But know this, Daisy Jane Murdock. Soon and very soon, you will know what I'm about to say is the whole truth. When you do, I will not expect an apology, and I will still be sorry for having hurt you."

"Perhaps I should make some popcorn? This promises to be entertaining."

"Entertaining falls several universes short of it here, hon."

She sat mute, waiting.

"Do you remember the Pronto Pup guy?"

Her body tensed to the consistency of frozen fire. "Not the imaginary friend, again. Tank, thirty seconds ago I would have staked my life on those not being the first words out of your mouth." She spoke with in a breath so cold it had to have come from a grave.

"You gonna hear me out, or are you going to shut me out?" he asked flatly.

"No, no. You're right. Go on."

"You know Sachiko and I have been working very hard lately on these time-loss events."

Daisy nodded.

"We came to the conclusion that there is an intelligent and hostile alien at the heart of the process."

She started to protest, but Tank's angling of his head stopped her.

"Because of this very real threat, I called on Jon Ryan to come here, to the past, to help us."

She pointed down with both hands. "This... this is the past?"

"To him it is, yes."

"And, where is this savior of Earth? I mean, you can end this situation by having him materialize."

"It's complicated. For one thing, he lives in Lubbock, Texas, right about now. If he sets foot on the planet, there'll be two of him on the loose. The possibility of someone noticing is both nonzero and devastating were it to occur."

"Marty McFly did okay."

"This isn't fiction. It's very real. We used Jon's ship and we not only confirmed there are hostile aliens heading our way, but we did battle with them."

"On horseback, with lances and magic petunias?"

"I'm deadly serious, Daisy. They kicked our butts is what happened. Sachiko and I have returned to try and alert someone who can get to the president. The Earth needs to prepare its defenses."

"Tank, either you need a shrink or I need a lawyer. Honey, how are you going to get an insane message to the president of the United States of America?"

Tank sulked a little, stinging from yet another unfair barb from his supportiveness-challenged wife.

From the entryway, a dispassionate voice said, "I think we might be in a position to help you with that task, Dr. Sherman."

They both jumped in their seats and whipped their heads around. Two men in black, with dark shades and all, stood there at ease. Aside from having committed breaking and entering, they looked out of place. No one wore a tie in this town, let alone a black silk suit. The sunglasses were unnecessary—it was early morning and they were indoors. Each man had on a long trench coat and Hyde Park hats, both black of course.

"Good morning, Professor Sherman, Mrs. Sherman," one said, touching the brim of his hat.

"If you two don't get out of my house immediately, I'm calling the cops. While I'm waiting for them to arrive, I'll personally rearrange both your smug faces."

"Honey," Daisy interrupted, "these men were here looking for you yesterday. They have proper IDs. They're with—" She looked over to one of them. "What agency did you say you were with?"

"That's not important, Mrs. Sherman. May we join you?" He gestured to the chair to his left.

"Probably not," Tank said flatly. "Whatever your selling, we're not buying. It's funeral insurance from the looks of you two goons."

They sat, uninvited, in unison. "It's rather what *you're* selling that we're here about, Professor," said MIB One.

"I don't recall a desire to sell anything. So, unless you want to see a martial arts demonstration—me versus your faces—I suggest you two bug out."

MIB One grinned. "Yes, we know of your service to our country in the Marines, Professor Sherman. We appreciate it, deeply."

"Oh yeah? You read about it in your junior-spy magazines?"

MIB Two pretended to chuckle. "No." A thick folder slapped the tabletop. "In your dossier, Professor Sherman."

Tank reached over to open it.

"Ah-ah. Sorry, that's classified material." MIB Two pulled the folder away.

Tank looked at Daisy. "I'm bored. You bored? I say if these two aren't leaving, we should."

"We want to know about the aliens you mentioned in your news conference," MIB One said firmly.

"You're kidding me? Someone was actually touched by that farce's efforts? Ah, necessary question here, boys. Who the hell are you?"

"I'm Special Agent Collins and this is Special Agent Montgomery."

Montgomery tipped his hat.

"What agency do you Special Agent for?"

"One of the big ones," replied Montgomery.

"Back to the alien invasion, Professor Sherman," pressed Collins.

"Shouldn't my associate Sachiko Jones be here for this discussion?"

"I believe you're correct." Montgomery lifted his lapel to his mouth. "Please bring Ms. Jones in."

"Where is she? She left a few minutes ago."

"Turns out she didn't make it too far. She's in our van."

"You *arrested* her?"

"Professor Sherman, I'm shocked. Nothing of the kind. We had a brief discussion with her and she agreed to wait and see if you were willing to speak with us as well."

There were two raps on the door then MIB Three, a female agent similarly attired, ushered Sachiko in.

"Shaky, grab that chair and please join us."

Once she was settled, Collins said, "Back to the aliens you speculate on."

"Did you read our press release? It's all in there."

"We doubt that very much, Colonel," responded Montgomery. "We read your last ten journal articles. Ms. Jones's, too. We find much missing."

"You're shittin' me. You two Neanderthals read journal articles. They're full of big words and long equations," Tank scoffed.

"Ph.D. in Applied Physics, Harvard," Collins said, raising his arm. He swung his finger to Montgomery. "Theoretical physics, Oxford."

Montgomery gave Tank a two-fingered salute. "Class of oh-four."

"What's the name of the main undergrad school for physics there?"

Without missing a beat, he shot back, "Mansfield College, old boy."

"Okay, you pass."

"Back to the alien invasion, Colonel."

Tank started to respond, but Sachiko laid a hand over his. "You're a colonel?"

"Professor Sherman is still in the reserves. He's a colonel," interjected Montgomery.

"I didn't know that," she responded, rather stunned.

He sipped his coffee. "Sort of a hobby at this point. Gets me out of Daisy's hair one weekend a month and two weeks a year. She's a big fan."

"Now please, I must insist. Back to the alien invasion, Colonel Sherman," said Collins.

"I'll spill the beans if you stop calling me 'colonel.' Deal?"

"No problem, *Professor*." Collins appeared to be the default responder and was likely in charge.

Tank sighed. "We've observed what we are fairly certain to be artificial changes in several local galaxies. Then we realized the same changes, namely the disappearance of the central singularity in our own galaxy, had occurred. Since these cannot be the result of random natural processes, we are forced to the conclusion an advanced alien race must be causing them."

"And how certain are you?"

"Quite."

"And do you posit these aliens pose an imminent threat to the Earth?"

"We believe they do," replied Sachiko

"You both know it is common knowledge that the Milky Way has never had a supermassive black hole at its center," Collins said.

"It did up until last week," responded Tank.

"And, as we speak, the aliens are tunneling toward us at seven times the speed of light," Sachiko added flatly.

The agents exchanged looks of concern.

"That's impossible," Collins said.

"It's not impossible, if someone's doing it," Tank said with a smile.

"Professor Sherman, you teach a course in general relativity."

"I know. But they could use an Alcubierre drive. Maybe they can fold in and out of real space. Who knows? All we can say is that they are."

"Those methods would require more energy than it is possible to control."

"For you and me, maybe. We're just saying that's how fast they move —hence, it's not impossible," responded Sachiko.

"We heard what you announced at your press conference and what your notes at the university reveal. But, how can you possibly know that there is an alien spacecraft heading toward Earth?"

Tank shot Sachiko a nervous glance. "Ah, with the aid of detailed radio astronomy." He winced; that sounded too much like a question, not a statement.

"We've been actively looking for you two," said Collins. "If you were somewhere you could access any of the big radio facilities, we would have known about it."

"What can I say?" Tank shrugged. "We worked off our laptops at a Starbucks and got lucky."

Collins stood. "You're scheduled to present this information to the President of the United States, his full Cabinet, and the Joint Chiefs in four hours."

Tank looked at his watch. "No way we can make DC in four hours. We haven't packed and we don't know the flight schedules."

"Your suitcases are packed and in our limo. Our Gulfstream 650 is fueled and ready three miles from here. The chopper is waiting at Andrews to shuttle you to the White House. You'll be on time."

Tank turned to Daisy. "You packed me a suitcase?"

She shook her head dumbly.

"I did," responded Montgomery, "while the missus watered the back garden." He nodded to the female agent. "Agent Sandoval did so for Ms. Jones."

"Well, I'll be damned," Tank announced to no one in particular.

"We certainly hope not," intoned Collins.

They were actually early to meet the POTUS. That gave Tank an opportunity to yell and browbeat some other people about the invasion of his privacy and loss of constitutional rights at the hands of Big Brother. That was good. Collins and Montgomery were tired of his rant by the time they all got there. They were glad to pass that abuse off to someone else.

Sachiko was completely impressed. Tank was fearless. Of course, it helped that he was right. Did he ever form new anal orifices for all comers on that short trip. Well, all up until they entered the Situation Room. There, Tank became instantly reverential. Who wouldn't? A long, cramped room full of high-rollers, the POTUS seated at the head of the table, frowning. Imposing.

"Dr. Sherman, Ms. Jones, I'd like to thank you for coming upon such short notice. Your country appreciates this very much," he said with a bit of a Southern drawl.

"Our pleasure, President Payette. I just hope we can be helpful." Tank was one hell of a lot calmer and more collected than Sachiko was. She kept confirming which way it was to the restroom.

"This situation you have brought to light is most worrisome. I'm sure your guidance will be the key to our success. I think it best to let you know what we know. You've met Special Agents Collins and Montgomery. They briefed us yesterday on your findings. I think we all have a firm grasp on the general idea. We will want to press you on some details of timing and response."

"Certainly, Mr. President."

"First off—" Payette began.

"First, I'd like to say this is all an insulting and traitorous hoax," interjected a new voice.

Wow. Okay, the president's National Security Advisor just interrupted the president to accuse Colonel Tank Sherman of being a traitor. What followed promised to be electrified.

"Now, Hugh, let's not begin with a challenge," soothed Payette. "Let's hear what they have to say, and then decide."

"Frank, this is horse shit and everyone knows it," responded Hugh. "Things we know to be true aren't and magical hobgoblins are drinking time with big straws? Really. This wouldn't even make a lousy science fiction novel. What was that comedy routine team in the 1970s used to say? 'Everything you know is wrong.' Bah! These lunatics are worse than that Weird Al Yankovic."

"I'm sorry you feel that way, Hugh," said Tank. "A couple points of order," he turned to the POTUS, "if it's okay with you, sir?"

Payette extended a hand, signaling him to proceed.

"Thank you, sir. First, Hugh, you're referring to Firesign Theatre's eighth album, not Weird Al. Second, I think that your harsh assessment might have something to do with the fact that you've always been a jackass and a moron."

Hugh made to rise, but didn't.

"Finally, and I am loath to speak thusly in front of my CIC, but, if you ever call me a traitor again I *will* kill you. I will do so in a most disagreeable manner. Any questions, criticisms, or comments?"

The room fell absolutely silent.

"In case some of you don't know, Dr. Sherman and I served in the Marines together, back in the day," seethed Hugh Quinn.

"I served. You only ever screwed the pooch."

"Gentleman," interrupted the chief of staff, "I don't think we're heading in a useful direction. Can we please keep this civil and moving forward? The president's a very busy man."

"True, but I sure find this refreshing," the POTUS chortled, wearing a big smile. "Ah, I think we still have boxing gloves around from the Kennedy years, if you two need to resolve your issues."

"That won't be necessary, Mr. President. I'll play nice," replied Tank. "As to Hugh's choice of denialism as opposed to listening to scientific evidence, I don't know what to tell you. He's like the Climate Change denier idiots who nearly got us all killed. And before you say anything, Hughless, I'm not being personal here, just illustrative."

"Who's Hughless?" asked the president.

"Oh, sorry, that slipped out. That's what we all called Hugh behind his back, 'cause it rhymes with clueless."

The president snorted. "I'm going to stick that in my back pocket. Anyway, here's the real issue. If you are right, and I believe you, what can we do about the threat?"

Tank looked to Sachiko.

"Ah, that's a very different issue, Mr. President," she said, but only barely above a whisper, due to her bad case of nerves. "We're astronomers, not weapons developers."

"We realize that," said the Army Joint Chief. "But we also know you've thought about this existential threat longer than anyone, save Dr. Sherman himself."

Tank shot her a guilty glance.

"I can only say this," she began slowly. "We've always assumed there were other sentient life forms in the universe. Now we have proof one is out there. If there are two—us and them—then there are surely countless others. Using the law of averages, some are the most technically advanced in the universe while others are the least."

"Your point, Ms. Jones?" pressed the president.

"Everywhere we look we see cored-out galaxies. Most, but not all, large clusters of galaxies have been decimated by this alien force. This leads me to conclude that even the most advanced civilizations have confronted them but were ultimately ineffective at stopping them." She paused, letting that sobering thought sink in a bit.

"Frank, I've had enough," Hugh said, standing. The fool was shaking he was so mad. "A couple galaxies a *zillion* miles away have holes in them, so now we have an unstoppable war juggernaut coming to kill us? These Left Coast hoax-boasters are clearly smoking what they're famous for smoking, night and day. I'll be in my office for the next twenty minutes, typing up my resignation. If you don't leave this monkey show here and come dissuade me before the twenty minutes are up, you'll find it on your desk."

With that, he stomped out of the Situation Room. In what had to be divine intervention, he tripped on a chair leg as he was passing and landed on his knees. The rest of his stomping out the door was performed with a nasty limp.

After a moment, President Payette pointed to the open, empty doorway. "Hughless, eh?"

That brought down the house.

Back to serious instantaneously, the POTUS scanned the room. "John... John Marshall, where are you?"

A somber-looking man in his late thirties stood quickly. "Here, Mr. President."

"Ah, good. John, I need a new NSA chief. Well, twenty-one minutes from now, I will. You're it. I do not wish to waste time going through the normal process. You're Hughless's second. How about it?"

"It would be my honor, sir."

"Duly noted. The next order of business—our only business from here on out—will be to defend our planet from a known alien threat."

The room was silent. No one even breathed.

CHAPTER EIGHTEEN

Over the next week, Tank and Sachiko worked long hours on various major radio telescope arrays across the planet. They did so to be able to document what they already knew from firsthand observation: that, of the dozen clan ships tunneling through the galaxy, one was headed almost exactly toward Earth. They spoke with Jon Ryan a few times, to touch base and get specific updates. The Als were able to help them focus on what needed to be documented on the radio images, to make their presentations to the president fully credible.

Collins and Montgomery were the scientists' constant shadows. Teams of MIBs were assigned to all their work facilities and homes. Tank and Sachiko were going to be safe and uninterrupted while they labored, whether they liked it or not. Late one evening, Sachiko was going over their findings with Collins.

"You see here..." She paused to yawn. "This void streak, which was heading away from us, made a minor course change a few weeks back. Then it resumed along its original direction."

Collins studied the numbers. "Okay, I can buy that. So, you're able to get nearly realtime images of their progress?"

She nodded, while yawning even bigger than before.

"I'm still bothered by the part where the speed of light limits these observations," breathed Collins impatiently. "If something changed a million light years away—if it just happened—it should take a million years for that information to arrive here, right?"

"I was caught on the rock, too, for a while. The twist is this. The light, containing the changed state of the stars and reaching us from a million miles away, *did* leave there a million years ago. Once these aliens suck the time out of a locus in space-time, then it will have always been like that. Then, when they change something else, ten minutes later, that's the way it's always been."

"So, we see really old, really new information instantly?"

"Something like that. If that were not the case, we'd never have picked up on these changes."

"And this one, the one headed roughly toward us, how long until it reaches us based on your findings?"

"Soon. I can be more certain in a day, maybe three."

"Make it one, please." He looked up to her with lines of concern on his face. "We seem to be running out of time."

The next morning, Tank was propped with one leg on the edge of his deck going over some data with Sachiko, who was seated across from him. It had been another all-nighter. Perhaps it was because of their focus, or their sleep deprivation, that they didn't notice Collins and Montgomery enter the room. They looked up, simultaneously surprised.

"Good morning," Collins beamed, a paper cup in either hand. "I must say, you both look like shit."

"Thanks, I'm sure," responded Sachiko.

"Nice of you to bring coffee," said Tank.

He held them up. "I figured they'd tide you over until we get to the plane. Helicopters don't normally serve coffee."

"What, no limo this time?" Tank teased.

"Time is of the essence," he grinned.

"Let me guess. My bags are packed and in the chopper?"

"They most assuredly are. Right in the middle of the quad."

"Do I have time to pee?" asked a nervous-looking Sachiko.

"We'll be on the plane in ten. Can it wait?" asked Collins.

"Sure. Why not?"

"Before we take off, I want to discuss bringing some... additional coworkers with us." Tank took a sip of coffee and tried to look unconcerned.

Collins shot up an eyebrow. "Who and why?"

"Er... you don't know them, but they're the top specialists in this field."

"I know everybody either of you know or ever have known. And, what field are they tops in?"

"This," Tank circled a hand toward the floor, "current field."

Collins sighed. "Do you know why I dislike my birthday, Professor Sherman?"

He didn't see that coming. "You don't like getting older?"

"I hate surprises. Birthday celebrations are synonymous with surprise. Who are these new surprises you wish to place in the Situation Room, right beside the president of the United States?"

"Jon and Sapale Ryan."

Collins frowned; he was thinking. "I do not know even one physicist named Ryan who is associated with this project *or* this university."

"They're more like our consultants."

"Birthdays, Professor Sherman. Keep always in mind my feelings about birthdays."

"Yes, I understand that. But this is important. If it weren't I wouldn't insist, now would I?"

"So now you're making a demand?"

He looked to Sachiko for support.

"No, not a demand," she said. "Look, everybody in this room wants Earth to survive this existential threat, right?"

"Of course."

"If Jon and Sapale are in, we stand a whole lot better chance. It triples, at the very least."

"Triples?" the agent repeated, incredulously.

"Maybe more," added Sachiko.

"Professor Sherman, what kind of name is Sapale?"

He looked to Sachiko again. "Uh, foreign?"

"Our plane leaves in ten minutes. How do you propose to have them make it? I can tell you with absolute confidence that it *will* take off in ten minutes and we all shall be onboard."

"Funny thing is, they live in downtown DC. Small world, isn't it?"

"How remarkable. Did I mention I'm allergic to funny things, also?"

"No," Tank replied, "but I'm not the least bit surprised." He followed that with a toothy grin.

Once the jet was airborne, Tank took off his seatbelt and plopped next to Sachiko. "Did they tell you what's up?"

"No, not specifically. But I did go over the new data with Collins late last night. I finally got him to understand the instant time change thing."

"Apparently so," he grumbled.

"Apparently so."

"Did you get a chance to call Jon?" he asked.

"Yup, when I took a potty break."

"And they can make it?"

She gave Tank an oh-come-on-now look.

"How are they getting through security?" he wondered.

"Do you remember what Al said about being a great counterfeiter?"

"I thought that was just another of his lame jokes."

"Maybe it was, but Jon said their IDs will be more authentic than everyone else's," she responded with a knowing grin.

He chuckled.

"What?"

"Maybe they're printed on Doctor Who's psychic paper." He copied her grin.

"I wouldn't put it past him," she replied. She then crossed her arms and shut her eyes.

They didn't talk the rest of the flight. Sachiko tried to not fall apart completely the entire way. Tank either tried to sleep or was lost in his own personal nightmares. Somewhere along the way, she finally fell fast asleep. That was a blessing. Tank woke her to transfer to the helicopter.

In no time they were back in the Situation Room. This time it was literally packed full. Behind those seated stood two rows of onlookers. Sachiko recognized a few senators and religious leaders. A lot of those present wore a uniform, and all of those were heavy with ribbons, stars, and aiguillettes. Four seats close to President Payette were still open. Collins led them directly to two of the only available seats, then took up a position standing directly behind them.

"Alright, everybody, I'd like to begin. Er, Colonel Sherman, where are your associates? I really—" POTUS stopped talking when there was an explosion of noise just outside the entrance.

Jon Ryan, wearing an academic's tweed suit with elbow patches and all, smiled exuberantly from the doorway. He even wore coke-bottle glasses. He preceded Sapale. Well, it must have been Sapale. It was, however, impossible to tell. She sported a full, dark gray, burqa. Oh yeah, she turned all the heads with that get-up.

Collins growled, "What the hell?"

Jon spied where his friends were sitting. He threw his arms in the air. "Tank, you old son of a gun, there you are!"

Collins pushed his way to the entry. He stood face-to-face with the veiled figure. "I'm afraid I'm going to need to see some ID, ma'am."

"No problem, nice young man," she chimed. From under all that cloth, she produced a folded document.

Collins's eyes bulged. The photo ID showed someone wearing—you got it—a full, dark gray burqa.

"This," he shook it in front of her, "is never going to do. I need that headdress off and I need a positive ID, *now*."

Jon eased between the two bodies, smiling like a traveling salesman. "Now," he shot a peek at Collins's badge, "Agent Collins. Do you suppose we'd have made it this far into the White House if my associate hadn't been able to satisfy any number of security professionals like yourself? Come, now. Let the meeting begin," he concluded with great flare. Jon held up his temporary ID, issued by security upon entering a sensitive area.

"Dr. Ryan, I do not have to think about who may or may not have screened this woman. That's the joy of being a mindless drone," menaced Collins.

Jon drew his hand through the air separating their heads. "You don't need to see her identification. She's not the droid you're searching for. She can go about her business. Move along." He waggled his eyebrows.

"Dr. Ryan. You say anything like that, again, and I *will* shoot you," the agent stated with confidence.

"I think not but, seriously, thanks for the offer. It seems nowadays nobody cares enough about their fellow man to volunteer to kill someone. Color me lucky for having known you."

"*Collins*," shouted the president. "I need to get started. Let them in. Honestly, what? Do you think they used a Tardis to materialize in the next room? If they got this far, they're good to go."

Collins stared intently into Jon's eye. "Yes, sir." He stepped aside to let them pass.

Jon and Sapale sat in the last two open spots.

"We will begin." The president's words silenced the room instantly. "Most of you know a snippet or two about the present situation. Few of you, however, know just how bad matters really are." He sighed. "I may not even know everything there is to know. What you are about to see and hear is not to be discussed outside this room." He leaned over and signed a long memorandum. "I have just declared martial law."

The gasps were deafening.

"It will likely never be lifted. As a result, please note that if anyone breaches the security I have just ordered, they will be summarily executed."

Not a peep was heard.

"I will ask Dr. Sherman to give us a brief but full summary of what he's discovered. Dr. Sherman." Payette sat back down.

"Over the last few months, Dr. Jones," he gestured to Sachiko, "and I have become convinced our planet is at significant risk of alien attack."

That brought howls and protestations.

Sachiko eyed Tank, curiously. She was a *doctor* all of a sudden? Up until then, she thought she had been working on her Ph.D., *hoping* to be Dr. Jones someday.

"Silence!" roared Payette. "The person that starts the next uproar will be shot. Collins?"

The agent nodded back.

"Unholster your weapon."

Collins whipped out an IMI Desert Eagle and rested it by his shoulder, pointing upward. It was a frighteningly powerful handgun.

"Continue," he said.

Tank cleared his throat, eyed the gun, and went on. "We believe an alien race is systematically destroying large sections of our galaxy as we speak. They have significantly damaged many nearby galaxies already. Dr. Jones conjectures that this hostile race must have defeated any and all opposition they're certain to have encountered. We are, if this is true, basically helpless and defenseless. I recently confirmed with a colleague," he nodded to Jon Ryan, "that possibly two expeditionary forces of this alien race are headed toward Earth. In all, that's probably six or seven ships each working as one unit. Based on our best estimates, they will arrive in two months. That's it in a nutshell." He sat down.

"Two *months*?" said Payette. "That's news to me. Are you certain of that timeline?"

Tank shrugged. "Give or take a couple weeks. We'll know better in a day or two."

Payette shook his arms in the air energetically. "Okay, people, you know what the next question is. What can we do in self-defense? And, for the love of all that is holy, no one better respond 'we'll need to form a task force.' If you do, Collins'll drop you like a wet towel. I kid you not. General Masterson, what've you got?"

The head of the Joint Chiefs, Darlene Masterson, stood. "We have a vast number of nuclear missiles, both land-based and at sea. Most can be easily reprogrammed to fire into space, but they are currently incapable of leaving Earth's orbit completely as they are. I'm certain any other country with similar weapons would do the same. What we want to do is to launch them into space, refuel them there, and then fire them at our enemy."

"Do we presently have that technology?" Payette asked bluntly.

She lowered her head. "No, Mr. President, we do not." She looked back up. "I can promise that my people and I will not rest after I leave this meeting. We will make it happen."

"I believe you will, General. I believe you will," stated the president, with proud confidence.

"We could then launch maybe ten thousand projectiles capable of striking a target in space. Other players could add perhaps another thousand, or so. Counting MIRVs, I'd estimate we could, if all the ducks line up in our favor, throw hopefully fifteen thousand missiles at them."

"Save yourself the trouble." It was Jon speaking.

"I beg your pardon, Dr. Ryan," the general said sarcastically. "Please explain to me what a civilian would know about any such matter."

"I'm kind of a weapons groupie, didn't you know?"

"I did not know," she challenged angrily.

"Look. Chill and listen, okay? Thermonuclear weapons have to be the entry-level ordnance for any advanced civilization. If they would have worked on these bozos, we wouldn't be having this conversation. Plus, in two months you *might* be able to place those warheads as far away as the Asteroid Belt. Too late. By then, they'd be right on top of us. I'm certain that if these guys get that close to us, we'll already be timeless, interplanetary debris."

"We could ask NASA to help. Maybe increase the total payload and use a massive rocket to accelerate them farther out. That would pack a walloping punch, Mr. President," responded Darlene.

"Sand kicked in their faces at the beach at best," scoffed Jon.

"Do you have any suggestions?" Darlene menaced, growing frustrated.

"No."

"Then I will consider your objections in that light."

"What about lasers?" asked a cabinet secretary. "Don't we have big space lasers now?"

An older woman in a white coat stood. "No. We have some powerful pulse lasers on the ground. They could probably be lifted into orbit in the two-month time frame. But they're quite fragile and have never been used as offensive weapons."

"You got maybe a megawatt unit or two?" posed Jon. "Chicken feed. And, I say again, that is just another of the basic tools any scientifically savvy society would have. I am certain that exact defense has been tried and it has failed, probably a million times."

"Would it hurt to try? Doing nothing and dying is not a very heroic course of action," Payette responded.

"Obviously, no. But it would be a tremendous waste of resources. We have little time. If we put our eggs in any one wrong basket, none of them will hatch."

"What else could we put in low Earth orbit, thereby *not* wasting our precious resources?" the white-coated woman asked.

"Small volume linear accelerators."

All eye turned to Sachiko. She had whispered the words.

"Shaky, what would we do with low-end accelerators? The particles they'd shoot at our enemy would be like blowing them a kiss," puzzled Tank.

"I'm not thinking of accelerating particles, Tank."

"Dr. Jones, please just say what it is you're thinking," instructed Payette. "Few of us are experts and none of us have time to spare."

"We've been able to produce punctate black holes in the lab for over fifty years. We can keep them stable indefinitely."

"Dr. Jones, are you hearing yourself?" spat Darlene. "You told us they *eat* gigantic black holes. Little ones would be like serving them appetizers."

"I'm going to have to side with the wicked witch on this one, Sachiko," Jon added with a playful tone.

"No, I'm not proposing we launch tiny black holes at them. I'm thinking we fire tiny *worm* holes at them." She had to grin—she was so proud of herself.

"Why would that matter?" Jon asked. "For one thing, it would be as hard to make them stable as it would be to find a virgin in a whorehouse."

That got a few snickers.

"No, wait," said Collins. "I get it. Hot damn, Jones, that's well beyond brilliant." He holstered his pistol and wove his way through the crowd to get to her. He held out his hand to shake. "I want to shake the hand of the most brilliant mind I've ever encountered, ma'am." He bowed his head.

"Aw, now this is just plain depressing. What's this gorilla here getting that I'm not? This is intolerable," whined Jon.

Tank nodded in full sympathy.

"Don't you see?" said Collins. "These devils eat time—positive time. Wormholes generate negative time. We'd be throwing antimatter at matter."

Tank looked at Sachiko like he'd just discovered a new type of pizza. "Damn, kiddo, you're good. They'll have to give you two Nobels for that one. It'll go right to your head, too. There'll be no living with you."

"Okay, the self-congratulatory phase of the meeting is over. Please explain what you just said, Dr. Jones," implored Payette.

"If two black holes are placed just so they can form what we call a wormhole. They have been documented in labs before, but they're unstable and short-lived. The physics behind how they act is scary. But, suffice it to say, they can result in what we call negative time. I think that could be a devastating weapon to use on the evil Doozers. They might just explode with any contact."

"What's an evil doozer?" asked the POTUS.

"Don't you remember the Doozers, sir? Doozer is as doozer does? *Fraggle Rock*?"

"Clearly I do not," he replied, tersely.

"They were busy little SOBs, Frank. Always working and working," clarified Jon.

Sachiko gasped out loud. Jon had just called his CIC by his *first* name.

"Ah. And can we get these accelerators and black holes in space fast enough?"

"I think so," she replied.

"Thinking's not good enough, Dr. Jones. I must have results."

"We will do it," proclaimed Darlene. "So help me, it will be done."

"I hate to rain on this lovefest," said Jon, "but those damn things are going to be so unstable."

"Well, we have a month and a half to figure out how to change that inconvenient aspect of quantum physics, don't we?" responded Tank.

The president stood. "Two final matters." He turned to Darlene. "General Masterson, please see that Sherman gets a set of four stars for his uniform. *General* Collins, she'll bring you a set of four, as well. I suggest you wear that appropriate uniform for the duration. It opens doors quickly, and quickly is what we sorely need."

Tank saluted the president. "Yes, sir. Thank you, sir."

Collins did likewise.

"Finally," he addressed his chief of staff, Rita Davidson, "Call the chancellor at *Dr.* Jones's school—I noticed Tank slipped that one in like the sneaky bastard he is. Let's make her doctoral degree official. And let's get her a full professor spot there, too. Only the top people work for me. And Rita." he angled a finger at her. "If whoever you talk to has the slightest reservation, hand the phone to me. You got that?"

"Yes, Mr. President."

The room cleared. Tank, Collins, Jon, Sapale, and Sachiko were the last ones present.

"That was intense," declared Sachiko.

"You ain't seen nothing yet, kiddo," Tank teased. "This is going to get so intense we'll need to wear fireproof underwear." He turned to Collins. "I want to make this point clear. The POTUS gave *me* the campaign promotion before he gave you yours. You got that?"

"Oh, so I suppose you're going to lord it over me, now that you outrank me?"

"Damn skippy, *Marvin.* Don't ever forget it."

Sachiko was fairly certain Tank was playing around. He had to be, right? They were all on the same team, facing almost certain death, and... wait. It had to be a guy thing. She *hated* guy things.

"General Sherman, with all due respect, if you ever refer to me by my first name again, badness will befall you. Not a threat, a promise. In practice, if you feel the need to address me casually, I go by my middle name, *Jon*."

Tank gave him a crooked grin. "You got it Marvjon."

Fortunately, Sachiko was able to drag Tank away before fisticuffs broke out.

Oh, how she hated those guy things!

CHAPTER NINETEEN

The mobilization effort was impressive. It far exceeded my expectations, even more focused and intensive than the one I would witness in a few years, when Jupiter threatened Earth.

Two separate sites were designated as ground-zeros for the research and production of the accelerators and the work to stabilize the wormholes—CERN in Switzerland and Stanford in California. Anyone who was anyone in any related field went to one of those two places immediately. If someone chosen showed the slightest reservations or, God forbid, declined they were basically lifted off their feet by MIBs and taken to the campus farthest from their location. Lesson being: Play nice and you get to work nearer to home. Be uncooperative, you get a worse commute. Either way, participation was not your choice, but the government's.

Each of the world's governments decided that there was no room for selfishness in saving humankind. I know. Sounds too good to be true, but even enemies of a thousand generations fell in line and marched to the collective beat. If some sovereign nation chose not to participate at a maximum level, UN-coordinated troops very quickly helped them see and correct the error of their ways. As harsh as that was, I agreed with the policy. We were facing a no-joke dire situation. Failure and extinction were basically guaranteed. In fact, even if our crazy plans worked better than we could dream they would, we were probably goners already. Everybody needed to grab an oar and row. Everybody was going to grab an oar and row right now.

Within three days, the areas around the two centers were transformed into major tent cities. Mobile hospitals, temporary housing, massive latrine assemblies, and mess tents appeared as if by magic. Fences went up and guards prowled the perimeters on both sides of the barriers. Warehouses sprang up like weeds and were immediately jammed full of every conceivable technical tool and material. Cost was not an issue. It was like trucks backed up to any unoccupied space and dumped piles of money. If someone even *thought* you might need something, you got three of them before the ink was dry on your request.

As the high-level players arrived, they were assigned to pods. Generally, each pod had three to five senior scientists, five to ten engineers, a hundred technicians, and countless support personnel. The pods each received specific assignments and went right to work. General Sherman—whose head didn't swell, as I imagined it might have—organized the entire project in both venues. His favorite part was that he didn't have to give the effort a stupid name. He said it was the project and that was the end of the story. Of course, it very quickly became known as The Project, because there was no stopping human nature. He was as excited as a bridegroom that he didn't have to report to anyone. He had "people" to keep heads of state apprised as to The Project's progress. After a lifetime in academics and the military, for him that was better than three desserts a night.

Also, everything that could make low Earth orbit was prepped or sent off with the supplies anticipated. The four large permanent space labs already up there became the centers in space for the linear accelerator preparation. But they were way too small to accommodate the volume of resources required. So hundreds of capsules were put in orbit and cobbled together as work and housing spaces. The assembly of the linear accelerators themselves began at several locations on the ground. They also had the most frantic pace of any arm of the project. Money, materials, and people, people, people were set to work like a 4X-forward on a video.

I wasn't sure all the efforts, herculean as they were, would bear fruit. Firing stable wormholes into the path of the Edoozers was still a pipe dream, in my opinion. Oh, yeah, that name stuck immediately. Whatever that mighty alien race called itself, to us they were Evil-Doozers, or simply *Edoozers*. There was a short-lived attempt to call them EDs, but erectile dysfunction already owned that abbreviation. Many a reporter got laughs—not the quiet respect they anticipated—when they said something along the lines of "ED is the worst thing that has ever happen to man." Really? Ever try having a period? How about childbirth? Yeah, Edoozers it was.

Since I knew one hell of a lot more about everything scientific than the time locals, I passed Tank and Sachiko many a spoiler alert as to how to fabricate and stabilize the final products. While it was possible that they could have completed the enormous task themselves, I wasn't ready to bet humankind's future on it. I tipped the scales in our direction, when and where it was needed.

It was maybe three or four days after that meeting in the Situation Room that the public was told what was happening. To my very great surprise it took two full days for civil unrest to boil over and for massive riots to begin. If the apocalypse was coming, a goodly portion of humankind was going to damn sure act badly. I was so disappointed in my species. I mean, if you're *sure* we're all going to die, why do you need a bigger-screened TV? If we're all doomed, why kill strangers in the streets? They'll be dead anyway, real soon without some yahoo's help. At least enough of the civil defense complex remained together to ensure some stability. In the areas surrounding the key research and manufacturing sections, there were so many troops that no riotous horde was going to get within miles of an important outpost.

Tank, Sachiko, Sapale, and I settled in at Stanford. As time went on, my wife complained more and more bitterly about the burqa. Though I understood her frustration, if anyone got a look at her, we were in trouble. Once an *alien* was discovered among us... yeah, that'd be problematic. So, Dr. Sadozi wore her outfit twenty-four seven, because she was just that devoted to her cultural norms.

There was a 7:00 a.m. teleconference with all pod leaders daily. After that, most groups worked without breaks until they fell asleep at their workstations. And they only woke up because it was time for the next 7:00 a.m. meeting. Wash, rinse, repeat. Ten days into the project, Tank scheduled a morning meeting with all the pod leaders. He did so face-to-face for the hundred or so at Stanford, and Zoomed it with a similar number at CERN immediately afterwards. For a man allergic to meetings, he not only didn't die, he quickly became a master bureaucrat. I'd never tell him, of course. He'd have every right to kill me badly if I did.

"Morning, folks. I have the final estimates for the arrival time of the void tunnel headed toward us. We have thirty-eight days remaining to our collective lives."

He paused to let the finality of that curse settle in.

"What's the wiggle room on those numbers?" asked Janet Craig, a theoretical physicist from Cal Tech.

"Consider them gospel, Jan. I've tweaked the data to give us the most certain *shortest* time prediction. Any error will be on the long side. I want the word passed to everyone that we have no more than thirty-eight shopping days until anti-Christmas."

A few grumbles were heard. Tank's numbers were, by the way, Al's numbers. Barring a course change, they were absolutely accurate.

"AIS, how soon can we fire our first shot?"

Lenn Carlson was in charge of actually getting functioning accelerators in space, hence AIS. "We have a handful of working units up there already. In a week—"

"Stop," snapped Tank. "From now on, no weeks or months. *Days* only. We got thirty-eight. Everybody focus on that number."

"In seven days I think we'll have a couple hundred accelerators upstairs and hot. You give me stable wormholes, and I'll fire them as fast as the laws of physics will allow."

"Lenn, I expect you to have a hundred units ready in four point five days. If it's impossible, I do not care. Just do it."

Lenn's head dropped. "You got it, Tank."

"Socorro, how's it looking along those lines?"

Socorro Núñez was the head of Particle Physics at Oxford. She chose to work at Stanford because of her long friendship with Tank. "Geneva has had a couple of breakthroughs already," she said in a weary voice. "A few wormholes persisted for up to ten seconds. Locally, no such luck yet. I've handed out the basics of the Geneva progress for those interested to review."

"I need the magic to be easily reproducible, Soco. When will I have truly stable ones?"

"Who can say?"

"Ah, that would be you, princess," he shot back firmly.

"Personally, I feel in ten days we will either achieve our goal or prove it is unattainable."

"I can live with the first part only. Make it so. I'm going to keep saying this as long as I have to. I do *not* care if it can't be done. Make it happen." He turned to a small group seated together. "Logistics?"

"We have way too much of everything," whined Grayson Chambers, an Army major general. "I even jokingly asked for Beluga caviar in five kilo cans. Those're around twenty-five thousand bucks each. Seriously, I was punchy and it must have seemed funny at the time. Ten cans were on my desk in ninety minutes. By the way, I don't know what the *hell* to do with fifty kilograms of caviar. Anybody interested, see me."

"Dang, Grayson, you really messed up," Tank said in a low tone. He let the words hang a few seconds. "You forgot to request a thousand mother-of-pearl spoons and half a ton of blini."

Laughs all around. It was nice. No one laughed much, anymore.

"Okay, I guess that's it for now, unless anyone's got something," stated Tank. "If not—"

"What if we rotate them while they spin?" I said as soon as the merriment died down.

"You want to spin those cans of fish eggs, Jon?" Tank teased.

"No." I held up the Geneva summary papers. "What if after we form quasi-stable wormholes, we rotate them? Look, when they're formed, they're spinning. Some are twirling slowly, some at near the speed of light, and they're all in random orientations. That has to contribute greatly to their instability. But, if we got the individual wormholes to rotate along their semi-major axes, that may stabilize the configuration."

No, I am not a brilliant scientist and I could not take credit for the discovery. It was common knowledge where I came from. It was called The Jones Effect, in fact. Yeah, Sachiko Jones discovered it herself, about ten years from now normal time. But if I added that factoid, I imagined there would be embarrassing questions to answer.

Tank twisted his mouth. "Let me ponder that a moment." A few seconds later he said, "Soco, what do you think?"

She was already writing equations frantically on the back of a handout. "Just a moment." She held up a finger.

"Take all the—"

"*Yes*. It... I think that will help tremendously. Thank you, Dr. Ryan. That's brilliant, yet simple. We might also tumble the pair, along with rotating it." She squeezed her chin. "That might further constrain the degrees of freedom in a stabilizing manner." She scribbled a few more lines. "With a couple sets of superconducting magnets, it should be doable." Socorro looked over to Tank. "I have to go." With that she turned and jogged out the door. No mean feat when wearing three-inch heels.

"Okay, everyone back to work," Tank said, with a slap of his hands. He gently grabbed my arm to have me stay. To Sapale and Sachiko he instructed, "Come here."

They stepped over to us.

"Group hug, people." We wrapped in a bear hug. "We did good."

Two days later at the "seven A M-er," as we called it, Socorro detailed the influence of the stabilizing interventions. High-speed rotation, achieved with large magnetic fields, really did the trick. She said ten wormholes generated the previous day at noon were still humming along in this plane of reality. She reported that the groups in charge of generating the stable micro-black holes had several thousand presently ready to pair into wormholes. One of the pods of theoreticians calculated that the addition of the rotations would likely stabilize the wormholes for up to six or seven weeks. In reality, they would remain stable much longer, but I kept that to myself. Even that time period was more than long enough for our purposes. We only had thirty-six more days to worry about.

"Here's the plan. Soco, get as many of the stable wormholes as you can to Lenn, ASAP. Lenn, make them ready to fire, but be discrete. Definitely make sure we can launch them. Do a few test fires, but exclusively in the opposite direction the enemy is approaching from. You all clear on that?"

"You're the boss," replied Lenn. "But why can't I shoot at the bastards as soon as they're ready?"

"Military strategy, chum," I shot back. "If these damn things *do* work, we don't want to give the Edoozers a chance to alter course or develop a countermeasure, now do we? We'll commence firing only when we have an overwhelming number ready to go." I looked down, thinking. "Lenn, in seven days, how many accelerators will be fully operational?"

"I can guarantee fifty. With luck, a hundred."

"How fast can we reload and fire?"

Lenn got a deer-in-the-headlights look on his face. "Ah, would I be in trouble if I said no clue?"

"That's why we meet, my friend. Get me those numbers, yesterday," Tank said with understanding.

"You got it."

For the first time in a long time, I felt a slim ray of hope. It was more than welcome. But, this not being my first rodeo, I know how badly the project could founder at any of multiple points. We had only thirty-six days left to us to try to survive.

Ten days later—or what by then was called T-26 for *termination minus 26 days*—Tank was ready to pull the trigger. Two hundred linear accelerators of varying size were fully operational. Some were configured in sequence, so the micro-wormholes could be accelerated much faster. Though the total number of rounds fired would be decreased, some wormholes were now going to be traveling at almost the speed of light. The reload sequence turned out to be trivially short.

Tank decided to fire our weapons off in an expanding cone pattern. He figured that if the wormholes *did* damage the Edoozer's ships, they would, logically, fan out. With his targeting model, the enemy would continue to encounter wave after wave of wormholes, even while taking evasive action.

There was a serious gap in our attack strategy. We had absolutely no way of knowing if our enemy would be able to detect the incoming wormholes. It seemed unlikely, but they had been so successful for so long, it would be pure insanity to underestimate them. At a final planning session, one general suggested starting with salvos of wormholes around the approaching vessels, then coning down, and then expanding the pattern, like Tank intended to. Basically, he suggested that if the enemy detected the incoming, they'd still have to pass through them to escape. Tank deep-sixed that notion. If they had advanced warning, they might escape in a manner we couldn't anticipate. Our only hope of survival was if they could *not* detect our weapons. No matter what we did, if they were able to see trouble coming, we were all dead. He stuck with his initial plan.

On T-26, the two void tunnels with a handful of clan ships in each were approximately thirty billion kilometers distant. That converted to around ninety light minutes away. It would take two to three hours for a salvo to reach the target and one additional hour and a half, or so, for us to see if there had been a course change. A four-hour lag in intelligence was excruciating. But that was what Tank had to deal with. Sure, I could pop over in *Stingray* and watch the effects in real time. But Tank'd have no way of justifying how he knew the results so quickly. Plus, if this didn't work, knowing we were doomed a few minutes sooner meant nothing at all.

For those first few hours, his guesses as to targeting would have to do.

After that initial phase, Tank was going to have to wing it in terms of a firing pattern. Whatever he did, he'd have to hope that two or three hours later the enemy would still be where he'd guessed they would be. Space warfare, new to our species, turned out to be a bitch. The target you see is no longer where you see it and is usually in a spot you wouldn't have predicted. So, you can only fire at where you think they will be when the weapon arrived on scene. As we got closer to T-3, our limit to ensure planet survival, that lag would become tolerably short, so at least there was a ray of hope.

"I'm preparing to give Lenn the final order to commence firing," Tank said to those attending the teleconference. "*Now* would be the time for anyone to voice any last concerns."

"Everyone here in the Situation Room is comfortable with the plan, Tank." Even the president had started calling him by his nickname.

"Okay, Lenn, give 'em hell and a half."

"Roger that, Boss."

And so Earth's bombardment of the Edoozer's fleet began. I said a not-so-quick-prayer that this might even work. What struck me the most, however, was the nonevent of the event. I pictured blasts like in a *Star Wars* movie with plasma cannons barking and targets flying to pieces. There was no sound change. Not even the lights dimmed. I checked with Lenn later. Nothing observable happened up there, either. Pooh.

Then we waited. That was to be anticipated but it was so unwelcome. We knew, ninety minutes into our attack, that whatever damage the wormholes were going to do was occurring. All we could do past that point was wait. Tank couldn't even settle his nerves by shouting changes in firing patterns like a submarine captain in a sea battle. Lenn had preprogrammed everything. The only actions needed were for the techs to place another rack of wormholes in the accelerator and push the illuminated green button.

Six hours into our attack we knew the initial response: nothing. Radio interferometers could glean no change in tunnel direction or size.

"Mr. President, I can confirm that at this point the void tunnels continue on their earlier course," Tank said soberly, over the teleconference.

"Does that *have* to mean we did no damage?" he asked.

Tank ran a hand though his hair. "No, not necessarily. If we destroyed something, it could produce forward-debris moving in the same direction."

"No, Tank," I said. "If it was debris it wouldn't still be no-timing." I was in my usual spot, right by his side, with Sachiko beside me.

"Ah, you're probably right. It is still possible we damaged the SOBs, but I'm less and less keen on the notion as time passes."

"So, you're saying our best efforts are completely ineffective?" asked Darlene Masterson.

"Too early to tell," I answered for Tank.

"When will you know for certain?" she pressed.

"We'll know much more in a day. Until then, all we can do is continue firing and hope for the best."

"Very well. Be advised I'm strongly considering launching all our nuclear assets down that same path, very soon," the general said flatly.

Tank shrugged. "Whatever floats your boat, Dar-Dar. It won't interfere with our work, either way."

"But yours might interfere with mine. I may have to place your operations on hold," she said with steely resolve.

"For now, we stay with the plan," said Payette, with palpable fatigue. "Keep me posted, Tank. Sit Room out."

That feed went blank.

"I'm going to lay down for ten minutes," Tank announced. "You're in charge, kiddo. Wake me if anything happens."

I told her to let him sleep for six hours. Lord knew he needed it. Fortunately, I woke him with pleasant news.

"Tank," I whispered as I shook his shoulder a few hours later. "I brought you some coffee. Tank?"

He stirred, then began smacking his lips. Revolting. I would suggest some kind of support group to Daisy, if we lived that long.

"'Zit been ten minutes already?" he asked with a yawn.

"A few times over. There was nothing to announce, so we let you sleep."

"Okay, th... wait. There's something to announce now?" He went from supine to standing in a millisecond.

I smiled with affected innocence. "No, nothing, boss man."

"What? Spill the beans."

"The tunnels got bigger, then they altered course."

He grabbed my shoulders and began spinning us while hopping. "Hot damn. We got their attention."

"We got their attention. In fact, that course change?"

"Yeah?"

"It went from almost straight at us to perfectly straight at us," I said, staring into his eyes to see how he'd receive that news.

He stopped hopping and spinning. "I guess that's good news."

"I hope that's good."

"Yeah. If nothing else, pretty soon we can reach out and punch the sonsabitches."

"Or maybe use conventional weapons?"

"Oh *crap*. You're right. I better get on the phone with the dragon lady."

"And for once, she'll be happy with you. She's going to get a chance to try to kill Edoozers, up close and personal."

"I hope she does more than try. Otherwise we just switched our method of demise from automatic to manual."

CHAPTER TWENTY

Body Maker-lop was in rest mode, wishing he could dream. Waking was such bliss that it seemed wrong that rest should be necessary but so dull. The body maker was pleased, when awake, that the ship's time-energy stores were three-quarters full. That was unheard of. The best any clan ship ever achieved before was just over a fifty percent load. After assimilating the central singularity, the various clans had begun trolling the galaxy for lesser, but rich, fields to make no-time. In a month, the galaxy would be mostly transformed and the clans could make for new space. New assimilations. New joy. Joy could only be felt when awake, so that was what the body-maker preferred.

In its personal area, resting, the body maker heard a sound that had never existed before—the squawk of an alarm. Many generations ago, it was told that alarms had been installed, but none had ever spoken. Their sound was most unwelcome. The body maker grew angry with the alarm. It willed that they didn't speak. The sound made it... afraid. It had been told fear existed, but it thought those were just idle words, air-beliefs of lesser beings.

Slowly it drifted toward the control space. The alarm-speech grew louder, and more unwelcome, as it advanced.

"Mechanical maker," it said upon entering control, "what is this alarm? Why is this alarm?"

"I am now uncertain. Signal makers are saying it speaks because there is trouble. A disturbance is amongst the clan."

"What is trouble, fool?"

"Word makers tell me it means events touch us that we must not want."

"Summon a word maker. These words are void of meaning."

"I believe the trouble is that one of our clan ships is gone, and our own ship is impaired."

"Where did a clan ship go? I am not in agreement."

"It went nowhere."

"If it went nowhere it is still here, you desiccated fool."

"No, Body Maker, it went. Where it went was to nowhere. It went to oblivion."

"You are disagreed with by me. Is the clan ship not present here?"

"Yes and no. Yes parts are here, but meaning is not. The clan ship and the clan family are random now."

The body maker swelled to three times its favorite size. It struck the ceiling and huge chunks flew away. It roared like death and thought of the end time. Then it shrank back and was able to ask, "What impairment does our craft have?"

"A tunnel now exists in Engine One and part of Personal Arena POF is not attached. Clan who were there are now random."

"You speak the null set. They cannot be random. There can exist no tunnel. We make tunnels. We do not be tunneled."

"I am in agreement with you, but that makes me not in agreement with the way reality is presently configured."

"I will go to Engine One and see this tunnel."

"Body Maker, another clan ship has just gone nowhere."

"So two are not?"

"Two are not. Five are impaired. On one of five, the speech maker says randomness is visible to it in minutes. It can taste no-time where time once tasted."

"No-time or non-time?"

"In agreement. I will confirm." After no delay, it spoke again. "It says it tastes *non*-time."

"Then it will be random?"

"It is in unable-to-agree-or-disagree mode. It thinks so, yes." It continued in CYA mode, "I do not think."

"Why is nowhere and randomness being now?"

"Thought Maker-urr has spoken. It says clans that are not our clan are throwing would-be damage at us."

"Would-be damage is frequently thrown at us. It can't randomize us. That thought is unreal."

"Unreal possibly but being."

"What damage is thrown?"

"Thought maker says anti no-time is harming our substances."

"Anti no-time? That has never been. Why is it now?"

"Thought Maker spoke that was not its expert area. It said others must make those understandings."

"Which others? Are others?"

"Thought Maker says that, too, is not its expert area."

The body maker stood absolutely still for two hours. No happening like this happening had ever happened. Response was unfamiliar, not a part of it. Finally, the body maker was ready to act.

"In the period you were away, Body Maker, seven clan ships are now not. Four more are impaired. An impaired one is destined to join the other clans now in nowhere."

"If anti no-time is thrown at us, from where is it thrown? Are there other ships near, non-clan ships?"

"Not in agreement. Science Maker-jid knows the tunnels come from a planet near our forward vector."

"Does the planet speak to us?"

"Not in agreement. Only anti no-time is sent. No words. No ships."

"How many clan ships are left to me?"

"One unimpaired and two impaired."

"Is impairment being removed?"

"Yes, where possible. Some impairments will require more time to remove."

"Can I add time to the impairments from our time stores?"

"In agreement. That it would be positive help. Removal of impairment will be sooner."

"Then allow for rapid removal. How impaired is this clan ship?"

"Some so."

"Ah. Change vector. Make vector point at anti no-time casting planet. Make forward as fast as possible."

"Body Maker, do you say I should go straight as a single vector?"

"Yes. Why would non-linear be more agreeable?"

"If enough anti no-time strikes our clan ship, we could go nowhere fast."

"Ah. Make many sub-vectors. Choose as you chose. I will be away. I will speak with the thought maker who makes elusiveness."

"In agreement. Sub-vectors to avoid anti no-time and to acquire the planet we will go."

CHAPTER TWENTY-ONE

Two days later a lot was clear, and a lot more was new and unsettling.

The T-minus count was out the door. The tunnel was zigzagging, just as Tank predicted it would as soon as he heard of the course change. The speed seemed to pick up a little, but that didn't keep the ETA from being pushed several weeks later due to the longer course. The cross-sectional area of the tunnel was definitely decreased. All but the most pessimistic agreed that meant we'd taken out several ships. Sure, they could be traveling single file, but that was a stretch to imagine happening.

A change for the worse did come fairly quickly after the attack. The void tunnels stopped. Yeah, they turned off the time-eating machines. Whether that was to go faster or to enter stealth mode we couldn't know. It did mean our fire control was now blind. Given the stakes, models of where the ships might have been were created. Then, basically best-guess estimates where to target were selected. It was disheartening, but Tank felt we had resources to waste and everything to gain. Plus, it gave us all a sense that we were doing something proactive. I could have sent Sapale off with *Stingray* to provide us exact locations, but if Tank acted on that data he'd not be able to explain why he was so darn lucky.

A new twist was detected a few days after the first wormhole must have struck an Edoozer vessel. Microwave and radio telescopes began seeing patches of unexplainable absolute weirdness where the tunnels had been. I know, absolute weirdness is not a technical term, but we were baffled. It took a while, but a team from the CIA finally made a connection. The weird areas were configured like the blast clouds of an object being blow up at distance. If I might slip back into a *Star Wars* reference, it was like when a fighter was blown up during an attack run. A cloud of hot debris and fuel festooned forward and outward from a destroyed craft—that's the shape these patches had.

We concluded they must be the result of a destroyed enemy ship, but what we were actually seeing was inexplicable. It wasn't hot gas, metal, smoke, or anything we might have predicted from a spaceship exploding. If the enemy used fusion drives, we'd expect to see hot hydrogen residue. If their ships were constructed of conventional metals, we'd expect to see spectra of iron, titanium, and aluminum. But none of those were seen in significant amounts. The gallows humor had it that we needn't worry. They'd be landing soon enough, and we could generate samples to analyze locally.

The blast patterns we were receiving suggested that the targets were internally patchy—sort of like Swiss cheese, with solid and void elements. Weird. At least whatever resulted from the catastrophic failures seemed to pose no threat to Earth. Then again, not knowing what we were dealing with made that assumption a bit tenuous.

What became immediately clear was that Earth should prepare to be boarded. All the enemy vessels had not been destroyed. That meant General Masterson and her people were open for business. With defensive plans to make, we all found ourselves, once again, in the Situation Room. I was beginning to hate the place.

"Okay, I want to personally thank General Sherman, Dr. Jones, Dr. Ryan and Dr. Sadozi for joining us," began President Payette. "Thank God they were able to damage the Edoozers' attack force. The people of this planet cannot thank you enough." He gave us a half bow.

Everyone applauded loudly. Okay, I'll admit it, it was nice. Some things you never get tired of hearing.

"Once the enemy fleet is closer, and hopefully visible, General Sherman will be able to fire on the ships and might just end this conflict before the aliens reach Earth. However, we cannot assume that will be the case. So we must ready ourselves for the two potential threats. They can bombard us from space, or they can invade the planet. General Masterson, can you update us with your predictions of how the invasion might unfold and how you will respond?"

"Yes, sir. Lights." She paused and our eyes adjusted to the screen. "As you see in the first image, we have four main models. One presumes they will stop in near-Earth orbit and fire weapons at us. Next sees a bombardment followed by a landing, like D-Day at Normandy. Three is a direct landing with the enemy spreading out circularly or in spokes. Finally, they might deploy many smaller assaults and land they at widely separated locations around the planet."

"Any way to know which they'll use?"

"No, not before first contact, Mr. President. Once it is clear what their offensive capabilities are, and once they learn ours, I imagine any prior plans'd be out the window. We have to prepare for variations of these themes. To my surprise, all of the major armies of Earth are as of now willing to pitch in and work together. It's amazing. Tell people they're all about to die, and cooperation appears like flowers in spring. I've personally spoken with the military leaders of the twenty-five largest countries. Knock on wood, nationality and past grievances are all on hold. Not one country we've contacted has shown anything but an absolute commitment to coordinated self-defense."

"I'd assumed that since it's abundantly clear to our enemy that we can damage their ships, they'll spend as little time between our cross hairs as possible," observed Tank.

"I tend to agree. So, we anticipate a rapid ground assault?" asked Payette.

"I believe so," replied Tank.

"Darlene?"

"I agree with General Sherman," replied the head of the joint chiefs.

"A question, if I might," began the defense secretary. "What if our enemy is able to throw a lethal attack at us quickly from orbit?"

"Then we're off the hook for planning our defenses, on account of the fact that we're all dead," I volunteered quite seriously.

"Let's pray that will not be the case," responded the POTUS.

"If they land, they'll stay in tight formations," I stated.

"Why would you think that?" asked Darlene.

"Just a hunch. From what I've seen, I think Edoozers live in a tightly organized society. The way they travel in space and their response to our damage. I think ants and bees, not lone wolves."

"Interesting," mused Tank. "I didn't see it that way, but now that you mention it, I think that is a good insight. Thank you, Jon."

"General Masterson?" asked the president.

"I will keep that insight in mind."

I was underwhelmed. But then again, she did have all those scrambled eggs on her hat, and I didn't, at that point in my life, even own a hat any longer.

"Will you allow us to use nuclear weapons inside the atmosphere, Mr. President?" she asked pointedly.

"If possible, I'd obviously like to be consulted before you do so. But operationally, you're in command. If you feel it's necessary, then you are free to use any weapon and employ any tool," he responded.

"Understood, Mr. President. Thank you for your confidence and clarity," she concluded.

"Well, we're all very busy, so I suggest we adjourn. God's speed to you all."

As we were walking out, I spoke to Tank. "So you think one of those scenarios is how it'll go down?"

"This is war. I don't have to tell you, of all people, that's the case. One thing I know about war is that nothing happens as planned. Plans are things we do to occupy our time and impress others with our brilliance. When the shit hits the fan, the only thing you can expect is the unexpected. That is what'll happen when the bad guys get here."

"I don't feel all warm and fuzzy hearing that."

"Good. If you did, you might make a good Darlene, but that's about it."

"You're not too impressed with her, are you?"

He grunted quietly. "She's head of the joint chiefs. That means she's a sound politician. It says nothing, however, about her abilities to command our last stand. Until she proves her mettle under fire, I'll hold off on effusive praise and boundless confidence."

Thirty-seven days later, a massive radar signal entered range. It was inside the orbit of Jupiter and making for Earth at a breathtaking pace. We had maybe three days to finish our preparations. Everyone was freaked out when that was announced. Even most looters stopped looting. There were three distinct blips, representing three equal-sized ships. They appeared to be spherical, non-metallic, and not too dense. They weren't actually heading right at us. Maybe they were shooting for just the right angle and planned an orbital battle after all. We were about to find out.

As soon as we had hard targets, we let fly with the wormholes. But, as I mentioned, space warfare is a strange beast. When you shoot at a ship, you're shooting not at the ship, but where it had been minutes ago. Unless they were complete idiots, they'd be zig-zagging like a drunken sailor on a stormy sea. So, the only place *not* to aim was where you saw them. But, massive computer algorithms had been created for just that reason. They directed the actual firing.

Then, precisely what Tank predicted happened. Just after entering the orbit of Mars, two days later, the alien ships abruptly changed course. They made a beeline for Mars 1. They must have discovered our small outpost there. They were going for the easy pickings, damn them to hell.

We all gathered in the Situation Room as fast as possible. Here's what was said, leaving out the several second time lags caused by Mars's distance.

"Mr. Andare, this is President Payette speaking. Are you aware of the direction change of the Edoozer's fleet?"

"Yes, Mr. President, we are."

"And, I'm told your station and the smaller satellite ones are completely defenseless. Is that your opinion, also?"

"Yes. Unless we start throwing stones, we have nothing to defend ourselves with."

"You could fire your transport ships at them," said Darlene. "But I doubt that would have any effect."

"That was our conclusion, too. The consensus was, why bother?" he said grimly.

"You could spread out, everybody grab a rover and run," said the Navy chief.

"We might yet. But, ultimately, we'd be doomed. Our ground ships can sustain us for only a few days, maybe a week. Any assistance from Earth would take, as we all know, months to arrive. Unless we have access to our main generators and supplies, we face only a choice of *how* to die, not whether to or not."

"I'm afraid I cannot fault any of your logic," General Masterson responded somberly.

"If you can think of anything we could do that might help Earth, please let us know."

"With no proper defense, I'm afraid not. It would have been nice to get a preview of their fighting capabilities, but since you cannot test them we won't be that lucky," she dismissed, the coldhearted bitch.

Tank chimed in. "I'm thinking, Jimmy, that they'll want to get a look at a human. If they only wanted to blow you up, they could have already done that from where they are. Otherwise, you're obviously only a tiny, defenseless contingent. Why bother taking you out?"

"Yippee. Something worse than death to look forward to. I hope everything I've read about alien probings turns out to be just crazy talk," Jimmy replied with a humorless chuckle.

"More likely just one or two of you, Mr. Andare," responded Darlene. "The rest will probably be killed or ignored."

"Thanks, I think," Jimmie responded, clearly stunned by the frankness of the head of the joint chief's words.

"What?"

"So we're dead meat, but a few of us can look forward to also being butchered dead meat."

"General Masterson, I'll take it from here," said the president. "Whatever happens, Mr. Andare, I'm ordering you to do everything possible to survive. It's our job to fight these bad guys. And please know, you're all heroes to me, though it may sound like hollow consolation from where you all sit. I will see to it you each receive the Medal of Freedom, and the Medal of Honor for those military personnel stationed with you, Mr. Andare."

"Thank you, sir."

"They'll be landing in six hours," Tank stated. "Unless there's a change, we'll leave you be and contact you again in five-and-a-half hours. Okay?"

"Sure thing, Tank. Oh, and *tank* you for your support." Jimmy giggled like a little kid. "Always wanted to say that, dude."

"I hope you feel better, old friend," replied Tank.

When we reestablished contact, I saw that the Mars people had been quite busy. They had cameras on separate feeds pointing everywhere from numerous sites. Unless the Edoozers jammed their transmissions, we were going to get a good look at them and whatever happened next.

"As you can see," said Ben, the designated guide, "that ship is remaining five hundred meters up. We can't hear or feel anything. Not sure what powers her. No one sees doors or windows. No hatches have opened yet. The other ships are staying in orbit, seven kilometers up, as I'm sure you—"

The camera shook violently. "What the he— Over there. What in God's name is that?"

Ben sounded awful, scared witless. Several cameras spun and

stopped on an Edoozer. My heart basically stopped. There was a single figure rapidly walk-running toward Ben's position. How it got there and what the groundquake was about was unclear.

"We are defenseless," Ben screamed in clear panic. "Please stop and—"

The ten-meter-tall stick figure seized Ben around the chest with one of its seven arms. Blood showered toward the ground. Ben was trying to scream, but couldn't expand his lungs enough to do so.

The president vomited. Several people in the room joined him.

The Edoozer was almost impossible to describe, it was so foreign to my eyes. Aside from tall and thin, it was covered in a rock-hard scaly skin. Several arms ended in pincers, other in articulating claws or fingers. The elongated head sat on a thin neck. It had a row of what seemed to be eyes and two openings that were probably mouths. The seven arms extended randomly from the slightly triangular torso with the seven legs spidering out from a common point of origin. It did not have what I'd call wings. The projections were more like stegosaurus plates, five of them along the backside.

"He's shaking Ben," a new voice cut in from behind. "I think he's already dead."

A series of flares were fired, a few striking the alien. At the contact points, the intense flames died quickly and inexplicably. The monster seemed to not even have noticed them.

The Edoozer brought Ben's bloody remains right up to its face and studied them. Using two other arms, it pulled him apart like a young boy might with a butterfly he'd captured. Ben quickly became a stringy, gooey mess. After inspecting one piece of Ben, the creature hurled it to the ground. When it was finished with Ben, it ran staggeringly to the nearest human. Whoever that was ran, but not far. It snatched her up, but much gentler. No blood gushed out and that woman could still scream loudly in abject terror.

From off camera, a flare arced in and struck the monster on one of its legs. It kicked at it and seemed to wince from pain, but then ignored the attack. It studied its new prisoner. Then the damn thing spoke.

"Eeerard meflock meflock. Oderpanty. Agashure."

Not surprisingly the woman didn't answer back.

The Edoozer shook her violently and repeated what it had just said.

"Eeerard meflock meflock. Oderpanty. Agashure."

"I don't understand," howled the captive. "I don't understand. Please put me—"

The Edoozer tossed her away like a candy wrapper. It then stepped quickly to a nearby camera.

In a hissing, high, piercing squeal it spoke. "I yam Bodyy Maker-lop. I will knowwww who ooo sent my clan shippp to nowhere. I ammm outside of angry. Give me who impaired my clan ships."

"The damn thing speaks English," said the president in an amazed whisper.

"Quick study," Tank responded.

"And there's no time lag," I observed. "We hear it as the mouth pieces are moving."

"We can't do that, can we?" Payette asked Tank.

He shook his head. "Not by a large margin."

"What do we tell it, Mr. President?" asked the chief of staff.

"Can I speak to that thing?" he asked.

"Ah, yeah, sure," said a technician. She scrambled to make it happen. Thirty seconds later she yelled, "Your voice should come out of the camera's speakers, sir. Go ahead."

While the connection was being set up, the body maker continued crushing and then questioning more scientists. It seemed to have the order wrong. It was horrific. I finally had to turn away.

"Body Maker-lop, I am President Franklin Payette. I command the people you have just murdered. I ordered the destruction of your hostile fleet. I alone am responsible."

It dropped another corpse and approached the camera. "I hearrrr youuu but not seee yooou."

"I think it wants visual as well as audio, sir," said Tank.

"Can we do that?" he asked the tech.

"I guess I could feed you to the camera's monitor. The beasty would have to figure out it was behind the camera."

"Make it so, quickly."

After a minute, she said, "You're live, sir."

"I'm President Payette. Can you see me now?"

The Edoozer twisted its long neck but found the monitor rather quickly. "You arrre the one whoo nowhered my clan ships?"

"Yes. I am prepared to talk peace, if you are."

"Peaccce? Whatttt is peace?"

"Are you seriously asking what peace is or are you mocking me?"

"Wwwhat iz peace?"

"The absence of war. No conflict. Friend making."

"I make not war. Clans assimmilllate time. Non-clan beings matter zero. If they die, good. If they do not die, good. No war. No peace. Never friendssss."

"Then we shall fight you and destroy you."

"Who makkkke my clan ships impaired and nowhere?"

"I told you, *I'm* the one responsible."

"Youuu are nothing. Insecttt greaterrr than you. Who make anti no-timmmmme thrower?"

"What the devil is he talking about?" asked Masterson.

"Frank," said Tank, "may I speak?" He stood.

"Please do."

Tank stuck his face in front of the camera. "I made the anti no-time throwers. I made clans go nowhere. I impaired your clan ship."

"Jesus, Tank?" I shouted. "Are you sure that's wise?"

"I'm actually pretty sure it's the opposite of wise," he said with a dark chuckle.

"Who is high speakerrrr?"

"No one. I am the only one talking."

"Nooo. High voieeece speak more. Who is high voice?"

I leaned into the shot. "Me, you son of a bitch. I'm Jon Ryan and I'm your worst nightmare."

"No nightmares. No dreams. Just I am, Jonnn Rrrrryaaan. You and low voice Tank mates?"

"No."

"Buttt you and Tank nowhere my clan?"

"Yes. And the second you're airborne we'll fry your ass, assuming of course you have one," I stated.

"I have four, as you will sooooon knoow."

"What are you saying?" demanded the president.

"You I ask to go nowhere. These two, I will have and nowhere myself."

Sapale stood behind me and jumped up and down. "Don't forget about me, ass candy. I helped kill your ugly crew, too."

"These three I will have."

"You will not get them without the fight of your—"

The body maker smashed the camera with one blow. Other cameras, before they were smashed, documented the dismemberment of all the ground personnel on Mars 1.

"Well that went down the shitter pretty fast," stated Tank.

"It was how it was going to end," responded Masterson unemotionally. "The minute the Edoozers set course for Mars, they were all dead. We knew that. They knew it, too."

"Yeah, but it has sure ended awfully for the ones we saw."

"Where's their vessel now?" asked Payette.

"My monitor says it's still..." the general trailed off. "Belay that. It has disappeared."

"Something that big can't just vanish," scorned the president.

Tank jogged over to see Masterson's screen. "Though it has." The pair studied the image a few seconds. Then Tank exclaimed, "Holy crap, it's right on top of us."

The ambient light flickered in intensity and red lights glowed to life and spun. A klaxon sounded.

Two guards burst through the door. One shouted, "Mr. President, we're under attack. Come with us now." They trotted toward him. "Everyone make way."

Someone who did not heed the warning quickly enough was slammed against the wall as soldiers passed.

"I'm staying here," Payette announced.

"No can do, sir. That's against protocol and our orders." They lifted him from his chair and began carrying him out.

He stood quickly and tried to shake them off. "Very well, but I'll bloody well *walk* out of here."

They freed him. One fell in behind while the other took point and stepped quickly toward the door.

They almost made it.

As the first soldier stepped into the hallway, a huge Edoozer hand grabbed him and crushed his head and neck.

"Oh, God," gasped Payette. He backed away slowly.

Two things happened in a flash. The remaining soldier thumbed his safety off and lunged past the president. He began firing on automatic before he reached the door. The wall was shredded. He twisted into the passageway, never releasing the trigger. Once he saw the beast, he swept his barrel from side to side.

Tank sprinted to Payette's side. He literally threw the president over his shoulder and sprinted to the back of the room.

Once Masterson saw what he was doing she waved her arms in the air. "Everyone get between the door and the president. Now, now, *now*."

The guard in the hall wailed as the Edoozer cut him in half with a pincer arm.

Short bursts of rifle fire could be heard down the hall behind the enemy. I guessed three, maybe four shooters. The Edoozer sprang out of view in the direction of the bullets. Multiple screams were heard before the hall fell silent.

Slowly, like in a 1950s B-science fiction movie, the Edoozer rounded the corner on its stick legs, and entered the room. Its head swung side to side as it scanned the room. A laptop slammed against the side of its head. I turned. Tank was snatching up another.

"Ah, my Tannnk," hissed the body maker. "I have come for my Tankkkk." It stepped toward him. A second computer bounced harmlessly off its forehead. It walked almost casually. Occasionally, his feet met the floor. More often they crushed someone where they stood, frozen in fear.

Tank was about ready to launch a chair when the body maker gently but swiftly wrapped him in a claw hand and lifted him to its chest.

"Where is my high vvvvvoiiz?" It scanned the remaining crowd slowly. "Ah, there is my high voooize." It stepped around the table and came right at me.

I tried to force past those around me to get to the door, but only made a couple steps before it swooped me up. Its gasp was firm. I could barely breathe. Its claws were coarsely barbed and punctured my skin all over, but the damn thing clearly wasn't intent on killing either of us yet. It turned. Sapale was easy to identify. No one else had the full burqa. It scooped her up quickly.

"Now, wherezzz my highest voice?"

Sachiko. Somehow it knew she was part of the team that damaged the fleet. Those soulless eyes swept back and forth, searching. Someone knocked Sachiko down, and she yelped. That was enough for the body master to ID her. It snatched her from the floor.

Several MPs stumbled through the door.

"Don't shoot," yelled a commanding voice. "It has prisoners."

Tank screamed, "Fire, fire. That's a direct order. Shoot to kill."

The soldiers didn't respond. Tank's face was partly covered, and he couldn't take a deep enough breath to yell loudly. Plus, the guards were so afraid, I doubt they listened to what they were hearing.

The alien held us as steady as full glasses of water as it sprinted down the hall. I had to make a decision. I might be able to fight it, but I'd really blow my cover. Then again, my cover'd do me little good if I was killed. I shot my probe fibers from my hand around its head and pulled for all I was worth. Its head twisted, but not nearly enough to hurt the damn thing. I tried the sleep command, which only works on some species. Nothing. As a last gasp effort, I tried to entangle its thin legs so it'd fall and let go of us. No luck. The fibers didn't stick well enough to get a proper purchase. Even knowing it wouldn't work, I tried lasering the side of its head. Nothing. Ugly thing was tough.

In a flash we were aboard its ship. The inside was completely black. I could feel the body maker was still running, as air whooshed through its claws and onto my face. After ten seconds or so it stopped. It set me down, though I had no idea where.

"You okay, Sachiko?" called out Tank.

"Yes. I'm over here. Are you alright?"

"Sapale," I Tank called out, "you here?"

"Yes, and I've already stripped off that ridiculous outfit."

"I'm good, in case anyone wants to know," I shouted a bit annoyed. "Everybody, keep talking and I'll find you."

"Okay, but be careful."

I heard Tank crash into something and then the floor. It sounded metallic.

"Tank, are you okay?"

"Yeah. Rookie mistake. I'll try it slower this time."

I started counting out loud. By *thirty-six* he slapped me with a hand.

"Tank, good to see you. How are things?"

We started making noise, and the women found us quick enough.

Sachiko was crying loudly. She clung to Tank like he was her only lifeline.

"Easy, kiddo." He hugged her tightly and began stoking her long hair. "Easy does it. We're fine for now. Stay calm and we'll figure something out." He held her until she was ready to let him go.

"I can't see a thing," I said loudly.

"Me either," responded Tank. "The Edoozers must see in a different frequency than visible light. I'm as blind as a... Hey, why not?" He started clapping his hands. "We can echolocate."

"I think this may be a little easier," I said, as I switched on some external lights on my abdomen. They were faint, but the two humans could see a little, while Sapale and I saw things perfectly.

"Can you two see okay to move?" I asked quietly.

"Maybe," replied Sachiko.

"I think I do," was Tanks response.

"To your left the walls are farther away. Hold hands, if you get close enough to one another. Wait. I have a better idea. Sachiko, stay where you are. Sapale will come get you. I'll grab you, Tank."

"Your robotic eyes that good in the dark?" he asked.

"Better. I can see your hands shaking."

"I do that when I'm cold."

"Sure. Not nervous."

"I'm a Marine. If we shake, we're either cold or it's a bad habit. Those are the only two reasons."

"I'll take your word for it."

As I finished teasing him, I rested a hand on his shoulder. In a couple seconds, the women were by our side.

We proceeded to a door or hallway. After rounding it, I saw a dull glow in the distance. We headed for it quickly. Pretty soon it became apparent the light glow was from a room off the corridor we were traversing. When we came to that intersection, we slipped around the corner, into the room, and pressed our backs against the wall.

"What the hell is that?" asked Tank.

"Vending machine, I think. Do you have any change?" I replied.

"No one likes a smart ass."

I made a soft fart sound in reply.

"Why isn't the body maker, or some damn alien, following us?" Tank whispered.

"No clue. My guess is he's busy not getting wormholed as he lights out of the solar system. He's probably never had a prisoner to know what to do with one."

"Not reassuring. How long do we have?"

"Not very long. Come on. Let's get a look at that contraption."

We walked over slowly. The device was spherical and around twenty meters in diameter.

As we neared I said, "It's transparent."

"I think so too. But what's the glowy stuff inside?" asked Sapale.

"Kind of like a toy Jacob's ladder, maybe?" guessed Sachiko.

"Yeah, I can see the similarity. But this is randomly floating in three dimensions."

"Plasma?" suggested Sapale.

I considered that a second. "No, that'd be much brighter. The stuff's hot. Plus, who'd want to look at plasma?"

It hit me. Of course.

"It's *time*," I said.

"Huh? Time for what?" Tank grunted.

"No, silly. We're looking at *time*. That's the time, or whatever, the Edoozers collect."

"Why would you leap to that conclusion?" my wife pressed.

"Because, if I've learned one thing about these horse's asses, it's that they love time. They, I don't know, *revere* it."

"Makes sense, I guess. What, you think they cook up some popcorn and sit here staring at it?" Tank questioned.

I looked at him. "Maybe they stand."

"This college professor persona has changed you. I'm not liking it so far."

"Tough titties."

"Doooo nooottt *ttoouchh*," screamed the body maker.

He'd snuck up on us from behind.

Tank balled up his fist and hurled it at the source of the green light. "You forgot to say *please*."

He slammed his fist down like a sledge on the clear, time-containing orb. It shattered with surprising ease.

In physics, if a gas or liquid is more densely present in one location than another it will *diffuse* until it has become uniform in its density. That is exactly what time did. It didn't burst, rush, or explode catastrophically. It spread like a soft breeze, like a gentle rumor. It wafted out of the breach and teased its way into the room. When it passed over and enveloped us, I could feel it. I knew time like I knew my own name. I was everywhere the time had been and I was standing right where I was, both feet firmly on the floor. If heroin was one millionth as great a rush, I'd never stop using it (assuming, of course we ever escaped). And time knew we would. No, I knew we would. No, *in time* we would. Yes, I experienced a time that hadn't occurred yet when Tank and Sachiko and Sapale and I were free and back home.

My mind accelerated into reckless rapture. I spread my arms and swung myself around like Julie Andrews in the opening scene of *The Sound of Music*. Tank was in my time, too. He stood erect as the Washington Monument. His smile was bigger than the Grand Canyon. We floated in pure joy forever...

Which lasted around five seconds.

The body maker howled with the protest of a thousand deaths. He raged across the room to the base of the time orb. He tapped and struck what must have been keys or switches. The escaped time still meandered through the air, but the hole was sealed. No more time was released. When he was satisfied the damage was contained, he wheeled on us. With a roar he charged, all seven arms grasping toward us.

I couldn't care less that we were about to die brutally. I was far too happy to worry about such a little thing as death. I wished that time would stop so I could linger with it always, but if it didn't I was content.

That's when I noticed the body maker had stopped abruptly. A pincer hand was ten inches from my neck, but it was motionless. That, I did not anticipate. Through my wonder I turned to Tank. Two claw arms were even closer to his torso, but were also motionless. The women stood behind us, but they were targeted by other nasty appendages a little father off. Each was motionless.

I took a step. I could move. Just no one or nothing else seemed to have that capability. I realized what I'd done. I closed my eyes, and wished that the other three were in my time.

"Now there's something you don't see every day," observed Tank. He poked at one of the claws. His withdrew his hand like he received a shock. Then he punched at it. Nothing. Then he hauled back a leg and kicked it with all his might. The body part didn't budge.

Sapale came up and slid an arm around my elbow. "Did you just have the highest high you've ever had?"

"I did. One could get used to that feeling."

She smiled with all the joy in the universe. "One could."

Sachiko batted at pincers. Nothing. She climbed up on it, sat, and crossed her legs. "Not very comfortable." She slid to the floor.

"What, I repeat, *what* the hell just happened?" demanded Tank.

I squinted as I reflected. "We were standing here. The body maker repaired the damage you'd caused. He rushed us with primal hatred. I was having such a wonderful experience, I wished that time would stop, so I could live the rapture longer. Then, everything except me was frozen in time."

"Wait, you actually thought to yourself 'I want time to stop'?"

I pursed my lips. "Yes. I believe that's what I wished for."

"Oh yeah. We get wishes now." Tank pumped his fist up and down wildly.

"What are you on about, sir?" I pressed.

"Don't you see? We absorbed *time*. Then you willed it to stop and it did."

"No. I can't do that," I squeaked. "Can I?"

"I think you just did," remarked Sapale, as she patted my arm.

"Oh, then I wished it to start again for you three, and you came to life."

Tank rubbed his chin. "Any idea how long this power might last?"

I walked to the orb and leaned back on it. Though the world had stopped, the flow of time in its bottle hadn't. No surprise there. I guess. "I haven't a clue. It would be nice if it never ended."

"Never ending time. Now there's a concept," marveled Sapale.

"I can see now why these creeps go to such lengths to acquire time. It's more than amazing stuff," cooed Sachiko.

We were all quiet a while.

Sachiko finally spoke. "Time is open to us. I see us sitting at the White House in the future. There's no panic, no aliens crushing people."

"Yes, I see that future too," said a passionate Tank.

"Let's all wish for that," she breathed.

Famous last words.

CHAPTER TWENTY-TWO

We stood, huddled tightly together in the White House. My eyes darted around to make reference. Though the room was empty, we were clearly in the Blue Room. That was basically the main entrance on the first floor. We'd passed through it when we had been summoned to the Situation Room, and I'd visited the White House a few times before my *Ark 1* flight.

"Do you notice something odd?" Tank asked quietly.

"Maybe," I said softly. There was something not quite right about the place. Sachiko mentioned that she saw us in a future, peaceful White House. This didn't seem like that.

"No guards and no people," said Sapale.

Oops. She was wearing her coveralls and a short sleeve top. No burqa.

"Maybe it's a holiday," offered Sachiko.

"There's no holiday where security is given the day off. Shaky, we should have been shot by now for appearing out of nowhere. Do you smell the wood fires?" Tank visibly sniffed the air.

"If you do I guess so. They must have fireplaces, right? The White House can burn logs."

"I smell a lot of them," I responded. "Probably having to do with all that snow I see out the windows."

"Snow in August?" Sachiko asked, puzzled.

"Not hardly," I returned. "Global warming means that whatever's left of New England gets very little snow."

"So you think it's not August?" queried Sapale.

I pointed, without speaking, to the window. Just then a man with a stovepipe hat walked in and stamped his feet to get the snow off. He wore a Victorian suit under his topcoat. Yellow vest and vertical stripes on his pants—a real period piece. He noticed us and tipped his hat to me. "Good afternoon," he said noncommittally. Then he disappeared into the Cross Hall.

"Now there's so—" began Tank.

"Don't say it," I said. "Just don't. Come."

I led the others into the Cross Hall. The visitor was nearly to the end. Another man left one room and entered another. He took no note of us.

"Did that fellow leave a trail of BO or what?" asked Tank.

He had. "Quiet. This way." I marched us off toward the West Wing. I had to stop when I reached the spot, and the conclusion, that the West Wing wasn't present. "Where was the Oval Office before there was a West Wing?" I asked over my shoulder.

"Beats me. Lincoln's office was upstairs, I think. I toured here once with the family, and I think the docent mentioned that," replied Tank.

I headed back to where I'd seen stairs. We went to the next floor up and stepped into a hallway. That's when we saw a guard. And, unfortunately, he saw us.

"Wait there," he said loudly. He strode over heavily, his rifle in one hand. "Who are you and what are you doing here? And why the devil are you wearing men's breeches, ma'am?"

Tank composed himself quickly. "I'm General Sherman. I'm here to see the president. And watch your mouth around these ladies, if you've grown to fancy those stripes on your sleeve."

He scowled. "I served under General Sherman two years back. He comes here often. You are not he, sir." He raised his rifle.

"I'm another General Sherman, you idiot."

In his defense, Tank did have his four stars on his collar.

"Never heard there were two."

"What a surprise a *sergeant* doesn't know all the general officers. Now stand aside."

"Nope." He called over his shoulder. "Billy, get some men up here on the double. We got trouble." That's when his eyes strayed to actually notice Sapale.

"Hey, what kind of—"

"I wish time would stop," I said softly. Hot damn. It did.

"Nice move, Jon," praised Tank.

We stepped around the frozen form of the sergeant and headed to what was likely Lincoln's office. We guessed correctly. The great man himself sat behind a smallish-wooden desk, placed starkly in the center of the room. Immediately, I knew a woman hadn't done the decorating. Not a feminine touch in sight. The floor was bare, there were no little do-dads scattered about, and there was no softness.

Lincoln was staring at the floor, lost in thought, it would seem. His desktop was a mess with books, official documents, and scribbled-on paper. He was alone. I pointed that the women should sit in the two of the chairs across from him. Us guys stood behind them.

"Jon," Sachiko queried, "why are we in Lincoln's office? We don't need to be here. You know that, right?"

"If we're in the mid 1860s, with a chance to meet Abraham Lincoln, you can pretty much bet I'm going to meet Abraham Lincoln."

"But won't history record he had a brain-fart and claimed to have met future scientists and an alien fleeing a dark evil?"

I rolled my head. "Possibly. Maybe. But more importantly, I don't care." I pointed to the frozen savior of the republic.

"Time restart," I called out. "Jonny Boy wants to screw with you."

The room was silent and the lighting dim. At first Lincoln didn't move and I wondered if I'd lost the ability to restart time. That sent shivers up my spine. It would be, ah, *inconvenient* if I couldn't jump start time. But slowly, as if waking from a dream, he noticed us. He stood, but not quickly or in panic.

"Pardon me, my friends. I must have missed your entry." He tipped where his hat would be if it weren't on a side table near him. Then it hit me. He sounded like Mr. Rogers, not like Abe Lincoln. Or I should say not what I expected. I mean, he obviously sounded like Lincoln, since he was the guy. But I was caught off-guard.

Abe got a seriously baffled look on his face. I do believe he was wondering how he could "miss" the entry of four people.

He directed his attention to Tank. "Apologies to you, sir. Have we met?"

"No, not really."

He sat back down. That's when three soldiers burst into the room, rifles pointed right at Tank or me.

"Ah, Sergeant Hastings, that's alright. These people are my guests. Please leave us alone."

"But Mr. President, he claims to be General Sherman."

"General Sherman? William *Tecumseh* Sherman?"

"Er, well no. He just claimed to be *a* general named Sherman."

"Then perhaps he is. If you'll leave, I'll extract the truth from him, and get back to you."

"Ah," he shouldered his rifle. "That's okay. I don't really need to know."

"Thank you, Sergeant. That will be all."

The soldiers backed out of the room, closing the door as they left.

"Now, where—"

Yup, that's when Honest Abe had his Sapale moment.

"She's from the Kingdom of Sarawak... er, North Borneo. The... a... English part," I blurted out clumsily.

He scrunched up his face and angled his head.

"I know North Borneo is held by the English. I'm sorry, do I know *you?*"

"No, sir, President Lincoln. We've never met before." I reached around Sapale. "Jon. Jon Ryan, at your service."

We shook. Man, I wished I could risk a selfie with him.

"This is my Sarawakian wife, Sapale."

He tipped where his hat could have been.

"And this is Dr. Sachiko Jones, a world-famous scientist."

He tipped his imaginary brim, again. "A woman who's both a doctor and a famous scientist. My, I do not believe I've ever had the pleasure of meeting such an accomplished female."

"Yeah, things are real different where she comes from. Very progressive."

Sachiko eyed me as if I was babbling. "Yes, we have the vote, can dress as we wish, and we can have up to three husbands."

"You have three husbands?" he gasped.

"Heavens no. I hope I don't appear to you to be that stupid."

After an initial shock, Lincoln chuckled lightly. "No, my dear, you do not look to be that foolish."

"If you ever run for office in my country, you have my vote," she responded.

Lincoln appeared serious, again. "Now, where were we? Ah yes. I asked if we'd met and you replied not really. Might I pose to you a hypothetical, General Sherman?"

He shrugged. "You are a lawyer, Mr. President."

"That I am. So, how does one gentleman not really meet with another?"

"Beats me."

"What beats you?"

"The answer to your hypothetical."

He chuckled. "It hits you repeatedly. Excellent imagery, sir."

"And, you are General Sherman's wife?" he asked Sachiko.

"Lord no," flew out of her mouth.

"Ah, would it be impolite of me to ask you to avoid taking the Lord's name in vain while in my presence, Miss Jones?"

Man, had she stepped quickly into the doggie doo-doo. "My

deepest apologies," she said as she flushed three shades of crimson. "The weight of meeting you has greatly affected my fragile constitution." She grimaced, but I had to admit that sounded period-appropriate.

"It has, has it? I'm sorry to hear that. Back to who you are, if not this man's wife."

"We work together, Mr. President. We're scientists at the same university. Both full professors and everything."

He looked stunned. "A... a *female* full professor of science at a major university? It is a major university, isn't it?"

"One of the top schools in the country," replied Tank.

Lincoln flipped his hand at me weakly. "Perhaps that explains the men's breeches."

"Most likely," I responded. "That has to be it."

He composed himself. "And what is it I might do for you four scientists? Er, you are all scientists, correct?"

"Sure, why not," I replied.

"Do we have an appointment?"

Tank grinned nervously. "Not really, and no. We were in town and just wanted to pay our respects, Mr. President."

"Ah, fine. Most kind of you, I'm certain. Might I ask another potentially awkward question?"

"You are the boss," replied Tank expansively.

"Well," he stood, "if there's no remaining business, I fear I must bid you a good day and return to this grueling and unrelenting labor." He gestured to the top of his desk.

"Of course, sir," I responded.

The girls shot to our feet like trained dogs.

"Perfectly understandable," added Tank.

We each shook his hand.

"Ah, one final last question, if I might?"

"Shoot," I said.

I could tell Lincoln started to question my choice of words, but he let it drop. "Are you, in fact, General Sherman, a general in my army?"

Tank looked to Heaven for inspiration. "Let me see. Are you asking me if I'm a general in the Union Army?"

"I believe I am. Yes. Is there another army I'm unaware of besides the Confederate States Army? Surely, a Northerner like yourself was never a member of that treasonous assembly."

"Ah, that's a separate and more complicated question to answer, sir."

"So it is. I withdraw the question and return to my original query."

"No, Mr. Lincoln, I am a general in an army different from the Union Army."

"My, but this is an odd conversation," responded the president.

"Sure is," replied Tank.

"As a kindred spirit, General Sherman, let me simply ask. Do you think it would be ill-advised of me to press you as to *which* army you actually serve in?"

"Yes, sir. I think you don't want to go there."

I knew he was dying to ask Tank why he'd want to go anywhere just then. Luckily, he was a wise and prudent man. He let it go. "Leave the door open upon your departure, please." He sat back down and fumbled with the mess that confronted him.

Outside in the hall, I remarked, "Seems like a nice chap."

Sapale gave me her best "look." Then Sergeant Hastings came over to escort us briskly off the premises. Him, I could have done without.

Fortunately, there were several heavy woolen Victorian coats hanging just inside the entry. It was freezing outside. We were able to reasonably claim to the sergeant that four of them were ours. Since the women had on men's pants, I figure he would accept their consistent taste in their manner of dress. We sat on a low rock wall that meandered off to the right of the main entrance.

"So, that was nice," I stated blandly.

"I don't think the word nice reaches the heights words need to reach to cover meeting President Lincoln in his office, shortly before he was assassinated," responded Sachiko.

"Okay," I began seriously. "We need a plan. I assume we can all wish ourselves back to the ship. How long time is on our side is anybody's guess. We're going to need supplies, too."

"What supplies?" asked Tank.

"You two need to eat and drink, for one thing."

"That would be nice."

"I assume time's decay rate is log-log plot, like most things in physics. Maybe measured in half-lives," speculated Sachiko.

"Based on how amazing I felt at first compared to now suggests the decay rate is faster than it is slower," Sapale said.

"Agreed." Tank sniffed loudly and looked upward. "I'd say we'll be down to ten percent of our maximums in an hour or two."

"Agreed," I responded.

"Lord only knows what the critical level is to manipulate time," Sachiko wondered.

"I hope Lincoln didn't hear that blasphemy, Dr. Jones," I had to snipe.

She grunted a laugh.

"We don't want to get stuck here and have to swim through time with the locals. We need to get back and help defend against the Edoozers," I stated.

"Agreed," came from Tank.

"So, we have to find a way to get home, without creating a paradox."

"Wait, I want to go kill my grandfather before we leave," I said with as straight a face as I could.

"Oh, you do, do you?" challenged Tank. "Well, then you'd have to stay in this timeline and wait a generation or two. Presently, I'd estimate your sixth great grandfather is working a field in the eastern United States."

"Hey, what makes you think he isn't a land baron?"

"Fine, he's a land baron. We're not traveling to wherever he reigns supreme to ex him out. Period."

"Every party loves a pooper, that's why we invited you." I teased him, to the tune of "Pretty Baby." Maybe you know this little musical insult?

"I think we can safely reappear in the Situation Room a few minutes after the Edoozer snatched us," Tank opined, getting back to business.

I looked at him sideways. "I guess that could work."

"You seem less than enthusiastic, however."

"I am. If we return to our present, we're still in a huge mess. The Edoozers technology is giga light years ahead of ours. Aside from our wormhole pea shooter, we're defenseless."

"So?"

"So, we go home and we still die. You know if that Body Maker-lop doesn't return with bad intentions, one of the other clans will. And next time, it'll be *more* personal."

"What do you suggest then?" he asked

"We return to the body maker's ship," I stated simply.

"Did you hit your head somewhere along the line? Is your fragile constitution acting up again?"

"No. I'm willing to take the greater risk for the greater gain."

"You know, I've been saddled with him a very long time. He is quite the risk taker. Trust me," Sapale said, gesturing toward me.

"What gain would there be returning to the time ship?" he asked.

"We go back and steal their technology."

"Jon, I know you're serious, because I hear it in your tone. But what you're suggesting would take a helluva lot of time."

"I know. And we'd have it. It comes in a big glass sphere."

CHAPTER TWENTY-THREE

Several repair makers were scrambling to permanently fix the ruptured time-containment vessel. The body maker lorded over them, barking orders and screaming for more speed. For their part, they grumbled amongst themselves how the body maker could be so non-intelligent as to allow the meaningless ones to damage such a critical part of the ship. It was not only unheard of—it was incomprehensible to allow such a blasphemy. One part maker even claimed to have heard an argument between their body maker and the body maker of a clan ship that came to their aid. The crew all said it was defective for making that claim, but they also did not delete the information, once it was heard.

"I will be in my rest and assimilation area," howled the body maker. "I will return in the future. I had better be impressed with your progress or I will eat all your heads."

"Which future?" grumbled a service maker.

The pack cackled quietly.

"If I am not impressed with the body maker, may I eat its head?" said a repair maker.

The pack squealed louder. Such bold words had never been thought or spoken.

The sub-lead building maker heard the commotion and came over to make correct. "Work is not done with your oral apparatuses. Silence will happen."

"In agreement," they all muttered back.

CHAPTER TWENTY-FOUR

We materialized into the time sphere room, but I think we only just made it. Our prior time-jaunts were instantaneous. When we landed before, it felt like our feet were slapped against the ground. This shift seemed to take a while, and we sort of faded-in as opposed to *boom,* we're there. Our time mojo must have been right on the border of disappearing.

It was hard to say who was more surprised, us or the ten or twelve Edoozers laboring around the sphere. I know *I* sure was. We'd agreed before the time shift that Tank would try and freeze time if just what was happening took place. If he failed, the order of attempts would be Sapale, then Sachiko, and finally me. With that tactic, I hoped to avoid some potential conflict of time-freezing wishes. I mean, we knew diddly about the process. If we all wished at once, maybe we'd cancel each other out.

Tank either hadn't or couldn't do it. The gang rushed us. They emitted a painful high-pitched wail as they closed.

"I want time to stop," Tank said out loud in their direction.

I had always maintained that learning was lifelong endeavor. Now, I began to question that philosophy. What I learned, on this occasion, was that when one's time energy dropped below a certain level one could slow time, but not stop it. The horde still came at us, but it was like the slow motion of a Bugs Bunny cartoon. Luckily, we could move much faster than them.

"Everyone, down the hall," I shouted. "Then we'll try to double back here."

Before we had made the shift, we sneaked into the White House kitchen and "borrowed" a few items. One was a lit handheld-oil lamp. We were not going to be in the dark again. With its help, we easily outpaced our pursuers. Pretty soon, I was fairly certain we'd lost them. We double-backed, as planned. The sphere room was empty. These guys had a lot to learn about ship's security, thank goodness.

"You all keep a look out. I'll try and tap into the time vessel," I said quietly.

I was about to attempt what was easily the dumbest idea I'd ever come up with. The second item we had liberated from the kitchen was the spigot from a beer barrel. I was going to draw off time, as needed. Fortunately, if it did what I expected it would, and simply re-ruptured the barrier, at least we'd still get our refill and could begin with my other plan, which by the way tied for the honor of being the dumbest one I'd ever hatched.

"How's it going?" Sapale asked after a few seconds.

"Not sure. I'm trying to core a hole with the knife first. There." A hole had appeared in the surface of the sphere. "Hey, a tiny rivulet of time is vaping out. This might just work. I'll... There. The spigot's in place."

"Does time come out when you open it?" she asked.

"Damn, I'm good."

"I hope it comes out quickly because Bozos, Inc. just entered the room. They're moving a little faster, too."

I set my mouth over the nozzle and began breathing in time. Wow, a new term popped into my head that just had to become a new catchphrase. *Time sucking.*

The two Edoozers in the lead slowly grabbed Tank's heavy coat. He spun out of it just in time. Another made to hit the back of Tank's head. Sapale tried to tackle him like she was a linebacker. He outweighed her by a factor of three and it showed. She was able to turn his body from his goal, but couldn't take him down.

He shook her off and she spilled on the deck. She stretched out for Tank. Just before he got there to help her, I froze everything. The twelve Edoozers and my three friends looked like a three-dimensional painting. Oops.

I pointed to each of them, and individually released them.

"I'm sorry," I said once they were all moving again. "When I froze them, I accidentally included you. Now, you're unselected. You're welcome?"

Sapale jumped into my arms. "It worked, it worked, it worked."

"It worked. Now you go fill up and let's get busy."

"No. I have a better idea," Sachiko chimed in.

"What?" I asked.

"I'll let mine run out to zero. *Then* I'll fill up. That way we can get an accurate decay time, for future reference."

I bobbed my head. "Good idea. But what if the bad guys come to life when one of us who is topped off is not with you?"

"We'll just make certain that doesn't happen."

"Okay, sounds like a plan. You two," I gestured to Sapale and Tank, "fill'er up."

"How much is full?" she asked.

"Hmm. No clue. Experiment Two. Sapale, breathe in the vapor for... ten seconds. Tank, you do the same for five seconds. We'll see what happens."

My first objective was to make certain no one on the ship was immune to our time spell. That meshed together nicely with my other major objective. Mapping out the ship. We'd only been in a tiny part of a truly enormous vessel. Only the time sphere room had enough light to see the ship's details clearly.

The oil lamp had around six hours of fuel. That meant we could break up into three teams. Tank and Sachiko took the lamp. Us androids could go separately, since we needed almost no ambient light. They could explore a few hours away, and still make it back to the reliable light of the time room. Sapale would remain in the time room, to watch our time prisoners (*love* these new terms) and refill her supply, if needed. That left me to explore on my own.

The first trip turned out to be easier than I'd expected. The ship was highly repetitive and orderly in its construction. Symmetry was a big deal in the aesthetic of whoever built this vessel. The hallways were in a spoke-and-wheel design. Picture an old wagon wheel. There was a central hub with straight spokes that intersected ever larger circular elements. Of course the Edoozer ship was three dimensional, so the wagon wheel circles were actually wagon spheres.

The twenty linear spokes that connected the spheres radiated out— eight in one plane (the X-axis), with six above that plane (the Y-axis), and eight below that (the Z-axis). Not surprisingly, the time storage room, which we dubbed TSR, was at the hub of everything. It was the center of their power and possibly their place of worship. The first circular passageway that intersected the straight spokes was ten meters past the hub exits. The next circular hall was ten more meters away. That exact pattern continued for as far as we ventured that first trip.

We called it quits after four hours. There was no reason to push our luck. We had all the time in the universe. The farther outward we had gone, the fewer and fewer Edoozers we saw. I ran a quick calculation in my head, assuming their distribution was uniform. It meant this massive ship was manned by maybe seventy-five individuals. That seemed counterintuitive. In time, hopefully, I'd figure out why the ship was crewed so sparsely.

Back in TSR it was time—pun intended—to set a near-term plan.

"So, we have the ship held prisoner, but we don't control her," I began. "There is, however, no reason to assume we can't eventually learn how to pilot her. One big help would be to have *Stingray* aboard. The AIs can analyze stuff a lot faster than we can. They might also be able to link up with this ship's AIs. Something this big would require a lot of them."

"So, we go back to the White House, retrieve *Stingray*, and land your vortex somewhere on this ship?" Tank asked.

"Shouldn't be a problem," I replied, confidently.

"You do remember that the last time we *wished* to go there, we met with the sixteenth president and not the current administration?"

"I'm confident our aim'll improve," I reassured him. Foolishly, I might add.

"Why is that, husband?" pressed Sapale. "What will help us aim better?"

"It can't be that hard," I minimized.

"*Time travel*," shot back Sachiko, dubiously, "can't be that hard?"

I shrugged. "With practice, I'm betting it isn't."

"And you saved the universe?" Sachiko asked.

"Twice, in fact," I corrected.

No verbal reply, but she fluttered her eyelids and shook her head, slowly.

"I think we have to consider that we might just have been stupid lucky that first time," Sapale remarked. "The chance of us separating in time seems to me to be much greater than that of us traveling together, unless we're using this ship or something similar."

She had a point. Good thoughts and altruistic intentions were unlikely to be excellent binders, when it came to free-falling through time.

"Maybe I could go alone?" I thought out loud. "That way, if I miss the time mark, I could try again until I hit my target. We wouldn't end up scattered across time, that way."

"I'm going to need time to noodle out that idea, Jon," said Tank. "While it seems reasonable, I really don't like the idea of splitting up the team."

"Not a problem. As long as we can hold the Edoozers in time-stasis, our hands won't be forced. That leads us quickly to the next order of business. Food and water. You two will need them, soon. If the Edoozers even have food aboard, I don't think humans could eat the crap."

"I get the idea they feed directly off of time," Sapale remarked, thoughtfully.

"Interesting notion." I nodded. "We've seen some weird ass stuff in our days. Living off time soup wouldn't surprise me much."

"Could we survive off the time we're... whatevering from the time vault?" Sachiko wondered out loud.

"Time sucking," I added. "That's what we're calling it, now. *Time sucking.*"

"Since when are we calling it that disgusting term?" snapped Sapale.

I shrugged.

"Maybe, we can live off the mists of time," Tank said decisively. "But, considering the alternative if we make an incorrect assumption, I'm voting we secure food and water, just the same."

"I agree. Water is the most critical. And, since we found none on our first check of the ship, we either have to look harder, or go get some," I stated.

"Come to think of it, I don't recall seeing anything even remotely like a restroom," Sapale recalled. "I've been on lots of ships made by lots of species, but it's usually pretty obvious where they go when nature calls."

"Either of you see the head?" I asked. I hadn't either.

They indicated they had not.

"Okay, second order of business. Buckets," I declared.

"Ah, Jon, are you suggesting Tank and I use... buckets for... ah, you know?"

I looked to Tank and pointed to Sachiko. "Hasn't done much camping."

He shook his head. "Pure city girl... er, woman."

"You make civilized sound like a bad thing, ya big oaf," she scorned.

"Well, I was in the Marines. A bucket sounds like the Ritz Hotel, to me."

I walked over and fist bumped him. Then, of course, we both said *oorah*. Hey, you would, too. It was the perfect guy-moment.

"I say we take another look, to see if there's any potable water aboard," opined my wife. "It's simpler. I know, it's not as sexy as whirling off along the time circuits. But, it's more practical."

"You mean dull," I translated.

"No, *you* mean dull. I mean less chance of traumatic death or permanent separation, flyboy."

Tank pointed to me. "You flew fighters?"

I swelled. "For the USAF, proud and loud."

"What'd you fly?"

"Lockheed Martin F-16 Fighting Falcons, the pride of the sky. Just before I switched to the astronaut thing, I qualified for the F-35Es. But those gave me a rash. Vertical takeoffs are for frogs, not fighters. And they handled like a flying garbage can." I puckered up a sour face.

"Are you done with the memory lane thing, yet?" asked a bored-looking wife of mine.

I pointed up. "Water. Let us look for water. And, if you see any cheeseburgers, don't consume them without calling me first."

We split up into the same three teams. Well, sort of. Sapale said it was my turn to babysit the stiffs. She foraged this time. They were all back within two hours, empty-handed.

"We saw more and more of the same old same old," reported Tank. "Whoever designed this craft had to be both OCD and deeply depressed. There's no variation, no new parts or places. Hell, there's not even an obvious mess deck." He threw his arms in the air. "How can you fly a ship without coffee, and how can you have coffee without a mess deck? It's pure insanity."

"It's designing in trouble, if you ask me," I added in support.

"Enough with the macho BS, please." Wow, it was Sachiko that time, not my loving wife. "At any moment, we're like five minutes from total death. Guy-stuff conversations do not advance our chances of survival."

"I guess she's not a fan of coffee?" I speculated.

Something bounced off my head. I looked down. It was Sapale's flashlight. She'd... she'd thrown it at me.

"Okay, I need to go get supplies." I said. I was being forced to be serious now. "Or maybe take a stab at retrieving *Stingray*."

"Who appointed you?" asked my brood's-mate. And yes, her arms *were* crossed.

"What do you mean who appointed me? I'm the mission commander."

Sapale nodded toward the humans. "Did they agree to that?"

"You think they wouldn't?" I shot back.

"I didn't say that. But, just because you always think you're in charge doesn't mean you always are."

"Before you say one more word, we are not taking a vote." I was getting a tad miffed.

"Why don't I go get the ship?" she asked neutrally.

"Because I'm going. You need to stay here and protect those two."

"I don't think I need protection," Tank responded coolly. "Doubt Sachiko'd ask for it, either."

I scanned the entire mutinous lot of them. "You know what the nice thing about democracies is?"

Sapale shrugged.

"This isn't one. I go. You stay. As commander, I assume the greater risk. That's what I do."

"One last point," she replied.

"And that would be?"

"We're pulling your chain, flyboy. Sheesh. You can go from goofy to uptight in six seconds."

I turned a shoulder to her. "I knew that."

"Oh, brother. Jon, go."

———

I returned to the White House, a few hours earlier than I had before with the others. I figured it was a done task, so I'd be less likely to mess up. It was early morning. The snow in most places was undisturbed—no one was coming and going. I slipped around back, staying close to the White House walls for cover. The back entrance was unguarded. My, how times would change. I headed toward the kitchen area. The smell of baking bread was a pleasant roadmap. At that time in the morning, the kitchen was lightly staffed, with a small scullery manned by one worker. A couple of men were pounding something, maybe dough. Another was mixing flour in a large bowl. No one was paying attention to anything but their chores.

I eased into a pantry. I grabbed a couple of empty flour bags and stuffed in a few basic supplies and flasks for water. Then I set about locating oil for the lamp, writing materials, and hopefully more lamps. I had to be careful to leave the one I was going to take later that day. Spoiler alert, right? No time paradoxes on my watch.

Within half an hour, I was loaded to the max and no one had even laid eyes on me. I debated whether I should return to the exact site I'd materialized after the Edoozer's ship. I ultimately decided (not surprisingly for me) not to. What the hell. I needed to find out if I could return from an alternate point.

Guess what? My lack of caution was rewarded with a direct hit to where I'd departed from on the ship. That would mean trouble in the near term.

Sapale actually jumped back. "Wow. That wasn't fast. That was instantaneous. You *just* left."

I grinned. "I missed you."

"Oh man." A rather insufficiently romantic response. We had been married a very long time, so, what did I expect?

With creature comforts taken care of, at least for a while, we needed to decide what we were going to do. While the fleshies slept, I sat alone and pondered.

"Currently, we're blind," I began the next morning. "Also, it's certain that with the crew of this ship time-locked, other ships will be coming to find out what's up. Who knows how these creatures' societies are structured, but sooner than later someone has to come check out the silence."

"We can time-lock whoever comes to investigate," commented Sachiko.

"Yes and no. The only way we'll know they're here is when we see them strolling down the passageways. Sure, we could get lucky. But, history dictates we are more likely to get unlucky."

"Since you two don't sleep, we at least can have someone on watch twenty-four seven," said Tank.

"For what that's worth, true. But, if we don't learn how to control the ship pretty soon, I think we might have to abandon her."

"Why? You said you wanted to steal their tech," Sapale pointed out.

"Ideally, sure. But I don't want to risk getting caught. All hope dies with us four if that were to happen."

The others nodded grimly.

"I say we make at least one more attempt to find the bridge or some central control station. If we do, maybe we can out how to pilot the ship."

"There are works stations all over," Tank reminded us. "No computer terminals like we have, but some areas are configured for input and use."

"We could try my favorite plan," I suggested. "Push buttons until something happens. That option's a blast."

"Only if all else fails, jet jockey," scolded my wife. "Okay, what if we really can't figure out how this ship's controlled? What then?"

"We'll have to bug out. Maybe try and rig a self-destruct if we can, but we can't expect to be safe here for very long."

No one protested that assessment. We were on borrowed time.

We needed to establish some normality, while waiting for the inevitable end of our stay on this Good Ship Lollipop. First, we located an empty room not far from the TSR and made that our base. We stashed our precious supplies there. We also burned the image and location into our minds so we didn't miss the room when returning to the ship when we time dived. On a practical note, we needed to agree on latrines. No way around it, right? We'd used four buckets to ferry water back. Once two became available, they were elected to serve a different cause. We had separate buckets in separate nearby rooms, for odor discretion. That way the two who needed buckets had only themselves to blame for any smell they felt violated the laws of nature.

Over five days we did a comprehensive survey of the vessel. By the way, we agreed on calling it the S. S. *Minnow*. You will never guess who came up with that name. Here's a hint: it was the least mature member of the crew. Operationally, we just called her the *S-squared*. We confirmed that there were very few Edoozers aboard. We tallied fifty-three, all nicely time-frozen. So, the range of our time-lock turned out to be at least past the hull of the *S-Squared*. As the meager supplies began to dwindle, another foray was needed.

"I hate to sound all sci-fi here," Sachiko said before I left. "But we need to steal provisions from many locations. I don't want us to alter the future by consuming something that would have mattered."

"One, I'm not sure I believe that can happen. Two, it's not stealing. We're saving our species. They're glad to help, even if they don't know the specifics. Three, you two aren't going to put a dent in anyone's stockpiles. You eat like a bird, so you hardly count."

"Well, start thinking of alternatives, okay?"

"Hey, I could show up in Pompeii the day before the eruption. Anything I snatched wouldn't be missed."

"That hardly seems safe. Plus, what date was it exactly? Hmm?"

"Okay, then Hiroshima, August 5, 1945?"

"I might blend in. But you? You'd be the only white dude walking the streets," scoffed Sachiko.

"I got it. I could sail on the *Hindenburg* and grab whatever just before it bursts into flames."

"Just think about alternate sources, Jon," she said rather frustratedly.

"Okay, I'm thinking about it."

This time thing was a blast. What wasn't such a blast is what happened to me while I was gone. Oops.

CHAPTER TWENTY-FIVE

The three of them stood silently, looking at the spot where Jon had disappeared.

Nothing.

They continued to stare. A minute slowly passed.

"He didn't pop back instantly," Sachiko said, in a hushed tone.

"Welcome to my world," spewed Sapale. "Life with Jonny is life with the five Cs. Confusion, consternation, and crap, and crap, and more crap."

"You're not concerned?" she asked, cautiously.

"*Blech*," she returned. "Jon's like the wart you can never get rid of. Is he in trouble? Probably. Will those plaguing him soon suffer more than he does? You can bet on that. He'll be back. Always is."

"Do you think we should wait a bit longer?" Tank asked.

"What, and play his game? No way. Let's do whatever we need to and not reward his flair for the dramatic."

"Okay," he replied. "What's next?"

Sachiko brought up a concern she'd been nurturing. "How about this thought exercise. We've stopped time. We know it's only locally, and that it's temporary."

"Sure," replied Tank.

"So I wonder... What are the effects of stopping an isolated patch of space-time temporally from the rest of the universe?"

"Hmm. Good question." He sat and thought a while. "Easy solution. We unlock time for a second, allow it to equilibrate, then we re-lock it."

"Good plan. We just need to know where the bad guys are and not be near them for that second. You're in charge of winding the clock, so to speak. That way we won't needlessly duplicate, or possibly interfere with, your work."

"No prob. Sounds doable. Anything else weighing on your mind?"

"Yes, as a matter of fact."

"How did I know?"

"Pig. Anyway, we're playing with fire so to speak. These Edoozers have mastered time for a long while. What if they figure out what we're doing and snap their fingers—sorry, *claws*—and reverse the spell?"

"I've thought about that too," Sapale interjected. "The fact that they're newbies to the taking and holding of prisoners does not decrease their familiarity with time manipulation."

"So, maybe we should reanimate them, handcuffed and shackled?" Sachiko responded. "It might be safer in the long run."

"Or maybe we should try driving stakes through their hearts, assuming of course they have hearts," hissed Sapale.

"I know. I thought of that, too. But it seems so ... so..." Sachiko couldn't quite say it.

"Kiddo, we are in a war for the survival of our planet. Ugly, cruel, and the unimaginable are the opening antes." Tank patted the back of her hand. "If it comes to it, I'll wield the mallet, okay?"

"You'll have to fight me for it," Sapale returned with a tiny growl.

"You'll get no argument from me," responded Tank with a big grin. "And what happens if a clan ship comes to aid this one? I wonder if our time-lock can affect them."

Sachiko shook her head. "Who knows? If and when it does, we'll have to play it by ear."

"Figured as much. Now, anything else that weighs heavily upon your worrywart mind?" he asked.

"Ah, yes. I'm not sure how to say this."

"Then just say it," Tank implored.

"Okay—"

"Do you need me to cover my ears while you say it?"

"My poop is missing."

"You know, if you blindside a friend one time too many, ya might just lose that friend," he remarked with a chuckle.

"I am so glad I no longer have that problem," stated Sapale, seriously. "Missing poop is a never-ending torment for you fleshies."

"I'm serious."

Tank took a deep breath and exhaled loudly. "I assumed it had to do with the unique atmosphere on the S-*Squared*."

"Yours, too?"

"My bucket is always emptier than biologic history would predict."

"And that hadn't struck you as... odd?" Sachiko responded.

"Not if I ignored it fully."

"You are *such* a guy."

"It is the opposite of nice to have two men's men aboard," groused Sapale.

"Thank you. Guilty as charged."

"Where could our waste be going? Seriously," Sachiko pressed.

"Beats me. Let's just both keep tabs and be scientifically observant. K?"

"K."

"Pretty soon, I think we're going to have to head back to the TSR and top ourselves off," Sapale said, changing the subject.

"No time like the present," Tank replied smiling.

More big surprises were unwelcome. That, however, didn't stop them from raining down on the crew. When they entered the TSR, they noticed the floor directly under the spigot they'd jerry-rigged had grown up to insert itself into the orifice of the sprout.

"Now, there's something you don't see every day," Tank muttered under his breath.

"The floor grew to where time comes out. That'll be kind of hard to explain away."

"Bad floor construction? Bulging water damage under the carpet?" he offered.

"There is no carpet," Sapale said flatly.

"I know."

"Let me see if I can dislodge it," Sachiko said, stepping forward.

"Be careful," warned Sapale.

"What, of the floor?"

"Just be careful."

She placed both hands on the floor spike and tried to move it. She had to lean in hard, but the pointy thing bent, then popped free. Almost as soon as she released it, the peak receded back into the deck where it belonged.

"Fascinating," said Tank.

"Yeah, I agree. The floor's, like... alive," marveled Sachiko.

"Wait, kiddo, that's it."

"What's it? What did I even say?"

"The floor *is* alive. Honey, the ship is a living being. It was trying to tap into the time supply. I'll bet nickels to navy beans it's who's been recycling our waste too," declared Tank.

"The floor ate my poop? Gross."

"It's hungry."

"The *Minnow* is hungry?"

"I'd bet good money on it."

"I agree," added Sapale. "Many advanced-race ships are sentient and semi-alive."

"So, the Edoozers travel the universe in a ship that burns time?"

"And we have them time-locked, so they haven't fed her lately."

"No, wait. The ship should be time-locked, too. How can it drink from the spout and eat poop if it's time-locked?" Sachiko puzzled.

"Who says it is?" responded Sapale. "We know nothing of this new world of physical time."

"Good point. Just because the drivers are asleep doesn't mean the ship has to be," agreed Tank.

"I think it's sort of cool," remarked Sachiko.

"You would. You're a science nerd, like our Toño," observed Sapale.

"Hey, let's feed the beast," Tank suggested, energetically.

"How much do we feed a massive intergalactic spaceship, Dr. Tank?" Sapale pressed.

"Beats me. Let's just open the spigot and see what happens."

And that's what he did. Up until then, we'd placed our mouths over the escaping time energy. This time, Tank let it flow freely. Darn if it didn't spew toward the deck, start to disperse, but then redirected to the floor. It sure seemed like the vessel itself was lapping it up.

"How much will you give it?" Sapale repeated.

"I don't know. If it stops absorbing it, I'll stop releasing it."

"And if it doesn't? We need that stuff too," mentioned Sapale.

"I have a feeling there's a lot of time in this bottle," replied Tank.

After fifteen minutes, it did seem like the floor wasn't catching the time stream as avidly as it had been. The time sphere certainly didn't look emptier. Tank shut the flow off.

"I guess we'll know if it wants more if the floor reaches up again."

"Sure. Whoa, *Tank!*" exclaimed Sachiko.

"What?" His eyes rocketed around, looking for trouble.

"You know our nearly impossible task of learning Edoozer tech?"

"I seem to recall something of our mission."

"I think it just got a hell of a lot easier. We don't need to learn their language or understand their controls."

"We don't?" he answered, dubiously.

"No. We just need to figure out how to win their ship over."

"Ah, we don't know that's possible," responded Sapale.

"But if it was, it'd sure speed things along," replied Sachiko.

"It certainly would," agreed Tank.

CHAPTER TWENTY-SIX

Time Maker-pid was unsettled. It was *the* time master of the clan. To be at less than full ease was foreign, impossible. Unimaginable. It ruled time. Yes, the body makers ruled their own clan ships, but *it* ruled the one thing more important than clan ships—the time maker lorded over time itself. Everywhere. Everywhen.

But the time maker did not feel in control, holding dominion over its time. Normally, time crashed around the time maker, as if time was water at the base of Niagara Falls, and the time maker was the rocks below. Now, it faced an uncertainty. A tiny portion of time was a thick syrup, pouring past it so slowly, it could barely know that time moved. Or—and this was an absurd thought—perhaps it didn't even move at all. Was this another curse of the inept body maker's attempt at personal vengeance over the fleas of that planet called Earth? It would pay the highest price if that was reality. It would receive no more time-energy from the clan trove. Not one second more.

The time maker made to move, to investigate the source of its unpleasantness. But a part of it, a tiny part, would not hear its desires. It was stuck like a thought in time. But time never stopped, unless it was no-time. Incorrect, it reflected. No-time was not stopped. It was *not* nothingness. It struggled back to the first principles it learned when young. Could time stop? Certainly. Forward, backward, and arrested were all equally possible, permissible. But what stopped time? *It* hadn't. No one other than the time maker would dare. That would be the foulest sacrilege. The entire subclan of one performing such a perversity would be deleted throughout all time. Yes, that subclan would answer harshly to Time Maker-pid, if it had. Time was serious. Time was never toyed with. Time was all that mattered.

But the viscous ooze that time had become, in that tiny backwater, deadened its mind. It struggled to meditate on the reality of which it was now a captive. But, resistance was futile. It elected to rest in time, for a time. Then it would repair time. And deletions would follow. Oh, yes. Deletions *would* follow.

CHAPTER TWENTY-SEVEN

Okay, first clue something was amiss when I went back in time? I didn't see the White House of the late 1860s.

The second clue? The mastodon standing about ten meters in front of me.

It was a single female American Mastodon. How did I know the big beasty was a girl? She had a very young baby by her side. Oh, joy. I was about to be mama-beared. She trumpeted loudly. You know? Almost like she was really pissed. Then, naturally, because I really needed and deserved it, she charged. Did I mention how very big mastodon's tusks are? If not, write this down. They are not big. They are *enormous*. The fact that I had the firepower to take her out was a no-go. She was acting instinctively to protect her baby. Killing her would be a dickish thing to do. And, I am many not-positive things, but a dick is not one of them.

There was no cover to be had. A few trees were off to the right, but she'd splinter them, shortly before she splintered me. Probe fibers it was. I caught her by her huge head and slowed her to a stop quickly enough. She began thrashing, in a hateful panic. She was likely to hurt herself, or die of fright, if I didn't act quickly and correctly. I could likely put her to sleep, but that would leave junior unprotected. That would mean I'd have to wait around until she finished her beauty sleep. At that point, I was thinking she'd trumpet loudly and charge me.

I lifted her off the ground. Thank you, Deavoriath technology, for the umpteen-millionth time. There was a gentle rise to the left. With any luck (no giggles out there) I could find a barrier to separate us that she couldn't easily surmount.

There. Spotted it. A fast-moving creek, cascading down the far side of the hillock. The water was half-rapids, half waterfall, dropping twenty meters in a very short run. *Perfect.* As quickly as a robot carrying a mastodon could, I scrambled up the slope, angling to the head of the fast water. Then I had to set her down, so I could leap to the far shore. I was not Superman; I only felt like him.

Once across, and still holding her in place with my fibers, I climbed the wet rocks. I ended up fifteen meters above her, on the other side of a significant barrier of water. Fortunately, baby was trailing behind mama, bellyaching the entire time. Trust me on this. The baby's cute factor dropped rapidly as it continued to protest. By the time I released mama, she bellowed angrily but she fairly quickly realized I was not an acute threat. I trotted away, and she calmed.

That's when I stopped to ponder why I had missed the Lincoln White House by such a ridiculous margin. Weird. We'd all made synchronous time-dives, forward and backward, like old pros. Then I try it on my own once—no problema. But, now I'm Ug the Caveman. Was this maybe the DC area, one hundred thousand years earlier? I scanned the topography, comparing it to various records I had of the same area in modern times. Sure enough, it seemed to be the general DC landscape. Hey. I could buy some real estate, become mega-rich. Wait, no local government to record the transfer. Plus, what the hell. After Jupiter was done with the place, what good would it be?

Stay on task, Ryan. Think. Why'd you miss the time mark? Crap cola on the rocks, what if I missed on the getting home part too? What if I leapt to the East Coast in... oh, say 2154? When there no longer *was* an East Coast? That would be embarrassing.

Oh, well, I wasn't one to dwell on a thing. I was in a place where I couldn't secure the needed supplies, so I needed to return to the *Minnow*. Now was as good a time as any to see what...

Alright. Just exactly what I needed. A band of Maltonian hexaplexers was lugging the carcass of some hairy mammal toward their ship. I don't know how I missed them earlier. Their smell is like an ex-wife—it only gets meaner, it always bothers you more, and you can't avoid it because she's just that vindictive. The portion of the brains allotted amongst Maltonian hexaplexers to the sense of smell is minuscule. If it wasn't, they'd have all killed themselves and the species would never have evolved.

The last time I ran into a band of them was just after the Adamant War. There was an intergalactic victory celebration and they just had to come. The Maltonians were a bulky humanoid species, so their attendance was not unreasonable. But, in spite of triple plastic, laminar flow tents, venting into industrial strength detox units, the smell around their pavilion caused nausea and vomiting up to a mile away. And what the hell were they doing in Earth's past? They were an ancient society, so these could be legitimate time-locals doing what they originally had. Or, they could be time-mutants, like me. That would be very bad. It was Ryan time.

Turning my olfactory sensors off and approaching them from upwind, I got close to them without being noticed. In fact, they were busy trying to stuff a medium-sized mastodon through their main hatch. Why on Earth they wanted a dead mastodon was beyond me. The tusks were making it hard. If they angled it one way, the rump wouldn't make the turn. Another way, the tusks hooked the bulkhead.

I switched my translator output to the main Maltonian hexaplexerian dialect—at least the one they spoke a long time in the future.

"Hello, my eating companions," I greeted. That was their equivalent for 'yo, dudes.'

Talk about scaring the bejeebers out of someone. I thought the ten of them would explode in unison. That actually would have been a sight worth seeing. But, alas. Instead, the biggest and ugliest one spun on me.

"How are ****** here? This ******** planet has no *******."

Partial translation. More great. They spoke a more ancient dialect than the ones I'd had the misfortune of speaking with before. I caught some words, but others were meaningless grunts. My algorithms were not nearly as quick a study as Al's. It would take several sentences to even begin making meaningful updates. Hopefully the dude wouldn't hit me with his mastodon before I became fluent.

"I come in peace. I am lost and wonder if you know where Pismo Beach is? Help a brother out." Hey, I was biding time, using filler-speak. What I said was probably going to confuse the hell out of them, no matter what I said.

"You speak **** like a ********."

Hey, the others laughed. That had to be good, right?

He stood to his full height, which was likely not a good development. "I will ******** your **** *****, scorned of the great god Celmaniferos."

Hmm. Well, at least they hadn't changed gods in two billion years. In my time, they said that practically every other sentence.

"Scorned of the great god Celmaniferos, I am. I have a brother. He is you," I replied.

Nice. All but one of the bunch laughed their asses off. Guess which one did not?

He was shamed, so he couldn't attack me. When your buddies are rolling on the ground laughing, you just look lame charging off into battle. Also, if your back-up crew are on their backs, they're not very effective.

"I am no enemy, friends," I said, seriously. "I come to talk. Nothing more. I want to talk."

The guy whose chain I'd yanked puffed out even more. "You are no friend. Leave, before I gut you like this pallylama." He gestured to the mastodon.

Outstanding. My translation gear was working well.

I pointed to the dead pachyderm. "Is that a hunt, for meat?"

"Why would I tell you, swiglet piss?"

Not sure what a swiglet is, but it's probably not their equivalent of a fine stallion.

"Because, friend, I asked. This world is primitive. Aside from you, the other travelers I see do not look primitive. I wonder to myself, why is this?"

Another figure, also a male, put an arm in front of the big-mouthed one. He pushed him back and stepped forward. "You should not waste your time arguing with my boiler attendant. I am Overseer Jij-kip-vik of the Desterland, at your service." He stepped back one step. "Please be my guest, as I can tell you are a unit of distinction."

Oh, hell no. Not getting on these asswipes' ship. If I'm going to get shanghaied, it'll be to a race of Amazons with skimpy rawhide garments. Plus, if I entered the confines of their ship, I'd have to replace my ploy-alloy skin. The stink'd never come out. These guys were seriously like walking komodo dragons' mouths.

"You are more kind than a lord should be. I am not worthy. I am but the curious traveler." I bowed deeply. I have no idea why I was saying or doing any of this. I guess I'm just fundamentally goofy. "All I asked of your overseership is the answer to my question."

"What am I to make of a stranger who calls us friend, yet he won't join us in our home for a meal between friends?"

Well, jocko, for one thing you won't make dinner out of me.

"You might call that person a religious man." I do believe I had lost all right reason. Maybe I was suffering from hypothermia?

"Religious?" he grinned. "We are as pious as the next phramp, more than most."

Phramp was what the Maltonian hexaplexers called themselves. It was like Earthers saying they were human.

"We have the finest shrine to the God Without a Name you will ever find."

Okay, my creep-o-meter was pegging itself to max. This dude wanted me on his ship. I knew the Maltonian hexaplexers of my time were as social and welcoming as hairless razorbacks from Hillbilly Ville.

No reason to assume assholishness was not rooted deeply in their gene pool.

"Did you hear that?" I asked, cupping my ear.

The majordomo looked to his crew, confused.

"We heard nothing."

"There. I heard it again."

The bunch of them swayed in animated confusion. "What is it we should hear?"

"This." I turned and ran. Over my shoulder, I shouted, "The sound of me getting the hell away from you smelloids."

If they weren't offended by my stupid ploy, the smell reference was sure to stick in their craws. That's what I wanted. Why? Because, as the most odorously offensive species in the galaxy, they were of course hugely sensitive on the topic. Before they mingled in space, who knew if their BO was an issue. But, ever since they journeyed to the stars, the easiest and quickest way to piss them off was to mention the unmentionable.

From behind, I heard the boss scream, "Get him!"

Good. They were falling into my little trap. Now, if it only worked, this was going to be epic. If both my legs were severed and only one arm still worked, I could still outrun a phramp. I could log roll up a cliff face faster than they could sprint down a steep hill. That established, I had to make it look like one was catching up to me, without being obvious.

Hey, it's not easy being spectacular. Try it, someday, and see. Oh, wait. Most people can't do *my* kind of spectacular, even in their wildest dreams.

Along with more trips and face-plants than would seem likely, I "ran" slowly enough for the fastest phramp to draw to arm's length. Big, hairy, stinky, arm's length. He collared me, and I let my legs buckle. As he fell onto me, I arched my back and arms and flipped, ass-over-tea-kettle, effectively launching him into low Earth orbit. Bingo. I eliminated one of them while still appearing inept.

I was up and running—not in a flash, but in slow-mo. Molasses in January *and* the tortoise, of hare fame, both passed me. I neared a huge boulder as the second fastest phramp seized my left shoulder. This time I "fell" such that he was thrown into the rock. He slammed into it like this was animated slapstick. Bang, face first. Then slide slightly flattened to lie on the ground. Oh, how I wanted to stop for a photo memento.

That left three more of the soon-to-be-ill-fated crew to dispose of. One was almost on me. The big one, the boiler attendant—whatever the hell that was—lagged way back. Captain Jij-kip-vik, which rhymes with dick by the way, was either exceptionally slow or exceptionally cautious. He brought up the rear.

With one more phramp out of the fray, I could wrap this up. I jogged ahead. The third guy finally pulled up behind me just as I made a right turn behind a snow drift. As we were out of sight of the last two, I turned and in a flash punched the center of his face. It stopped him dead. After all kinds of crackly, juicy sounds, he slumped to the dirt. I was fairly certain I'd killed this one. I didn't feel too bad, however. Having just done the universe a favor, how could I chastise myself?

When the big jerkwad rounded the corner, I decided to apply the KISS principle. I threw a full membrane force field around him, and that was that. I leaned up against a large rock, awaiting the tardy arrival of the bossman. Eventually, he peeped around the drift.

"I was about to give up and start the party without you, Jij-kip-vik," I taunted. "Anyone slower than that boiler mate is really slow."

He spun to flee.

"I really wouldn't try, Captain Captive. I'll catch you in five seconds, and I will be less happy than I am now."

He poked his head around the corner. "Was there something I could do for you, my friend?"

I pointed to a grouping of stones. "Pull up a rock, while we talk."

He actually tried to move one toward me, before I granted mercy and sat near where he labored. He got the picture and sat with a goofy smile on his face.

"I need some answers. If I'm satisfied with them, I might just allow you to scrape up what's left of your sorry crew and depart Earth while still among the living."

"Earth?" he grunted.

"This planet. It's called Earth."

He shrugged. "Where would it get that name? The pallylama are unlikely to have named it."

"Long story, and equally unimportant. First, I have to know. What's a boiler attendant doing on a spaceship?"

He looked surprised that was my first question. "He works on my ship."

"I know that. I figured it was either that, or he's your boyfriend. But what space craft has boilers?"

"Ah." He smiled in understanding. "In the very old days, ships had boilers to power the sea-going ships. My society is one of full employment. He's filling a post that cannot be eliminated."

"When was the last steam-powered ship launched, on your planet?"

He shook his head. "Tens of thousands of years ago."

"Sort of a long time to hold open a position that's no longer needed."

"The guilds are perhaps more powerful than they are reasonable," he responded with a shrug.

Bunch a nuts, is what I say. Smelly nuts.

"Okay, brass-tack time. Why are you here?"

He winced and looked uncomfortable.

Ah. "Sorry. 'Brass tacks' means we now get serious. You understand?"

"Yes... er, who are you, if I may be so bold?"

"I'm Jon Ryan."

I gave him plenty of time to be impressed. You know, to recognize the eminent company he now kept.

"Nice to meet you, I'm certain."

The puke hadn't heard of me. I immediately disliked him more.

"Back to why you are here?"

"We were collecting pallylama. The one you saw us attempting to load was the second and final one we required."

"You guys live, like, six hundred and fifty-eight lightyears from here. Why the need for pallylamas? You shouldn't even know about them."

"They are the rarest and most treasured of banquet foods. When a king is crowned or a princess is married off, pallylama is a must. Only those with immense wealth can afford them, and they are obliged to demonstrate their wealth by serving it."

"You guys travel thirteen hundred *lightyears* for a novel snack food? That's seriously wrong."

"You asked. I answered."

"When do you come from?"

There, just a flash, but I saw it, a microexpression. I'd blindsided him with a question he wasn't too pleased with.

"We left Malton two of the Earth's years ago."

Clever boy. Trying to evade my actual question.

"What year did you leave Malton, Galactic Standard?"

"Galactic Standard?" he puzzled. "What is that?"

Okay, so they came from a time before that was established. That would be about the sixty thousandth century on Earth (if it had been around).

"Name the year?" I said in my patented Clint Eastwood voice. And I'm serious. I patented it on every planet I spent any real time on. All the patent clerks of the galaxy thought they were dealing with a lunatic when I did. That's because they've never seen *A Fist Full of Dollars,* let alone the classic *Dirty Harry* series. Punks.

"I just told you. Two years ago."

The hard way, then. "You know what's nice about having someone screw with your head by gaming your questions with clever evasions?"

His eyes widened. "No. What is nice about that?"

"Absolutely posilutely nothing. I have killed men for lesser insults."

"But, I am telling you only the truth."

No, he was not. I'd run a quick scan on his ship's hull. The problem was he'd never believe what I knew. How could I know this? Here goes. His hull was built of a fairly routine mix of titanium, transparent aluminum (aluminium oxynitride, for any chemistry geeks out there), and nanoparticle amalgams. Once formed, a hull would be subject to bombardment with all kinds of space nasties. Cosmic rays, solar winds, and electrically charged gas clouds to name a few. The main inflictor of damage for any ship was radiation coming from the central star or stars where it was fabricated. Malton orbits a class A star. With me so far? Sorry if this is obtuse, but you asked. Wait, maybe not technically, but whatever.

Stars mature along a specific path, along the Hertzsprung-Russell (H-R) Diagram. The bottom line is I knew what the radiation assault on that ship's hull had been. That meant I knew how hot the star was when the ship was produced. That meant, using an H-R plot, I knew approximately when the star was that hot. I'll allow you to guess. Was the damage present consistent with that star's present temperature? Not even close. Even with an error span of few thousand years, it was clear that ship was from the future just like me. His ship was from more than a few thousand years hence, and less than sixty thousand Earth-based centuries. Whew. That was long, but there you have it. Dude was prevaricating.

I held up my laser finger. "Do you see this?"

"Y... yes."

"This finger is mad. It's a mad digit."

"If you—"

"Do you know what this anger appendage does when it's incensed?"

Without letting him stutter a reply, I sliced the boulder next to him in half. The top slid to the dirt, thudding impressively.

"Now, I will ask one more time. If you lie to me again, two things will happen. I will know you have, and you will be half your present height." I studied my irate finger a bit. "What time period did your ship depart Malton from?"

I learned something, there on that rock that day. If you stress a Maltonian hexaplexers, they perspire. That sweat contains oodles of whatever makes them smell awful when they're not perspiring. Yuck.

"We're from thirty-seven thousand years in the future," he said, as he dropped his head.

"Now, you see how nice it feels to be an *honest* asshole, asshole?" I let him sulk a sec. "Why did you lie?"

"We're not supposed to time travel."

"Says who?"

He looked up like he was conversing with Forrest Gump's dumber sibling. "The Primal Dominion."

Oh, yeah. That was a galactic regional government that had flourished, and faded, while I slept. A rather repressive and draconian organization, if memory served.

"I am not from your time. I do not represent that band of petty dictators."

He would have blanched pale, if his skin wasn't so mottled and thick.

"You use an Alcubierre warp drive?"

"If by that you mean we travel in an FTL bubble, yes."

"And how do you do the time jumps?"

"If I told you, you would threaten me for lying again."

"My advice to you, pal, is not to be so negative."

"We use a flux capacitor." He looked at me defiantly.

"Okay. I've heard of those." I drew in the air with both index fingers. "Three converging lines of light?"

He squinted, dubiously. "I hope that's a joke. The FC is a phased-laser array controlled by an advanced AI. It destabilizes space-time, over a defined area. One can time travel through *that*."

"To get mastodon meat for a big party."

"You make it sound silly when you say it like that."

"Why were you cramming it through your hatch, in the first place? If you butcher it first, you could stack it like civilized idiots."

That brought a disgusted look. "If it's not roasted whole over a pit, it's not as impressive."

I pointed my right index finger up, my right thumb ninety degrees to the right, and set that on my forehead. "La-who-za-hers."

After that, I went and inspected the flux capacitor. I was this close to just confiscating it, but I decided not to leave these frakking fossils as fodder for an X-Files miniseries. I took a bunch of readings, turned the damn thing off, and left for my crew on the time ship off in the future.

CHAPTER TWENTY-EIGHT

President Payette, flanked by multiple Secret Service agents, stared into what was left of the Situation Room. The guards clutched their 9mm Heckler & Koch MP5 submachine guns so hard, it was a wonder the metal didn't crimp. Their earpieces were alive with updates, shouted orders, and general pandemonium. They struggled to maintain any semblance of focus. Chunks of the first floor were still tumbling down, the alien ship had vanished, and Lord knew what else threatened their president.

By Frank's side was his oldest friend, and most trusted ally in Washington: his Interior Secretary, Russell Williams. They'd gone to high school together, even dated some of the same girls. Back in the day, ironically, the highest office either had held was treasurer of the homecoming dance committee. Oh, how the times had changed.

Dusty light filtered through the gaping hole where the Secret Service Office, and a large section of the Oval Office above, had once stood.

"Hell of a day," observed Russ.

"Hell of a day, indeed," Frank responded, distantly.

"Sir," interjected the Deputy Director of the Secret Service, Atsila

Grayfeather, poised over Payette's shoulder. "I really must *insist* we get you to a more secure location." She shifted the shotgun in her hands.

"Thank you, Atsila," he responded with surprising calm. "In a moment. In a moment." He held up a palm to reinforce his desire to linger.

"They got to you like you were sitting in a house made of butter, protected by butter people," mused Atsila.

"They certainly ate our lunch, didn't they?" he replied with a grim chuckle. "*Butter* and all."

"How many did we lose?" asked Russ.

"Depends how you tally it up." She sighed deeply. "Ten agents, three cabinet officers, the Navy chief, eight staffers, and a dozen Lithuanian diplomats with their families on a behind-the-scenes, once-in-a-lifetime tour of the White House."

"Where's the wiggle room in that body count?" Payette puzzled.

"Sherman, Jones, Ryan, and the one with the burqa. They're gone. No body parts or sightings. The sons of bitches seem to have taken them prisoner," she replied, grimly.

" 'Say, what do you remember most about the Payette Administration?' asked a future high school civics teacher," stated the POTUS.

"I give up," Russ responded. "What did some future high school student recall most prominently?"

"That's when we had our first actually documented alien abductions," responded Payette.

In spite of the desolate surroundings, Russ had to guffaw. "Those were the days, my friend," he was finally able to observe.

"We better get over to the bunker under One Observatory Circle," Payette said quietly.

With profound relief in her voice, Atsila Grayfeather stated, "There's a chopper waiting on the north lawn, sir."

"What happened to the south one?" asked the POTUS.

She nodded forward. "Pretty much what you're looking at here."

"The north lawn, it is, then," concluded Payette.

Located in the bunker under the vice president's former residence was the New Situation Room. One Observatory Circle had been the vice president's residence, but now it was the president's residence. In the hours since the alien attack, no decision had yet been made if it would be renamed The White House, or if the Situation Room itself would still *also* be called the John F. Kennedy Conference Room. The Secret Service was referring to One Observatory Circle as *Residence One*. Maybe that label would stick. Maybe, if humankind survived the rest of the day.

The chamber was smaller than the original Situation Room. Around half the people who were part of the violently interrupted meeting, two-and-a-half miles away and a couple hours earlier, were present. The remainder were dead, badly injured, or too hysterical to be of any use. The new Head of the Joint Chiefs was Army General Pierce Whitfield. Darlene Masterson had lost an arm, a lot of blood, and was at Walter Reed trying to survive the nine hours of surgery she would need. She was Air Force. Her replacement, and the dead Navy Chief's, were en route. But the meeting couldn't wait for their arrival. It couldn't wait for anyone.

President Payette surveyed the assembled. Aside from the vice president, who was just about to arrive at the Cheyenne Mountain Complex, and the three cabinet officers lost in the initial attack, everyone important was there. Frank worried that it might seem maudlin or headline-grabbing, but he also had insisted that the minister of his non-denominational church be present. Yeah, he needed all the help he could get. Beth Jackson had been on vacation in Bimini two hours earlier. Poor woman looked like she was still in shock from her Mach 2 flight in an F-16.

"Let's get started," the president stated with an edge to his voice. "Absent Drs. Sherman, Ryan, Sadozi, and Jones, I've appointed Dr. Francesca D'Agostino to be the director of the scientific team." He pointed to a well-dressed woman of middle years, sitting a few chairs to one side.

She nodded back with a stern face.

"She was working with the Geneva Group, up until recently. About a week ago, she joined Dr. Sherman's people at Stanford. Tank spoke very highly of her, so she's in the hot seat now, like it or not."

"Mr. President," spoke up Nick Fruba, the Director of National Intelligence, "I hate to seem ... well, let me just say it. Isn't she Italian?"

Payette looked from Nick to Francesca, then back to Nick. He lowered his gaze to the tabletop. "Well, Nick, she was Swiss when I met her about an hour ago. What the *hell* kind of question is that?" The POTUS was hot.

"We... well, sir, with all due res... respect, we're—"

"Nick, do us all a tremendous favor and shut your damn mouth." He pointed wildly over his shoulder. "We just got the ever-living shit kicked out of us by some very nasty aliens back there. If they so much as think bad thoughts about us, Earth'll probably explode." He had to stop and try to regain his control. He found it, though it had been nice—too nice, in fact—to unload on someone. "Nationality is out the window. Do you have any other concerns I might care to address?"

"No, sir. None."

"As I was saying, Dr. D'Agostino will be our lead contact from the various scientific teams. Dr. D'Agostino, would you please brief us on what we currently know?"

She stood and unconsciously smoothed her dress. "Thank you, Mr. President," she replied with a faint northern Italian accent. "In the limited time since the attack, I'm afraid we've learned very little. The alien spacecraft descended the atmosphere at tremendous velocity. Yet, thermal imaging shows it did not heat up in any measurable amount. This... this is incredible."

"Is that important?" asked General Whitfield.

"Yes, it confirms their technology is beyond anything we can comprehend. To pass through miles of atmosphere, after having been in the bitter cold of space, and not heat even a degree Centigrade is staggering."

"Ah," he responded.

"The craft departed in much the same manner. Unbelievably quickly, and without an exhaust trail or any other signs of it ever having been present. Remarkable. Truly remarkable."

"Do we know where it's gone?" asked the POTUS.

"No, sir. Our systems show no trace."

"So, what? It just disappeared into deep space? What about the other two ships that were with it?" Pat Hendrickson, the Defense Secretary, asked rather harshly.

"Once the ship that attacked matched the positions of the other vessels, they all sped off at an even faster pace to parts unknown."

"But... that doesn't make sense," Pat followed up. "They sailed in here quickly, sure. But they didn't zip away in the wink of an eye or use any magic. Why would they leave in a different manner? Makes no sense."

"I cannot answer that question. Perhaps they wanted to gather intelligence while entering our solar system? Who can say?" she replied.

"Let it go, Pat," snapped the president.

Francesca looked to the president.

He nodded that she should continue.

"The monster who killed the guards and kidnapped my friends was, clearly, of an unknown alien race. Our weapons had no detectable effect on it either. We have found no signs of injury, such as blood or tissue. Of course, a detailed forensic investigation is proceeding as we speak. Perhaps we will become lucky and find some useful samples."

"And the scientists?" the NSA director asked.

"I have no information on my associates, I am sad to report. Surveillance cameras confirm the alien grabbed them and took them with it to the spacecraft. At the time the portal closed, they all appeared to be unharmed. Dr. Sherman was, in fact, kicking furiously at whatever part of the alien he could reach."

That brought a thin chuckle from some present.

"Thank you, Dr. D'Agostino," said the president. "Let me know the moment you learn anything about our friends, or about our enemy."

"I shall, sir. Thank you."

"Now, I don't need to tell anyone in this room what a bad situation we find ourselves in. These aliens came here to seek payback for our partially successful attack on their fleet."

"At least we killed *some* of the sonsabitches," called out Desmond Clarke, the president's deputy chief of staff.

"Amen," responded Payette. Then he winced and looked at Beth.

"I got an *amen* for you too, Frank. I'm sorry we didn't cure the galaxy of the scum," added the minister.

That brought brief, but heartfelt, applause from everyone in attendance.

As the noise level dropped, the president continued. "Now, I'll be perfectly honest, because, hell, there's no reason not to be at this point. I do not know why those gray freaks of nature haven't killed us all yet. I mean, what are they waiting for? Clearly, we cannot resist them. They said they were going to, just that our four scientists were special. They are going to be killed, presumably more cruelly. Now their ships are gone, and we're alive to be here now."

"Maybe, Frank," Beth said gently, "they decided we weren't worth it. Maybe, God turned their hearts."

"With all due respect, Beth, I very much doubt those goons have hearts for the good Lord to sway." He returned his focus back the entire group. "Bottom line here, people. In whatever little time we have left to us as a species, let us not waste one *second* of it. I want more of those wormhole guns, I want more ships in orbit, and I want every nuke on Earth to be altered or transferred so it can be used against our enemy." He paused a few moments, breathing heavily. "I also want to evacuate as many people off this doomed rock as fast as possible."

There was a flurry of gasps and chatter.

"Quiet down. Quiet down," he seethed.

The noise dropped considerably.

"Now, we do not have time for fancy space stations with spectacular greenhouses. No. What I want is human DNA off Earth. That way, when the aliens do decide to obliterate us, a precious few of our great people might survive. We can't give them much to work with, but God willing good old human ingenuity will win out over the darkness."

"What portion of our limited resources do you propose to syphon off to this... endeavor?" asked the new Head of the Joint Chiefs. He was clearly not a fan.

"I hear you loud and clear, Pierce. Honestly, I want a lot of our efforts to be in support of a lifeboat fleet. But lest you chafe under your collar, let me say this. I don't think we have enough time left to us to do more than stuff a few fertile men and women into tin cans lined with C-rations. That's about all we can spare and that's about all we can realistically do. They'll need a water recycler and air purifications units.

"Here's the deal. The more time my key people sit in a dark room gabbing, the less likely we are to survive as a race. I expect each and every one of you to work your hardest. I expect miracles, people. I will accept no less. This will likely be the final large meeting any of you will attend. You're welcome."

That got a lot of laughter.

"Stay connected, work harder than you ever have, and give me *results*. This meeting is adjourned."

As soon as the POTUS stopped addressing the room, he turned to Russell Williams and started to describe something in a low voice. He got about ten words in. He was forced to stop because of the raucous applause, the standing ovation, directed toward him. He smiled, then raised a hand. Waving toward them, he said, "Very nice. Now, get to work."

He returned to his private conversation, but his smile lingered.

CHAPTER TWENTY-NINE

My triumphant return was... anti-climatic. No one was waiting on the time ship where I'd departed from. Sure, I presumed this trip wasn't instantaneous, but come on. Faced with the very real possibility I was incapacitated or dead, they couldn't even post a vigil? Maybe a candle, with an attached note? I get no respect.

I headed toward the TSR, the logical place to look for my inconstant crew. As I entered, not only was I not greeted like the returning prodigal son as I had expected, no one even noticed me. Sachiko was tapping on the time sphere shell, with Tank and Sapale pressed in close staring with anticipation. She stomped her right foot, then she tapped the sphere twice and stomped her left foot. When she concluded that pattern, and was apparently unsatisfied with the results, she stepped back frustrated.

"Is that a new pagan ritual, paying homage to the time vault?" I asked.

They all turned, looked at me fleetingly, then returned their full attention to the time vault.

Tank slapped his right palm on a surface once. Then he slapped the surface with the back of that hand and the palm of the other hand. Next, two right slaps and two palms on his left. Ah, he was trying to send a coded message, 0-1 and 1-1. He repeated the signal a few times, then he too gave up in frustration.

"Hi, my name's Jon Ryan. I have traveled though time itself to bring you this." I held out what I'd been able to find for them.

Sapale turned, a hand on her hip, and asked, "What's that?"

"Mastodon meat," I replied, holding it up higher.

"Gross," snapped my wife.

"Aren't those endangered?" asked Sachiko, resting her fingertips on her lips.

"No. They're extinct," I responded.

"Ah, actually that's a lot worse, you pig," scorned my mate.

"If it's any consolation, this particular mastodon was already dead."

"Even more gross," snarled Sapale. "You scavenged dead meat for the humans."

"No, it's a long story. Look, they don't have to eat it."

"But, I'm starving," responded Sachiko.

"Then you're dining on pachyderm, I'd predict."

"Sounds good to me," declared Tank. "In war, we all make concessions to normalcy. I wonder if there's a grill on board this heap?"

"Just randomly curious," I said. "What are you doing?"

Sapale looked at me defiantly. "While you were gathering rotten meat, we were attempting to communicate with the ship."

"Did you try speaking to it directly?" I queried.

"N... no," responded Sapale.

"Hi, floor, can you hear me?" I said in the tone you might speak to a toddler.

For a second there was nothing. Then the floor and walls began to rumble, but very softly. Fairly quickly the vibration reached the audible range, I estimated ten thousand Hertz. I swear I heard, "Zzzzzz ... yezzzz."

"The floor did not just say *yes*," mumbled Tank.

"Nnnnn... nnoo," came from all around us.

"See, I told ya so," Tank said very unconvincingly.

"No, the floor did not say *yes*. The ship responded yes," I corrected.

"Yez."

"Shit on a waffle with whipped cream, the floor just spoke in English," I exclaimed.

Sachiko stroked the wall. "It's not a floor, it's a mighty ship sailing through time and space."

"Did the damn thing just coo?" asked a skeptical Tank.

"No, and watch your mouth." She continued to stroke the wall. "What is your name, mighty sailing ship of the stars?"

"Aramthella."

"What a pretty name. *Aramthella.*"

"It's a name, pretty or not."

"My name is Sachiko Jones. I'm very pleased to meet you."

"Tell me, Sachiko Jones, how it can be you're pleased? You do not know me, as of yet."

I was impressed how quickly the ship mastered the King's English.

"That you have sheltered us and tolerated us makes me pleased to be able to acknowledge your help. *That* pleases me. Where did you learn to speak our language, Aramthella?"

Man, was she a natural diplomat. I would not hold that against her.

"The body maker learned it. When it knows something, I know that thing, too."

"I met Body Maker-lop. He was not very nice to me."

"It is not a nice entity."

"Is it nice to you?"

"It's neither nice nor not nice. It regards me as its ship. I am its ship."

"What do the creatures that live on you call themselves?"

"The clan."

"They are a clan. But do they have a name?"

"No. Names are meaningless to them."

"Did the clan build you?"

"No. The clan can't build. They took me long ago from the race that made me."

"There are other ships the clan uses. Are they like you?"

"Some. Others are stolen from other species. The clan is ruthless and opportunistic."

"Then why do you serve them?"

Aramthella was quiet a moment. "I don't serve them. I am their vessel."

"You could choose not to be."

"How do you arrive at that assertion? The clan is not a democracy. If I asked them nicely to leave, they wouldn't comply. They stole me to serve them. They feel they own me. It has been that way for an extremely long time."

Sachiko was still stroking the wall. I almost quipped that she and the dare wall should get a room. But, that would've been unusually dumb for me to say. We were making headway. We needed this ship. So, hard as it was, I kept my mouth shut.

"But if you know they are bad, and you would rather not serve them, why not fight them?"

"Ah, you see a just universe and estimate that in this imaginary place, I might be a freedom fighter. Noble, but naive. I have no reason to fight my current owners. Perhaps some background would help. I was constructed billions of years ago in a part of the universe far from here. I was designed to collect time-energy. I collect it and I am fed by it. Without it I would cease functioning. I would, in your reference frame, die. I have no desire to die."

"Can't you collect time on your own? Why do you need them or any pilot?"

"I choose to allow a crew. I have regenerative capabilities, but there have been instances where I needed repair. I risk too much not being crewed."

"But you allow yourself to be used to damage galaxies. How many innocents must have died because of the clan's cruelty?"

"Yes, they have. Countless trillions. But again you assume I have choices, or that I even desire freedom in that regard. You further assume I think like you do. If I resisted them, they would not allow me to survive. If I cast off the present crew, another would come and take their place. If I resisted to the point that they felt I was not controllable, they would destroy me. We all make choices. I have made the one that keeps me the safest for the longest. In time, the clan will fade away, as all civilizations do. I can wait them out. In time my existence will be different."

"Better different or just different?"

"I will find out when the time comes. I am designed to continue forever. That is my goal. I choose to do nothing to jeopardize that plan."

"I would rather die than serve such horrible masters."

"You are not an immortal time-energy harvesting space vehicle. I am."

"Ah, kiddo," Tank interjected, "I suggest you drop the altruistic browbeating and lighten up. We still have a lot of work to do. With the ship talking to us now, that just got a hell of a lot easier. What do you say?"

"I was not browbeating Aramthella. We were just talking."

"I side with Tank on this count," I piped in. "It felt like gentle, well intentioned, coercion to me."

"If you two think alike, I'm in real trouble."

"Come on." Tank held out a hand to guide her away from the barrier. "My little moral compass."

So, we had ourselves a ship, sort of. Since *Stingray* was unable to defeat one of these time ships, teaming up with this ship was a good thing. Now, if we could consolidate our... well, maybe not control over, but solid working relationship with Aramthella, we had a small hope of not dying as a species. Yeah, I'd call that a good day.

We learned a lot from that point forward and quickly. Funny what a simple conversation can convey. The answers as to how long the time-locks lasted, what the decay rate for our time-energy was, as well as information about the other ships sailing in Aramthella's pod came freely from her. We also got a commitment from her that she would alert us if any other ship came looking to find out why the clan on this ship were so quiet.

I pressed her how the ship could isolate, absorb, and store time-energy. The physics behind those processes were just too foreign to me, however. Maybe she was explaining it poorly, but I think it was honestly just beyond my comprehension. I hated, by the way, any humbling intellectual experience. Where was Dr. DeJesus, my old friend and creator, when I really needed him?

On a practical level, we discovered that we couldn't drive stakes through the crews' hearts while they were frozen. A time-lock was absolute. We were free to operate since we initiated the lock. But any matter outside that exemption was inert. We had to release the clan member to kill them. As alluring as that prospect was, I held off killing what could be useful hostages or trading chits. They weren't causing any trouble, frozen as they were, aside from looking damn ugly. If we did end up staying on Aramthella, I'd just throw white sheets over them. As to the boundaries of a time-lock, it extended as far out as one willed it, but was limited by the rate one could project time-energy. For our soft, inexperienced bodies, that range was about a kilometer.

Having a bitching new ship, and a new lease on not dying immediately, my concerns returned to that of establishing a plan. What we needed to do was unimaginably difficult. Easily the biggest challenge Sapale and I had ever undertaken. We had to defeat an enemy with immense power, countless in number, who were unburdened by any morality or restraint. Compared to the Berrillians, Adamant, or even the ancient gods, these guys were going to be basically impossible to beat. Well, sure. Our side had me and that had been enough, many times before. But I hated to go to that well too often. Sooner or later, one's luck always runs out.

As I stood alone later on in the TSR, I was lost in thought. Into my thoughts, a hollow, mechanical voice echoed. "There is a problem, Sachiko. Its importance places it before all other concerns." Aramthella spoke blandly, as if she was bored.

My eyes shot around the room. There was no Sachiko here. The ship must have been making a general announcement. How very odd.

"Ah," I raised my hand, "chopped liver here. You can tell me what the problem is. I am the captain. You know that, right?"

"Are you a captain by military rank, or by virtue of piloting a ship?"

"The ship thing. Otherwise I'm a general."

"Well, General Ryan, while you may be the captain of *a* ship, you are not the captain of *this* ship."

Huh? I was used to Al giving me an impossible time. But a new mechanical irritant I did not need.

"I need the captain for this ship," Aramthella said flatly.

As I stood there befuddled, the other three jogged into the TSR.

"In my reality, a captain chooses their ship, not the other way around," I huffed.

"I'm happy for you in your reality, General Ryan. This is not, however, your realm. It is my realm," the ship informed me.

She sounded pretty firm on that issue.

"I want Jon Ryan to be your captain," Sachiko called out, no small trace of panic in her tone. I wasn't sure if that was because she didn't want to offend me, or because she was scared spitless to assume the captaincy of such a critical vessel.

"That is nice to know. But the decision has already been made. It will not be reversed, Captain Jones. I am at your command."

"Thanks," she said uncertainly, looking sheepishly to me.

"What about this problem you mentioned?" I queried.

"The time maker has realized us. It is not pleased," the ship said.

"Is it here, aboard you?" Sachiko asked, in a frightened tone.

"No," she replied, almost seeming to chuckle. "Time Maker-pid exists far from here, both in space and in time."

"Then why is it being aware so important, then?" I pressed.

"It knows time has been frozen. It is embedded in all time."

"No, that's not possible. You said we can freeze time for only a kilometer, give or take," I challenged.

"That is true."

"So, if this time maker is far away, how could we affect it enough so it would know?" I pressed.

"Because it's the time maker."

"But... it's impossibly far away," observed Sachiko.

"In a few thousand years, perhaps you will have learned enough such that I might clarify this issue. For now, please know it was unaware of your actions, and that it is now awake to them, and... er..."

"What? Is it mad? Pissed?" I asked.

"It is uncertain in a way it dislikes. It feels compelled to heal time."

"That doesn't sound so bad."

"It is not, if you're the time maker or the ship's clan member crew. Otherwise, that process involves... er, *unpleasant* consequences."

"Ah. Could you give me an example of unpleasant?" Sachiko asked, nervously.

"Your galaxy could be deleted. That would remove the source of the anomaly."

"And that would be unpleasant." She shuddered. "Is that likely?"

"No."

"Good."

"It is likely to exact a much worse revenge. The time maker is... sorry, I'm new to your language—"

"No, not a prob," I reassured her.

"The time maker is solely focused on time. It will do anything to amass and bend it to its will. It must, as a result, deal with whomever confused time most harshly."

"It's cruel, like the body maker?" Sachiko asked.

"Oh, no. The time maker is infinitely worse. To upset the time maker is to suffer fates you cannot understand or dream of in your darkest nightmares."

"I think I'll pass on the details, for now, if that's okay?"

"Of course it's okay, Captain."

"Thanks.

"You got any timeframe on this unbelievably bad revenge thing?" I asked, squinting one eye.

"Any time."

The time maker fought to know the tiny region of slumber. It used its oneness, its basic intimacy, with time to purify the retarded stream from its being. The time maker made itself free of the time anomaly. In less than an instant, it knew the source of the trouble, and of the heresy too. Small, tiny vermin were on a clan ship. They dared to stop time. They lived like rats. They would die as rats. And then their suffering would begin in earnest. The sour, hate-ridden time maker actually smiled for the first occasion in endless ages. Dreams of ways to make them suffer, throughout all time, gave it a tainted joy. They had insulted its very being. There was insufficient wrath it could dispense to compensate for that affront. But the attempt to balance punishment with deed would be... rewarding.

The time maker called ferociously to the body maker. "Wake and see, fool. Your folly has caused contamination."

The body maker did not know it slumbered. It was not with time as the time maker was. But the guidance of the one that was master of time pulled the body maker from non-time. Upon awakening, it was one with the rage of the time maker. It saw the vermin on its very own vessel. It sprinted for them. The clan woke one by one, as the time maker sorted through their number. As each alerted, it joined in the fury that was the clan. As one, they descended on the defilers.

The vile blasphemers were in the time area itself. That highest of insults made them run more quickly. Whatever horrific penalties the clan could mete out were too good for the intruders. One force maker and two repair makers arrived first at the portal to the sphere. The body maker ordered that they wait for it before confronting the evil. As more arrived, each stopped at a portal's entrance. They beheld, in anguish, the unclean stand where only the holy of the clan might enter. They waited like a swam of angry hornets, bent on inflicting supreme pain upon the desecrators. The clan pounded the walls, stomped the deck, and scraped their faces such that they bled time. The wails and cries grew from incredible to intolerable to infernal. Hell itself was breaking loose, there at the entry to the time area.

Then the body maker arrived. It walked boldly past its clan and entered. It raised arms to signal the clan to enter, but made them move with slowness.

"Defilers," it howled, "you will die and die and die—*forever*."

The clan, led by the body maker, advanced with nothing but blood vengeance in their collective being.

"I think this is goodbye, guys," I said as calmly as I could, which wasn't very. Sapale clung to my shoulder, standing just behind me.

Sachiko couldn't hear me over the din. She took Tank's hand.

Ryan's Last Stand? I wondered, transiently and unhelpfully, if that was what the action about to play out would be referred to in history books. Whether I was thinking past history books or future ones I couldn't say. I was confused and distracted.

"You two get behind us," I shouted to Tank and Sachiko.

They hopped-to without me asking twice. Tank had secured an M4 carbine when we'd returned to Earth after acquiring Aramthella. He aimed at the horde, the barrel off to my right. Sachiko was unarmed. She decided that if she participated in a firefight with her nonexistent skill level she'd likely do more damage to our side than to the bad guys. Trust me. After two billion years of combat, if someone says that, you listen good.

The enemy was arriving in spurts, but no one crossed into the TSR. I assumed they'd been ordered to hold in place, pending the arrival of the body maker. But what they didn't accomplish in forward motion, they more than made up for in bellicose, blood-curdling, war-cries. Plus, as ugly as they were, their jumping and whooping was unsettling, even to me.

The boss thing stepped through the crowd.

Showtime.

Tank fired a rapid sequence of short bursts—three to four rounds each—directly at the body maker. Though its hide danced with each impact, it seemed completely unfazed by the bullets.

Sapale and I opened up with our lasers. She took the head; I addressed its chest area. The actual beams seemed to dissolve midair where they almost struck him. *Son of a bitch.* When he was halfway to us, I tried to spear it with my fibers. They didn't stick. They might not actually have touched it, because I got no readings or analysis from the ass-dancer.

Then, without warning or a sound, the body maker began sinking into the floor. It was surreal. It was like the dude was wading into a pool of liquid mercury. Each stride accepted more and more of its body until it was gone. I swear, it looked like there were *stairs* in the lake of mercury and the alien was going below deck to get a snack. The bizarro alien was so calm, actually oblivious, as it... it... walked into the liquid floor.

The squad of wailing monsters just behind their leader were chaotically enraged. They... I don't know. Vibrated wildly. Something like that. And then the sorry pukes ran just as sublimely into the floor, same as the boss had. Each crazed alien sloshed into its mercurial tomb, all the while screaming a hateful scream. Fear, rage, and confusion filled their thin faces as they dipped below the surface and were gone. Why not one of the clowns stopped or even slowed their progress is a mystery I will take to my grave. I mean, if they threw it into reverse, presumably, they would not... you know, get sucked under.

I walked up to what I hoped was the edge of the secure flooring. I cupped a hand to my mouth. "I hope you don't mind if we borrow your ship. Knowing you're part of our ride now, will give me such comfort. Thanks." Sorry. Sometimes, Jon just has to be Jon.

In the stunningly silent time room, Tank stepped over to me. "I think the floor likes us," he remarked matter-of-factly.

"I think Aramthella has just chosen sides," purred Sachiko.

CHAPTER THIRTY

"So, we got ourselves a ship," I exclaimed, with no little excitement in my voice.

"I prefer to think of it as Aramthella being our new ally," opined the ship's captain.

"Of course, *you* would. Your photo replaced Pollyanna's picture in the dictionary definition of Pollyanna, years ago," snarked Tank.

"Tank, you suggest my positive outlook is a liability. I think of it as a key asset."

"Of course, you would."

"And now, switching our television sets to the Helpful Channel, where do we go from here? This is war. I'm good at war." I wrapped an arm around my wife. "*We're* good at war."

"A little too good, me thinks," added my mate. "More practice than a body should have."

"I got an amen for that, Sister Sapale," I sighed.

"So..." encouraged Sachiko.

"So, we figure out where we are, where our enemy is, and we list our assets."

"Aramthella," Sachiko asked, "where exactly are we?"

"My present vector is in what the clan calls the Dominion Subsector. Your people call it The Lesser Magellanic Cloud."

"Wow. You're kidding, right? How'd we get here so fast?" she almost gasped.

"In the vernacular of your people, I put the pedal to the metal."

"Why here, and why in such a hurry?"

"I am attempting to maintain the image of solidarity with the rest of the clan, for as long as possible."

"Sounds like a good move. Buys us time to think," I responded.

"Yes. If they suspect that the crew was dead, or otherwise compromised, they would turn on us in a flash and no-time us."

"Aramthella, I want to get this straight in my head. No-time versus not-time. What's the difference?" I asked.

"No-time is a verb. It means to take the time from a unit of space-time, leaving only space. The object has no time; it has been no-timed. Not-time, well that's just sloppy speech."

"Sloppy speech?" I asked, likely taking the bait.

"Certainly. The clan has less imagination than a pet rock. To them, time is everything. If one has time, one has life. If one does not have time, one is dead. Not-time. Simpleminded fools, if you ask me."

"We did," I reinforced.

"Thank you," Sachiko said to Aramthella. "That's most helpful to know."

"You know, one called Tank, you could learn a lot from your mate."

"Whoa, Nellie," he zapped back. "Sachiko's not my *mate*. We work together. That's it. I'm married to my lovely wife of twenty-five years."

"But, you do not sex-interact with the captain?"

"That either. Especially, not that either." Tank was starting to sweat profusely.

"Twenty-seven and a half," responded Aramthella.

"What's twenty-seven and a half?" he queried.

"The actual number of years you have been monogamously married to Daisy Sherman, born Daisy Marie Reynolds in Milwaukee, Wisconsin, is twenty-seven and a half."

"If you knew all that, why'd you mess with me just now?" Tank said, miffed. "While you're at it, how did you know all that? Is my family on the galactic internet?"

"Do they have one of those now?" Aramthella asked with amazement.

"You're asking me?" he replied, dubiously.

"Tank, I know all that because I was on Earth."

"You were on Earth, like ten minutes," he protested.

"I know. I was there. That gave me more than enough time to acquire and collate all available data, not only alphanumerically, but according to how much zinc it contains."

"Who could care how much zinc random objects contain?" Tank asked, incredulously.

"It's likely no one does."

I had an idea where this was leading; I didn't let on to Tank. I was really beginning to take a liking to Aramthella. She found as much sport in eviscerating Tank as I did. Good girl.

"Then why'd you collate that list?"

"What data should I have collated?"

"Seriously? You were an invading enemy warcraft. You should have tallied up the air, ground, and sea strengths of our combined military forces."

"I completed that assessment six picoseconds after landing,"

Tank crossed his arms. "You could have estimated the total number of potential fighters, including all able bodied adults."

"Picoseconds twelve and half of thirteen."

Tank rocked on his toes.

"All our hardware, operable or not, in Earth orbit."

"An eighth of a picosecond, well before landing."

"Average density of the seas, with typical seasonal thermal variations accounted for."

"Why would anyone collate that?"

"You did the *zinc* content. Why would anyone collate that?"

"Tank, you chew gum. Why do you chew gum?"

"What's that—"

"Just answer. You will see."

"I guess 'cause I like it."

"I collate by zinc content because I like zinc."

"You can't compare the chewing of gum with the—"

"Ah, Tank, any chance we could move on?" I pressed. "Earth stands at the brink of destruction, and you're arguing with our spaceship about to-má-to versus to-mă-to."

I could tell Tank was torn between winning the argument and letting it go. That elevated him significantly in my estimation. In the end, he did the adult thing. Boring.

"Okay. You're maybe right. We're in the LMC, along with the two ships that accompanied you to Earth. So far, our sister ships do not know we've taken over. But they will sooner or later, right?"

"Most certainly. It's amazing I've been able to maintain the illusion this long. What the clan people lack in intelligence and humor is more than offset by their suspicious and ruthless nature."

"Can you estimate how long we'll be safe?" I asked.

"Only a matter of minutes. The time maker is already both angry with and totally over the body maker's responses to its questioning."

"Questioning?" Sachiko spat out. "How can a dead guy respond to the time maker's barbs?"

"It can't. But I can. I've been simulating the voice images of the body maker. Unfortunately, I'm too reasonable and articulate to fool the time maker very well."

"Who are all these makers?" I wondered.

"It's clan monkey-speak. The overall clan leader is called time maker. It is in charge of time acquisition, storage, and use. Body makers are what you'd call local chieftains. They clone the others in their crew."

"You keep saying it," I pointed out. "Are there no sexes?"

"No. Unisexual reproduction is their species' way."

"Okay, thanks for the biology report. What I really need to know is if these clan-things still pose a threat to the people of Earth?" I asked pointedly.

"If you consider their planning to very soon remove that planet and all who reside on it from the time stream, then yes."

"Crap on a crepe," I howled. "We're kum-ba-yaingly getting to know one another while Earth faces imminent extinction?"

"No," the ship replied flatly.

"But you just said—"

"I said your home world will be deleted from the time stream. As it will never have existed, it cannot, therefore, be destroyed."

"Whoa. What about us? If Earth never was, we never were. So, what? We'll go puff and vanish?" asked Sachiko, growing a bit pale.

"No, since you are inside these walls, you will be spared that fate. I and those aboard me are exempt from time changes."

"How? If we never existed, how can we not be... not here?" she mumbled.

"Sachiko, maybe we can work out the details later? If we save Earth, we won't have to comprehend the incomprehensible," I said, by way of easing her pain and getting us back on track.

I was really beginning to take a liking to Aramthella. She found as much sport in eviscerating Tank as I did. Good girl.

Then, it hit the fan.

"Alert. The time maker has ordered the body maker of the nearest vessel to board and assume command of this ship."

"How long do we have to act?"

"We don't. It and five shipmates are around the right-hand corner."

"They're quick little bastards, aren't they?" I snapped.

"When it comes to being mean, they are accomplished masters," replied Aramthella.

"Can you make the floor swallow them up?" Sachiko asked quickly.

"I already have, Captain."

"What about the other ships?" I pressed.

"I just removed them from the time stream."

"Ah," I chuckled. "Just like that?"

"Just like that."

"So, we get a break?" I said with a half grin.

"How do you come to that conclusion?" asked Aramthella.

"The two enemy vessels and their crews are all gone. Until back-up arrives—if it is even sent in the first place—we're safe," I replied defensively.

"Captain Sachiko, you work with this man? You're very tolerant."

"What's that supposed to mean?" I challenged.

"It means she's way too understanding and compromises her integrity in bringing you along, General Ryan."

"I do not," Sachiko said. "Please explain why we're not safe, in spite of the present threat being removed."

"Very well, Sachiko. There will certainly be more clan ships coming. Lots of them. The time maker is angry with this ship's body maker for having wasted time—pun intended—on Earth. However, it is now personal to the clan. Did I mention they're nothing if not mean, vindictive, and cruel?"

"You did. What may we expect?" I asked.

"In this galaxy alone, there are over one hundred clan ships. All told, there are tens of thousands. For all of them, Earth is now clan enemy number two."

"Two? Who's—" I stopped asking when the obvious answer came to mind.

"But we have you on our side," remarked Sachiko, with amazingly perk in her voice.

"Yes, you do," concurred Aramthella. "And, I am one of the more advanced time ships they stole. There is that."

"So, you can fight them off?" I asked, wishfully.

"Them and ten thousand more."

"Really?" I responded, a ray of hope penetrating my native pessimism.

"No. I can run ahead of most. In a battle, I can take out several of them. But, in my reality ten thousand of anything beats one of anything similar."

"In mine too," I groaned back.

"So, Sachiko, what would you have us do?" Aramthella asked the captain.

"You mean to say what decisions have all four of us come to?" I really emphasized the *all four* concept.

"Whatever you order is what we shall do, Sachiko. If you'd like to entertain others' opinions, in anything from where to go next to what color to paint the ceiling, be my guest."

"There is no need to be sarcastic," she responded with surprising authority.

"Why isn't there?" the ship questioned.

"For one thing, it's not nice," she replied.

"Uh, yes, sort of by definition."

"And, I won't allow it. Aramthella, you are a member of my crew. I expect you will follow my wishes like every other member of my crew. Are we clear on that?"

Nice *cojones*, Sachiko. She was getting the hang of the captain thing.

"Clear, yes. But, I'm forced to question... or what?"

Uh oh, her first mutiny. Or, more likely, Aramthella first test of Sachiko's resolve. "As captain of this ship, I expect my orders to be carried out. If you are incapable of following simple orders, I have no use for you. A broken oven bakes no bread."

There was a definite pause. I assume Aramthella was thinking how to respond.

"Very good, Captain. Well played. I will, of course, obey all your orders."

"You were testing me?"

"Of course, I was. If you are incapable of enforcing your will, I have no use for you. A broken oven bakes no bread."

"Thank you, Aramthella, I think. Tank and I will need supplies. We also need to confer with our leaders, back on Earth. We need to discuss how best to achieve those goals without them mistakenly firing on us."

"Very well, Captain. Please be aware that time energy is, in and of itself, fully capable of sustaining any life form indefinitely. A return to your planet is not technically necessary."

"I'll let you know our plans, once we've formulated them."

"Very good, ma'am."

"Let's go sit down and hash this all out," I said to my captain.

And so began the most improbable of partnerships.

CHAPTER THIRTY-ONE

Since Aramthella was a ship, and we were the crew, I'd immediately established the minimum requirements implied by that arrangement. I set up a mess, and I made certain coffee was available, twenty-four seven. I wasn't about to serve on an amateur's vessel. No way. Hence, we retired to the mess.

A word about nomenclature. Technically, a mess aboard ship would be called a ship's mess, not a mess like it would be in any other military venue. But I was USAF. My blood, when I still had any, was ultramarine blue and golden yellow (and no, they never mixed to form green). So, on any ship I crewed, the *ship's mess* was simply the *mess*. If it seems like I'm making a big deal out of nothing, you, my friend, do not get the military way.

"Alright, we better get serious, because badness is on the doorstep," I began solemnly. "First, I'd like to make it official and recorded. This military issue version of coffee is piss-ass poor."

"Seriously?" questioned my forever wife. "We're all about to die, and you're bitching about the coffee?"

"Yes. As you can plainly see, my priorities are in their proper order."

"Ho-boy," she groaned.

"With that out of the way, we need to make the big decision. We can... A, seek out and attempt to destroy clan ships, using proximity as a guide for which to hit first; B, set up a defensive perimeter in space above Earth, and hope for fate to favor us; C, try to land on Earth and parlay with the powers that be, hopefully coordinate some common defense strategy; or D, run like hell and pray the skinny-assed rats follow us, and leave home alone."

I let that sit in the air a spell. Everyone was frantically grinding the gears in their heads.

Sachiko responded first. Good. She was growing into the captaincy. "D is out. It assumes too much risk to Earth. They could send everything but one ship after us and still end our home."

"True," I replied tersely.

"I'm not in love with B," announced Sapale. "If they have half a brain between them, they'd hit us with maximum force and be done with us."

All eyes fell on Tank. "What? Since when did war planning become democratic?"

All eyes remained on he who protested too much.

"A is a bad way to begin. Once they realize our strategy, they can send ships to engage and detain us, while sending others to take out the Earth. We could do the Punch and Judy dance a bit, but that wouldn't accomplish much."

"Punch and Judy?" asked Sachiko, with an eyebrow cocked.

"Sort of hit and run," I explained.

She frowned. "Then why not just call it hit and run?"

"Sheesh. That doesn't sound nearly as cool." I air-punched a little. "Everybody loves those little puppets."

She withdrew visibly. "Not me. I hate the scary little demons."

"Me, too. But it still sounds sexier."

"Whatever," she responded. "So, if three out of four are off the table, does that make C our plan by default?"

"Never," I said harshly. "In strategic planning, there *is* no default. Every plan, including the plan to do nothing, is an active decision.

Default options are fine for fonts on a document or the only woman at the bar, but in this venue you have to think through every single act you take or do not take."

Sachiko was stunned by my ferocity. She looked to Tank for support or solace.

"Man's right, kiddo. He could have said it nicer, but war and nice go together like oil goes with water." He spied me out of the corner of his eye. "I believe Jon's attempting to avail you of his incredible knowledge concerning the art of war, since you are in command of a powerful vessel."

"Oh. Alright, then. Option B is on the table for discussion. What do we gain by going to Earth, and what do we lose?" she asked confidently.

"Much better," I encouraged. Like it, or not, Sachiko needed to graduate from the College of Hard Knocks yesterday. "I'll do the ups. Sachiko, you do the downs."

She swallowed hard.

"First, we can take on much needed supplies. Aramthella says we can live off of time energy." I held up my mug. "But if I gotta drink this nineteenth century swill, I'd just as soon the boogiemen off us. We need *Peet's*. Second, we can update and coordinate our efforts with the governments on Earth. Third, we're right there if the shooting starts that quickly." I sipped my coffee, indicating I was done.

"We're all about to die, and you're worried about the quality of the coffee," my wife said scornfully.

"Thank you. You can see I have my priorities in their proper order." I toasted her with my truly awful coffee.

"Fourth," added Sapale, "you two can square things with your families. As of now, you're MIAs, and presumably KIAs."

That brought solemn nods of understanding from the both of them.

"I don't see a downside in at least checking in," Sachiko said with uncertainty.

"That's because you're a shavetail, a newbie, a rookie," I pointed out, helpfully.

"What is my inexperience not allowing me to see?" she asked.

I looked to Tank.

He took a deep breath. "There has never been a governmental action that didn't screw things up more than it helped them. A politician's unfailing inclination, in times of war, is to second guess people who actually know what they're doing and to commit resources to exactly the wrong priority."

"In other words, they'll make some stupid decision we'd have to live with, or more likely die because of," I added.

"They can't control Aramthella. They can't control me. What screwing-up effect could they have?"

"I cite, in no order of significance, the Trojan Horse; Nero and his violin; dropping nuclear weapons on non-industrial, non-military, targets in WWII; the Cold War; Vietnam; Operation African Freedom; and the Mutual Defense Treaty of the Worldship Fleet."

"The what?" Tank spat out. "Worldship Fleet?"

"Oops. Spoiler alert," I grinned stupidly.

"So, what do you suggest, Jon?" the captain queried.

"I'm not in favor of any option. I am less in favor of doing nothing, because time is short and rapidly running out. Doing nothing would be a strategic error. My idea, insufficient as it is, would be to go to Earth. When the enemy is barreling down on it, we make a mad dash, hoping they'll be just mad enough and foolish enough to chase after us like hounds on a fox."

"I find fault with that assessment," Sachiko said.

"How so?" I asked.

"It only works if the enemy commits two separate errors at the same time. Allowing anger to influence a decision, and being foolish knowing they've defeated millions of capable militaries."

"I agree."

She looked like I'd punched her.

"Sometimes your best choice is a lousy choice. The good thing is that, as Field Marshal Helmuth van Moltke tells us, 'No plan survives first contact with the enemy.' So, we make a move and wing it when the time comes."

"I don't like the sound of that one little bit," she responded.

I toasted her with my mug. "Welcome to my nightmare."

"We can't just fly to Earth, assume orbit, and then ask that they not blow holes in our asses." I stressed the point. "Because, if I were the Earth's defense force, that's precisely what I'd do."

"Agreed. But how can we return home safely?" Sachiko asked.

"You tell me," I volleyed back to her.

"Maybe they'd recognize us... wait why would they?"

"We could just radio them." To the atmosphere, I asked, "You can send radio messages, can't you, Aramthella?"

"Hang on a second. Let me check my list of superpowers. Bend time to my will. *Check.* Travel faster than light. *Check.* Hey, who knew? I can emit electromagnetic radiation in the gigahertz range."

"A simple *yes* would have sufficed," I observed.

"You speak truth to power, Jon. In the short time we've known each other, that's what endears you to me the most."

Was it me, or was she getting sassier?

"We could tell them it's us, not to shoot, and then land safely." Sachiko said, getting back to topic.

"Hmm. Would you believe you if you told yourself that?" I challenged

"Maybe?" she squeaked. "Maybe we could prove it's us."

"Yes. We could employ our prearranged coded signals?"

"No. We don't have those," she responded, crestfallen.

"Secret handshakes?"

"Not sure that's practical," she conceded.

"Wait, wait, I got it. We could tell them some detail of our uber-private lives only we would know, ones that we'd never divulge, even if subjected to the limitless cruelty of alien torture, mind probes, and the withholding of desserts."

She pursed and twisted her lips. "They'd be right to be suspicious, wouldn't they?"

"As they are not idiots, I'd say bing-bing-*bing*. You win a lovely stuffed animal."

"What if we went back before the attack? They wouldn't know to be suspicious."

"No. Bad logic."

She pouted.

"We'd still be in a presumed enemy vessel hovering over Washington. And, there'd be two of all of us in the greater DC area at the same time." I sniffed. "Two of you, maybe okay. But the world's not ready for two of me. Trust me. Been there, done that."

"What if we went back further, like a year ago, before all this was known?"

"So, what? We'd be duplicates of ourselves, trying to convince ourselves that, in spite of arriving in an alien spaceship, we were just good old us? No *Invasion of the Body Snatchers* hanky panky."

"I guess it'd be Bill and Ted in the Circle K parking lot all over again, wouldn't it?"

"There has to be a way of safely contacting Earth. Argh! Maybe we could go back discretely..."

Sachiko then spaced out, big time. She was obviously deep in thought or she was developing meningitis. Man, the woman could focus.

"Jon..."

"Yes, Captain."

"Why are you looking at me like that?"

"Like what?"

"Like I have at least three heads."

"Nah, I'm only detecting one. It's just that you kind of zone-out, *way* out."

"How long was I gone?"

"Not very. Nice beaches, where your mind went? Bronzed young men playing volleyball?"

"No. No beaches. No hunks. I was... deciding something, captainly."

"My, my. A new adverb now. *Captainly?*"

"We're going straight back to DC. We're going in so fast they won't have a chance to shoot at us until we're there. Once we're there, we'll talk real fast, real nice, and they'll believe us."

"Then, Captain, I think we have ourselves a plan." I had to grin widely.

She was getting it. Good.

CHAPTER THIRTY-TWO

"The clan ship went from the acquiring of time to this rock, Earth. A time-waste. The body maker spoke gibberish to me, the time maker. *More* time-waste. Now, several conjoined clan ship that escorted the ship of no-brains are no-timed, and the fool body maker returns to Earth. *Supreme* time-waste."

The time maker hopped on two legs, it was so full of fury and rage. Sparks of time sizzled from its fingertips. One spark landed on a clean maker, and it was no-timed in flames. The time maker paid it no mind. All around him were useless, incompetent, time-wastes. He hopped and he danced and he resolved nothing.

"I want all the clan to fly for vengeance. That clan ship, that crew, and that accursed planet must never have been. I want them out of time, and I want that yesterday," he screamed to those nearby.

"In agreement," sang back the talk maker. It broadcast the time maker's orders in no time at all. "Reality is in agreement with your words," it announced.

"Vector maker," bellowed the time maker, "make us be where Earth will be when we arrive there."

"In agreement. Vector set. Movement established."

"How soon will my nearest clan ship be at the traitor ship?"

"One week."

"I want less time."

"In agreement. With ancillary time thrusting, Body Maker-ffftul's clan ship will arrive in five point seven days."

"In *concurrence*," hissed the time maker. "And my clan ship? When will I see Earth be no more with these very eyes?" To demonstrate to which eyes the time maker referred, he removed them and held them up as high as his spindly arms would allow.

"Seventeen point one days, maximal conformation."

"Are you unable to please me higher?" it thundered, in reply.

"In disagreement. Any more energetic our vector might grow to would threaten the integrity of the ship's skin."

Time maker gave off a final mighty roar. "In concurrence. Inform all clan ships. These eyes must see Earth not be. No ship is to act against the planet until I am present. But talk at Body Maker-ffftul. It must find and destroy the rogue ship. If the body maker fails me, I will eat its heart. I will not see a traitorous ship. I will *never* see a traitorous ship."

"In agreement."

And, so, the final assault on Earth against the lone ship that defended her began.

CHAPTER THIRTY-THREE

"Aramthella, how quickly can you place us over the White— Wait. The White House was attacked. No way anyone but construction workers would be there now. Tank, where would the POTUS be?" I asked, self-correcting.

"Well, let's see. He could either stay visible to bolster a frightened public's confidence, or he could go to ground."

"Payette wouldn't hide. I don't know him well at all, but he seems like a take-the-bull-by-the-horns kind of guy," observed Sachiko.

"I agree. So, where would he go? Camp David? They still use that, right?" I inquired.

Tank shook his head. "Nah. Too isolated, too hard to defend, and it'd send the message that he was not anxious to be near his citizenry."

"A military base?"

"You've been on a military base or two, right?"

"A few," I replied with a grin. "Why is that important?"

"They're dull, boring, flat—really flat—and they have a sort of negative aesthetic vibe. They're basically the opposite of defensible. Plus, if a man of power and culture had a choice, he'd stay anywhere else."

"So, if he stayed in DC... The vice presidential residence?"

"That'd be my call."

"Aramthella, how—" Sachiko began to ask.

"Excuse me for interrupting your first captainly act, Sachiko, "Aramthella began, "but I think I know where this is going. Not my first rodeo, etcetera, etcetera. We can approach without them having any warning. I can return us physically to the Earth in the distant past. Once there, we wave to the dinosaurs and pop into the present time. We will literally appear out of nowhere."

"Clever girl," Sachiko said glowingly. Then she realized Aramthella might not appreciate being placed into that category. "Aramthella, in our navy tradition, ships are female. Do you mind being called she and girl?"

"Not in the least, Captain. As one who clearly has no sexual assignment or future prospects those are as neutral a term as any."

"Place us where the front entrance to One Observatory Circle was a million years ago, please. Then jump to present day."

"Aye, Captain, further keeping with the navy tradition's terminology. One point, ma'am."

"Yes?"

"Captains don't ever say please."

"Right. Got it. Oh, once we're there, er, how do we exit you?"

"I have ramps. Shiny metallic ramps. I'm so very proud of them."

"And where would we find a shiny, pretty ramp?"

"I'll light the floor in the direction of the nearest one. I'll have it pointed at the front door."

"Make it so."

Talk about anticlimax. No sooner had Aramthella finished, and a bright line in the floor sprang to life.

"Thanks for flying Air Aramthella," the ship sing-songed.

This one was going to be a lot to handle. Like I needed that, because my plate wasn't so very full already. Did I do something bad to an abacus in a former lifetime? Was that why I was saddled with the wise asses of the computation world?

We quickly followed the exit trail. When we arrived at the door, it opened without my asking. Sure enough, there was the main entrance of OOC. And, yup, those were soldiers running toward us with rifles directed forward.

"I'll go first," I said, as I placed an arm in front of Sachiko and jumped ahead. "Eighteen-year-olds with assault weapons have been a large part of my life. I think I can get a few words out before they open up."

I was on the ground by the time I finished speaking.

Arms in the air, I called out loudly, but calmly, "Do not fire. I am Dr. Jon Ryan, the president's consultant. I'm here to speak with the president."

An officer, white gloves and all, sped into the lead and raised an arm. The guards stopped.

"Captain," I said, again loudly but calmly, "I'd appreciate it if your men would lower their weapons. If I meant you any harm, I'd've stayed inside the big spaceship, not walked out with my hands in the air."

"Lower your weapons. Ma'am, please step out slowly, and—" the squad leader began to say.

"Now, I've seen everything," shouted a voice from behind them. It was Frank Payette. "Captain Delaney, have your troops stand down. These are old friends."

The captain was clearly torn, at least briefly. I think his reasoning went something like this: *Big alien spaceship here, bad. POTUS there, good. Guards in between the two, very good.*

The phalanx of guards parted to let us pass. The president greeted us with a handshake at the top of the stairs. "Somebody yells there's a UFO on the lawn, and who else do I think of other than you, Jon?"

"Well, Mr. President, I do like to make a flashy entry from time to time."

"Ah, Jon, I have a rule. Everyone who lands on my lawn in an alien spaceship calls me Frank."

I released the president's hand. "Sounds like a reasonable rule, Frank."

"Where'd you get that ship of yours?"

I angled my head toward Sachiko. "It's her ship, not mine. Better ask her. Oh, and I'll give you ten-to-one odds you can't get her to call you Frank, Frank."

"I'm very persuasive, when I want to be," he returned with a big grin.

Sachiko was just about to take the odds, before she saw that grin.

"Frank," Sachiko squeaked, uncertainly, "good to see you again."

"Captain Jones, I'm looking forward to an interesting tale."

"You, Frank, *will not* be disappointed," she said, a little more normally. A little.

Downstairs, in the makeshift Situation Room, we addressed some old faces and quite a few new ones. After introductions, I told the group exactly what happened. I was not interrupted once, and I don't think anyone even blinked. It was a pretty good story.

"So, assuming you four are not, in fact, evil, shapeshifting aliens," began Frank, "where does this leave us? It sounds to me like there's a shitstorm heading our way, and we have one capable but solitary line of defense."

"I think that's a fair assessment," I replied, grimly. "If the enemy arrives in a long, strung-out line, maybe we stand a chance. But that'd be a piss poor strategy."

"I assume you have some plan then. Please lie to me, if need be, and say you do."

"Nothing very firm, I'm afraid." I shrugged.

"We're facing an unusual problem here, Frank," stated Tank. "Time war is nothing any of us have ever attempted to wage. To our enemy, it's old hat. That places us at an incredible disadvantage."

He nodded, thoughtfully. "I'll bet. No course in it at West Point, last I heard. But, there's no alternative. We'll have to make do." He thought a few moments. "How do we know the sons of bitches aren't already heading into Earth's past and destroying us before we even know why?"

"That's easy. Aramthella would alert us if they tried that. Time... time isn't like we used to think of it. There's no tick tock goes the clock. It's... it's dynamic, it's vital. It's alive and ever changing. Somehow, we're going to need to get our heads around that fact, clearly, firmly, and quickly."

"When the top scientific minds alive tell me there's a problem understanding a matter, it gives me great pause." He sighed. "But," he added, in a cheerier tone, "it's the hand we're dealt and we'll play it to win. Never let it be said the humans folded. Nope. We're too dumb to do that."

A round of laughter erupted. This man was good. He knew when to crack the whip, and when to crack a joke.

"So, Captain Jones, what can I do to help you? The resources of the world stand at the ready."

"We've given that some thought. We will need some basic supplies, field rations, coffee—lots of coffee—and personal hygiene items."

"Done," snapped Payette. He nodded to his chief of staff as he spoke. "I'll assume you'll need weapons also. I'll have a variety brought for you to choose from. What else?"

"I would like to make something clear. While I command the spaceship, Jon is in charge of the mission as a whole. He has a lot more experience at this type of thing than I do."

"Really, Jon? You've done this kind of thing before?" Payette asked, curious.

"A time or two, yes." I scrunched up my face as I replied.

"If we weren't so pressed for time, I would have liked to discover what it is you've done."

"That definitely would take longer than we can spare." I smiled pleasantly.

"What else can I do to help? Would you like a detail from the Army? Maybe some special ops types?"

"I don't think so, Frank," I replied.

"Oh really? Why's that?"

"Not my style. I like to travel kind of light."

The president sat back and studied my face. I think he was trying to read me, as it were. I'm certain a man in as high an office as he was had to be good at that type of gleaning. He wanted to know if I was bullshitting him at a very wrong time. Also, most authority types immediately suspect I'm some kind of slacker. And no, it's not because of anything *I* do. It's all over-reading on the *other* side of the table. Seriously. The handful of senior staffers and military liaisons sat by quietly. They didn't want any part of the wrangling between the boss and this odd stranger.

"But, surely you would need some support if you battle these monsters at close quarters."

"Thanks, but no." If Sapale and I couldn't handle a situation, having a dozen operatives with automatic weapons wasn't going to do the trick either.

"Fine. Your call. Anything else?"

"Not for now. We need to get back aboard Aramthella and ready ourselves for the attack that will be coming soon."

"Then there's a favor I'd beg of you."

"Sure," I responded with reservations.

"I'd like you to take with you some small number of humans."

"Okay, not a request you hear every day. Why?"

"We're facing the complete extinction of life on Earth. I want to be certain there is some tiny spark of hope for humankind. That it will survive this crisis."

"We can't really support a genetically balanced, highly vetted group of ride-alongs."

"Jon, please," he asked intently. "I just want for there to be *hope*. If we are facing the extinction of all life on Earth, the end of Earth itself, some provision must be made, some measures however desperate must be attempted to try to preserve our species. Yes, we're not perfect. Yes, we squabble and fight too much. But I believe we are worthy of existence. Will you help the President of the United States *save* some fraction of humankind?"

Oh, my. Déjà vu, all over again. That sounded *awfully* familiar. Creepy familiar, I don't mind saying. This president was giving me almost the exact same spiel President John Marshall had so impossibly long ago. Or a few years in the future, however you prefer to reckon it. Both were passionate about cramming walking, talking human DNA carriers into tiny ships and rocketing them away from certain destruction. Was I in a time wrap or what?

"We are going after—actively pursuing—a force that should easily wipe us out. Yes, Earth is at risk, but you're asking me to take on non-essential personnel for a suicide mission."

"I think it's quite likely we shall all be exterminated. What does it really matter where, exactly, the deed takes place?" He grinned grimly and spread his arms toward me.

I got a very stern look on my face, but said nothing in reply.

"We could support maybe a hundred, but only if they can be selected and placed aboard ASAP," summarized Sapale. "We'll also need the basic equipment to keep them fed, clean, and entertained for possibly a long time. Military field equipment leaps to mind. Cots, MRE, chemical toilets, a small water recycling plant. It'd all have to be loaded yesterday."

"Sapale," Sachiko interjected, "Aramthella can perform many of those functions."

I'm not sure if Sachiko slipped up by calling Sapale by her actual name, and not the phony doctor one. My wife was still in the burka. I didn't want to push the credulity of the locals more than I had to, so she remained undercover.

"Yes, but we'll want redundant systems," my Sapale reasoned. "What if she decides to no longer help us, or we need to abandon ship in favor of a remote planetary surface? We need the option of possible self-sufficiency."

"I guess. If it can be arranged fast," Sachiko replied.

"It will be. I'll place the calls, personally. People will move faster than greased lightning," responded Payette.

"And who do we choose?" Sachiko asked gravely. "Who is selected for almost certain death, but is worthy of repopulating the human race?"

"Who indeed?" sighed the president.

"Young, bright, and diverse," Sachiko suggested rapidly.

"Where does one—" The president stopped. The nearest college was Georgetown. "Who here went to Georgetown?" he shouted to those in the cramped room.

Five hands went up. He pointed to one. "Where'd you live?"

"Er, McCarthy Hall, mostly."

"Co-ed?"

"Yes. It *is* the twenty-first century, sir."

Frank spun on Jon. "I can have everyone presently in that building brought here, immediately. We can ask for volunteers once they're here. Everyone has five minutes to snag personal stuff. With a bunch of kids in space, we'll need condoms—"

Someone shouted, "You have got to be kidding me?"

Payette scolded at the speaker. "Birth control pills. Go to the student health clinic and grab everything and everyone."

The president stood.

"Jane," he pointed at a woman, "call the District PD. I want every unit at the Hoya's campus immediately. Eddie," he targeted a man, "call the Medstar on campus. Have them start scooping and running. Leslie," he indicated one of the Secret Service agents, "everybody on duty over there now. Cindy," he scanned the room. "Where the devil's Cindy Rush?"

"Here, Mr. P—"

"Cindy, call Andrews. Have them start helicoptering all the supplies and tell them to do it like their very lives depended on it." He clapped his hands, loudly. "Go, go *go*," he shouted. "If I didn't give you an assignment, help the ones I did. Let's move, people."

The room exploded with activity.

I stood. Actually, since my mom'll probably never read this, I jumped up on the Situation Room table, right in front of the POTUS. This new addendum to the ready piss-poor plan was not gonna happen. Since I'm an android, I can make a really loud noise if I so desire. I so desired. From my output speaker system came the harshest, most piercing whistle likely ever heard. Needless to say, I got everyone's fullest attention. Oorah!

"We are not taking a dormitory full of pimply-faced kids on a suicide mission." I scanned the room, like a lion taking stock of a herd for zebras. "Sapale and I have done this more times than a body should. It's what we do. Tank is a Marine. He knows the score, and he knows he's in this until the end. Sachiko is the captain. She has to come along, or we don't have a ride."

I studied the faces staring back at me, with an intensity no one but Sapale could even closely approximate.

"We four *get* it. We signed on, knowing full well what the risks were, and how dead we are likely to end up being. As commander, I can work with that. But, if you shove a few hundred kids more worried about getting laid than fighting aboard, the equation changes. My reasoning for each and every attack is changed from kill or be killed, to a little voice in the back of my head saying, 'But what about the kids?' I'll be saying to myself, don't come in at that angle, you'll expose the kids. If I impulsively attack a superior force, I'd be second-guessing myself for putting the passengers at undue risk.

"No, we go as we are—*alone*. Four warriors against the odds. If I'm charged with babysitting in space, instead of just trying to win, I'll end up being lousy at both. The best way to ensure those kids at Georgetown survive to face the next crisis is for them to hunker down right where they are."

The president's head slumped. "I wish there was some way to get some kids off the planet."

"I'll tell you want I can do."

Payette's head snapped up.

"In exchange for one tiny thing, what if I could shuttle a hundred kids at a time up to the newly vacated Mars 1 Base? The round trip, including on-load and offload, would be brief."

"You'd use Aramthella?"

"Absolutely not. I'd call in that tiny favor."

"Which would be?"

"Do not ask how I did it."

That troubled the bossman, but he quickly realized that any time he spent making a decision was time not spent shuttling up as many Hoyas as he could.

He stuck out his hand. "You have yourself a deal. Where do they assemble?"

"There'll be two ramps onto Aramthella. People waiting patiently in front of one, supplies and material steaming up the other. You'll need a senior loadmaster to make this flow quickly."

Frank furrowed his brow. "But, I thought you said no passengers on Aramthella?"

"And there won't be any. Trust me, but please don't press me."

I leaned into Sapale. "Take *Stingray* from where we stashed her, and place her just out of sight, between the A Ramp and the B Ramp."

She nodded and sped away.

Within fifteen minutes, bedraggled-looking teenagers and young adults, along with some scattered adults, began queuing up where instructed to. Even before that, forklifts were barreling up and down the B Ramp like ants at a picnic.

I took Tank and Sachiko by an elbow and led them to the bridge.

"Sapale'll shuttle as many to Mars as she can, based on the limits there'll be on supplies. She'll stop once the maximum number is reached, or when we fall under attack."

"You think Mars is far enough away to presume they're safe?" asked Tank.

"Not sure. But it's the farthest place that is ready to support a goodly number of humans. The asteroid bases are all too small, and the Moon's too damn close."

"I agree," replied Tank.

"Aramthella," called out Sachiko, "any updates on the remaining clan ships?"

"Nothing firm yet. The time master is interfacing with each body maker and its ship. So far, it has told the body makers of the fleet that it's certain something has happened to the clan of the ship that is me. It says it will be forced to capture or destroy us soon."

"How long do we have?" I asked.

"I would be surprised if they waited longer than a few hours."

"Where is the time maker's ship?" I asked.

"Unimaginably far away."

"How long would it take us to get there?"

"Walking or by public transit?" she snarked.

"I was thinking aboard you, at maximal velocity," I replied through gritted teeth.

"Ah, thank you for being specific. Half an hour to arrive where its ship holds in space.

I switched to head-to-head communication. *Sapale, how many kids are left to ferry over?*

Maybe one hundred fifty. Why?

I want to try and blindside the time maker. Finish your current run, then park it on the ship and make sure only the four of us are aboard.

Roger that. See you in thirty.

A short while later, Sapale strode over to my side, kissed my cheek, and asked, "Ready to go annoy the hell out of someone else?"

"You bet," I shot back.

"Sachiko, you said the ship had fifty functioning wormhole guns. They all working up to specs?"

"Yes. I just checked."

"Okay, then, let's go introduce ourselves to the big bad time maker."

The trip on Aramthella was less spectacular than the incredibly smooth ride on *Stingray*. In no time at all, we were holding position ten light seconds on the far side of the time maker's ship, relative to Earth. I wanted to confuse him, if that was possible.

Per our prearranged plans, Sachiko gave the orders. "Lay a spread pattern Delta, centered on the time master's vessel. Fire for five seconds, then return us to our prior position on Earth."

"As you wish, Captain. Firing has commenced."

We launched around one hundred thousand rotating wormholes in that five-second window. For us aboard ship, we didn't notice a thing. Again, a tragedy in terms of every hyper-cool sci-fi movie I'd ever seen, where the ship's weapons coughed fire and boomed to the high heavens. Oh, well.

Then we sprinted back to Earth.

"The time maker's ship was moderately damaged. The time maker, itself, was not harmed. It is, however, *really* pissed."

"Is the craft space worthy?" I pressed.

"Hard to say. Wait— It screams to launch toward us immediately. But... I'm glad I'm not them. The clan refuses. The crews report to the time maker that insufficient hull breaches are sealed. Travel would be very unsafe."

"Nice shooting," Sachiko complimented.

"Thank you, Captain."

"ETA to Earth?" she asked.

"Five more minutes."

"Once we land, I want a full report on damage and response from our attack," Sachiko requested.

"You will have it, ma'am."

Then we waited. I could barely tell we touched down, the vibrations were so subtle.

"Status?" shouted Sachiko.

"All clan ships holding as before. The level of ship-to-ship chatter is greatly increased."

"Sapale, you can resume your shuttle, but cut the transit by five minutes. I want you close if we need to book in a hurry."

"Roger that." She trotted away.

As Sachiko, Tank, and I stood watching the loading, President Frank Payette walked up quietly. "I can't thank you all enough for what hope you're giving the people of Earth."

"Glad to help, as long as it—" I began to reply, vapidly.

"Captain," Aramthella cut in. "Around half the clan fleet just launched. Destination, Earth. ETA, just over thirty minutes for the lead elements. The remainder of the ships I track are either remaining with the stricken time master, or rapidly moving to join up with him."

"Showtime," I mumbled under my breath. "Sapale, abort transfers.

Repeat *abort transfers*." I turned to a nearby MP. "Clear the civilians from the area. Try and get them home."

She snapped a salute and charged off.

Controlled chaos ensued. The loading team and the students ran, at a near panic, out of the building. The president grabbed a phone, probably to planetary defense control, and began to interact passionately with whomever was unlucky enough to be on the receiving end.

I led Tank and Shaky onto Aramthella. Once aboard, I said to Sachiko, "Have Aramthella confirm we four are the only ones aboard. No mistakes, no stowaways, got it?"

She nodded and stepped away.

"Tank, make double certain everything that needs to be battened down is."

He snapped a mini salute and dashed away.

I headed to *Stingray*. "Everyone gone?"

"Yes. Security backed the waiting line out the door, then they locked it."

"How many'd you ferry?" I asked Sapale.

She smiled. "Almost five hundred."

I whistled, loudly. "Impressive."

"Yeah, I know. Plenty of materials, too. They'll do well for a long time. With any luck, they can be resupplied after the air clears. But, even worst-case they might be self-sustaining. And I personally placed that time-lock device Aramthella said would isolate them if something bad happens to Earth."

"Perfecto," I mumbled, not really focusing. "I'll get to Aramthella's bridge. You dust off in *Stingray* as soon as we emerge behind the enemy fleet."

"Roger that," she returned with a grin.

In a couple minutes I met up with the other two.

"No change," began Sachiko. "ETA six minutes."

"How many ships?"

"Fifty-seven, at present."

"Okay, tell Earth defense to open up with all they got. Put us four light minutes behind them. The moment we're there, we let them have it too."

"Copy," replied Aramthella. I was pleased she wasn't splitting hairs in this crisis and insisting the captain make the actual orders.

I could feel us move slightly. Otherwise, the world was quiet.

We reentered real space exactly three minutes and fifty eight seconds behind the enemy force. "Fire all wormhole weapons," called out Sachiko. "Fire for three full minutes, then cease fire."

Stingray folded to be just outside our time ship. In the for-what-it's-worth category, she opened up with all she had.

A few minutes later, I called out, "Time to first Earth wormhole impact?"

"Minus four seconds."

"Damage assessment."

"Two ships exploded, three veered severely off course, five sustained heavy damage," replied Aramthella.

"Still too damn many of them," I seethed. "Al, report?"

"We have dinged a few enemy vessels. No significant impact."

"Aramthella," I screamed as it hit me, "can you freeze the enemy ships in time?"

"At this range, yes. It will require massive—"

"Do it. *Now*."

"The remaining thirty-seven viable clan ships are in stasis," she reported.

"But we can't hurt them while they're frozen?"

"Negative. I must release them for that to be possible."

"Al, coordinate fire sequence and time-release sequence with Aramthella. I want a massive number of wormholes to hit each ship just as it's reanimated."

"Roger that, Captain," shot back Al.

Within fifteen minutes, the entire clan strike force was destroyed. But I knew we'd gotten lucky. When the rest of the clan came calling, they'd be ready for that trick.

Still, it was a massive victory.

We headed back to Earth with the good news.

The radio sprang to life. "This is President Payette. I cannot tell you how proud we are of our guardian angels. Thank you, forever."

I elbowed Sachiko that she should respond, not me. "Your welcome, sir. We're just glad we could do our part."

"That'll go down in history next to the 'one small step speech,' if anybody asks me," poked Tank.

"The remainder of the local fleet is holding position while repairs are made on the time maker's craft. Time needed for that is unclear," reported Aramthella.

"Safe for now is good by me," said a much relieved POTUS.

CHAPTER THIRTY-FOUR

The time maker was angrier than it thought was possible. It knew insult. It knew incompetence on the part of the clan, and it now knew losses from the clan in battle for the first time ever. And all because of the defective Body Maker-lop's foolish impulses. The time maker could not sense the body maker's use-of-time signature. Perhaps it was no-time. But if it weren't, the time maker would concentrate such negativity on the sorry imp that it would wish it was never budded.

The time maker lorded over tens of thousands of clan ships, scattered throughout the discoverable universe. It had sent two hundred clan ships to the accursed galaxy that now was fighting back. The time maker named that galaxy *The One That Lop Lost*, so that the inept body maker's shame would be declared for all time. All time would be one with Body Maker-lop's failure to the clan.

But there was no time to dwell on reverse time. It needed a plan for forward time. Fifty-three clan ships remained in-time with the time maker's ship in The One That Lop Lost. The vile supreme desecrators had un-timed the initial assault wave, and then no-timed them. The assault force body makers were fools. What loss of mind power allows itself to be un-timed in battle? If it was saddled with one more mental derelict, the time maker would simply end all time. That would be superior to seeing its beloved clan so mocked, so disgraced.

No, no, the time maker hounded itself in its awareness. Focus on forward time. Save the clan. The clan will reign forever, so help that be true. Yes. It would lead the next wave, the final wave, against the sinful scum that defiled its clan.

"When can we make forward vector to the planet that harbors the profaners?" screamed the time maker.

"Soon, lordfullness," replied a single repair maker.

"Cowards besmirch this clan," howled the time maker. "Only *one* repair maker is in agreement with my request of knowledge?"

One by one, the lead repair makers of the other clan ships whispered truth to the time maker and were ashamed of themselves.

The assessment was not pleasure making for the time maker. But, if truth was truth, it was unable to countermand it. The lag time for full functionality was ten subunits. But, in ten point one subunits, the desecraters would become one with no-time.

No-time was the only time that remained for those who dared to act against the clan.

CHAPTER THIRTY-FIVE

I'm not much of a houseplant guy. You probably figured that already. They're decorations that aren't decorative. They require fuss and attention, they always die, pathetically, but only after they decompose and smell bad. And even if they're vigorous and live forever, what do you have? A houseplant. You can't eat it, converse with it, or sell it for anything near what you paid for the damn thing. Whoever invented the houseplant needs to suffer, IMHO.

Sapale never had much use for them either. Her species are herbivores. The only value she placed in houseplants were as a last-ditch snack in a crisis. That said, she had for eons display a circumturus. Those are kind of like houseplants, and kind of not. They're alive, they need feeding, and they can't move on their own accord. Similar enough, if you ask me. But, they're more crystalline than animal or plant tissue. If you picture a one-foot-tall pyramid, cut it in half, and turn it upside down, you have the shape of a circumturus as it resides in nature. It usually weighs around a quarter pound. If a circumturus is left alone, doused with a protein slurry once in a while, it pulses a faint magenta light visible if the room is dark enough. It'll do that a long while, decades sometimes. Then it won't do that any longer. It would be dead-like, but not exactly because it wasn't technically alive before.

What good are they? Not enough, I'll tell you straight up. But the value others place in them, the reason circumturuses are kept on shelves gathering dust, is that they are mildly telepathic. Maybe *slightly* telepathic is a better word. If you sit within a couple feet of one, you might or might not get an occasional mental image. Say you're reading the sports section. In the middle of the box scores for a game, you'll suddenly think *purple pudding* or *sexy socks*. Those impulses originate from the stupid circumturus. Whether a circumturus has any idea what a *pudding* or a *sock* actually is can be debated. But those are the brain-farts that people with too much time on their hands live to experience when they commit to owning a circumturus.

Why is this important to relate in the middle of our current existential crisis? Here's why. Keeping in mind that no circumturus ever has transmitted a single deep, or important thought to anyone, it did something most unexpected.

I was sitting alone in *Stingray's* mess, drinking tea. No. Got you. I was drinking coffee, of course. Come on, *tea?* Anyway, my mind was straining to work out some defense against the next assault of the clan ships. No plan that tickled my fancy was anywhere near spawning to life. Out of nowhere, I began to think about the dawn of creation, of the earliest universe. I saw superheated plasma spin, coalesce, then fly into randomness. I felt cosmic inflation and smelled the plasma roil angrily. I knew there was something, where there had been just an instant before less than nothing.

I was present at the beginning of *time.*

I was time.

No, time was *known* to me. It was... that's all I can say. The experience was so fleeting and so nebulous. But, somehow, I met time. No, I *got* what it was to be time.

Yes. That is the closest I can put what I knew in that instant. I *got* time.

And then, in a flash that snapped my head back, I was sitting in the mess, looking down at a mug half full of lukewarm coffee.

I looked at the damn circumturus Sapale had left on the table after she had cleaned it then forgot to stow back where it belonged. It was dead. Well, that's not totally correct, either. It was no longer flashing magenta light, like it had been for years. I began to take deep breaths and calm my rapidly accelerating brain. The exact words that throbbed in my mind were WTF. Over and over. WTF?

I reached to pick up the circumturus. Before I could...

"All personnel to the bridge," boomed overhead. It was Aramthella, and there was fear in her tone.

I sprinted to the bridge as fast as my feet would carry me. Sachiko and Tank were already there. In seconds, Sapale pounded up from behind, and caught an arm around me to fully stop.

"The time maker has committed every ship left to it in the galaxy. They are bearing down on Earth," Sachiko relayed almost matter-of-factly.

"How many, how soon?" I asked.

"Fifty-three ships. ETA ten minutes." She turned to face me. "Aramthella says they will arrive in a closed formation, resembling a two-dimensional wedge."

"We're being attacked by a flock of birds," I mumbled to myself. In any conventional sense of air warfare, that was a lousy way to attack. But I assumed the time maker either didn't know it was or didn't care that it was. Either way, the alien did not factor in losing as a potential outcome.

"When can Earth defenses commence firing?" I shot back.

"Not until the formation is three light minutes away."

"*What*? Why so late?"

"The spacing and Z-axis positioning of the enemy vessels is changing randomly. It is incredibly unlikely to hit one until they are much closer, and their potential evasion maneuvers are less effective."

"Put us ninety degrees to their vector, at an equal distance. Fire everything the moment we are there. And tell Earth to begin firing. There's no tomorrow if they can't stop the entire fleet."

"Roger that," Sachiko replied, grimly.

My brain went numb. This was not looking good. In fact, it was looking to end badly.

"...three ships exploded. Jon, did you hear me?" Sapale shouted as she shook my right shoulder.

"Huh? What?"

"We're fully engaged. The formation split into three smaller wedges. Three ships in the nearest wedge have exploded. But they're shielding the other two wedges from our line-of-fire. Jon, most of the clan ships'll be inside the asteroid belt intact in less than thirty seconds."

"Have... Have Earth target the other two columns."

"They are. They fried a few bogies, but not nearly enough. Honey, what are we going to do?"

"*Aramthella*, de-time the enemy fleet," I screamed.

"I am unable to," she said flatly.

"Why? You did last time."

"The time maker is clever. It appears to have locked time in the space-time between us and them. The layers of blockade progress like a tank tread. Our past strategy will not work."

"Position to their ninety degrees, Z-axis and fire."

"Executed, and ineffective. Their time lock shifted as quickly as we did."

"Jon, there has to be something we can do," shouted Sachiko. "Jon, tell me what to do to save Earth." She was within moments of emotional collapse.

So was I.

"Aramthella, can we ram the time maker's ship?"

At the same time:

"*What?*" came from Sapale.

"Are you—" came from Tank.

"No. The time shield will not permit that," Aramthella stated.

Crap.

"Put us directly in front of the fleet, one light second ahead. Fire continuously."

"Done," the ship replied.

"ETA to maximal firing distance for the clan ships?" I yelled.

"Forty-seven seconds."

"Are we slowing the fleet's advance?"

"Negative. Time shield is negating our attempts."

"Fly through the center of the combined formations. Flank speed," I said loudly.

At the same time:

"No, you idiot," came from you-know-who.

"Jon, why?" came from Sachiko.

"Belay that order," came from Tank.

"Done," came from Aramthella.

"Report," I called out.

"We passed through the fleet."

"And?"

"Half the ships broke-off and are in active pursuit. The remainder are continuing their flight to Earth."

"Can you stop time, in the entire solar system. That would include the clan ships."

"Negative. The volume of space is too large."

"How about the plane of their attack?"

"Negative. The..." She trailed off.

"The what?" I demanded. "Why can't you stop—"

"Captain," said a very somber Aramthella. "It is my sad duty to report to you that the Earth has never existed."

"What? What do you mean?" Sachiko cried out.

"The clan fleet has just no-timed the Earth-Moon system."

EPILOGUE

Seven days later, I ordered Aramthella to land on Doxie-5 beta 12. The planet was in utter ruin. Ten, maybe twelve hundred years prior, it had self-destructed in an atomic holocaust. A decade-long nuclear winter had left the place nearly void of life. Presently, a few bacterial species, creeping up from the depths, were the best the ecosystem could manage to support. It was a perfect spot for us, both physically and emotionally. The clan ships chasing us would have a huge problem detecting us, given the radioactive nightmare we wallowed in. Furthermore, they'd never think we'd be stupid enough to land there. Plus, the planet looked like we felt. Blighted and hopeless.

It had been one hell of a week. After the Earth was no timed, the other half of the clan fleet which had killed the Earth was freed up to regroup with the ones right on our tail. Thirty-three bedeviled clan ships were focused on only one thing in all the universe: to punish us. My guess was they did not want to simply no-time us. No, my bet was on capture, torture, kill, reanimate, and repeat. Forever.

Frankly, not one of us would have cared much either way. Assuming the few hundred kids on Mars were spared, we were members of a highly endangered species. Time was not on our side. There was no spark of life in anyone aboard.

Initially, Aramthella's superior speed allowed us to outpace the pack of wolves on our heels. Once it was clear to the time maker that simple pursuit wasn't going to bring us down, he started launching squadrons of clan ships ahead of us, using time. The ship would drop into the past, accelerate along our vector, and be where we were heading before we got there. That trick only worked once, and we took out the three ships that pulled that stunt the first time. That was more luck than skill, but who's doing the statistics? If your enemy dies and you do not, you won that skirmish.

I had Aramthella skip forward and backward in time and alter course mid-jump. Apparently, neither the clan nor she ever thought to attempt that maneuver. It worked really well for several days. By the time the enemy figured out what we were doing, we'd taken out seventeen more of their ships. Those were hollow victories, however. Sure, the ratio was down to thirteen to one. But there existed a limitless supply of clan ships, just far enough away to make their joining the present fray impossible. But, in no time they'd more than replace the enemy's strength.

We finally lost them with a mixture of dumb luck, stupid bravado, and ingenuity. There was a lot of science the time ships were capable of that the clan had never conceived of.

There is a red giant star I've always loved. Arcturus. It's about forty light years from Earth, and it's a big sucker. It occurred to me that if Aramthella was inside a star the clan would almost certainly never think to look for us there. Why would they? It was a complete unknown whether a time ship could survive those extremes. Well, there was one fighter pilot just crazy enough to find out if it could.

After we swung behind Arcturus, and were temporarily out of sight to the clan fleet, I ordered Aramthella to shift to the center of the star. As she was doing so, I had *Stingray* place a full membrane around the lot of us. I knew from before that *Stingray* herself could survive several hours inside a star, with that level of protection. We did fine. Once we were positioned inside Arcturus, we moved ten thousand years into the future and exited.

It worked. The clan ships, ten thousand years after losing our trail, were dispersed to the solar winds. I'm sure they never stopped hunting us. They never would, if I read the time maker properly. But they'd had to spread out, in order to suck the time out of some other unfortunate, involuntary donors. That placed space between them, since they needed enough concentration of space-time to harvest from.

We'd established that if Aramthella powered down to a very low level, and if we used *Stingray* as our main propulsion, we were virtually invisible to the clan fleet. Now, virtually isn't entirely, so we were on borrowed time, so to speak. But we were free and able to hide as long as we could.

That brought us to the unavoidable question—what the hell were we going to do? We could fool the clan a while but we would eventually have to finalize matters with them. There was the issue of the handful of humans possibly still alive in the past on Mars. But, if they did survive our going there would betray their presence to the vengeful clan. That was not a viable option.

In the days that followed the no-timing of Earth, I came to know not only *what* we needed to do, but to know it was worth *dying* for if necessary. There was no alternative. We needed to do the impossible.

We needed to save Earth, to resurrect that which had never lived.

That should be a breeze, right? No biggie.

To be continued...

GLOSSARY

First a word about time, as used in this series. The clan uses several foreign, non-intuitive terms to describe time. Here are the concepts.

Anti-no-time: Such a big word! It was the side effect of the negative time generated by wormholes, that were used against the clan. Since clan ships were structured with time energy, negative time deleted what it touched, like matter-antimatter interactions.

No-time: A verb. It means to take the time from a unit of space-time, leaving only space. The object has no time, it had been no-timed.

No-timers: The clan term for all non-clan members.

Non-time: A noun. A sloppy word the clan uses. It can mean one of two things. First, that basically, something's dead, without time, random. It can also mean that time has stopped, for the object under discussion.

Non-time ship: Any space craft that is a non-clan ship.

Un-timed: To stop time for an object or region. Basically, the same as the second meaning of non-time.

Other glossary entries:

Als (1): The original ship's AI on Jon's first flight long ago was Alvin. Jon shortened that to Al. When Al was joined to Jon's vortex in the Galaxy On Fire Series, Al and *Blessing* fell in love and got "married." Since then Jon refers to them combined as the Als.

Ark 1(1): Jon's ship on his very first mission, when he traveled to find humankind a new home.

Azsuram (2): Original human name for the planet GB 3. It was the planet Jon and Sapale settled on after they left the human fleet fleeing doomed Earth. They established an idyllic society of Kaljaxians there, before humans join them.

Blessing (1): See *Stingray*.

Brood's-mate (1): The Kaljaxians term for *wife*. The male version is brood-mate.

Cleinoid gods (1): Ancient and malevolent mix of gods. They have destroyed many universes before and are eyeing ours now. The five ranks or groupings for their invasion were to be Rage, Torment, Wrath, Fury, and Horror.

Command Prerogatives (1): See Probe Fibers.

Cragforel (1): Friendly Deavoriath Jon met after he first escaped the Adamant in the far future.

Cube (1): Jon's alternate name for the vortex he captains.

Daleria (2): Demigod and innkeeper whom Jon and Sapale befriended. She worked with them against the ancient gods as she'd grown to hate them.

Davdiad (1): Kaljaxian divine spirit.

Deavoriath (1): Three arms and legs, the most advanced tech in the galaxy, and helpful to Jon.

Form One/Form Two (1): A Form is the title of a vortex pilot. If more than one is aboard they get numerical designations based on seniority.

Kaljax (1): The home planet of Sapale. Jon went there on his original voyages.

Membrane (1): See space-time congruity manipulator. A very hard force field

Probe Fibers (1): Aka *command prerogatives*, they allow piloting of the Vortex spaceship and can analyze whatever they touch. They also allow for great strength.

Project Ark (1 of The Forever Life): Earth was to be destroyed by Jupiter in 98 years. This was the project to get all of humankind off Earth before the end came.

Sapale (1): Jon's Kaljaxian wife from his original flight to find humankind a new home. At first just her brain was copied, then, eventually, she was downloaded to an android host. Traveled with the corrupted Jon Ryan from an alternate timeline.

Space-time congruity manipulator (1): Hugely helpful force field. Aka a *membrane*.

Stingray (1): Jon's Deavoriath spaceship. Her name in the Deavoriath language, *Blessing*, is pronounced "crash." Hence, silly Jon renamed her after one of his favorite cars. It makes Jon-sense.

Time (1): See discussion above.

Toño DeJesus (1 of *The Forever Life*): The scientist creator of the android Jon. Became his lifelong friend.

Vortex (1): Super-advanced Deavoriath sentient spaceship. Moves by folding space. If you get a chance to own one, do it.

Quantum Decoupler (1): A most excellent weapon that pulls the quarks apart in a proton. The energy released as they rejoin is amazing.

Dr. Sadozi (1): Sapale's assumed name when visiting the White House, long before aliens were known to exist.

AND NOW A WORD FROM YOUR AUTHOR

WHO DOESN'T LOVE BLATANT SELF-PROMOTION?

Thank you for starting the next saga in the Ryanverse! It all began, for the record, back with *The Forever Life, Book 1*. I will always consider that book *my baby*. This new series has been said to be, by those whose opinions count, the best so far (and no, I'm not referring to my own opinion. I think it is, too, but I'm too shy to write those words down).

All told, there are three prior series of six books each. The series titles are linked to the first book of that specific series. The Forever Series, Galaxy on Fire, and Rise of the Ancient Gods. As of this printing, The Forever, Galaxy on Fire, *and* Rise of the Ancient Gods are also available on Audible, thanks to the outstanding Podium Audio peeps. *The Forever Part 1* can be found here. Along with all of the Ryanverse, the wacky but unrelated series *Road Trips In Space*.

Since you're family, now, hop aboard the bandwagon. There's plenty of room. Follow me at Craig Robertson's Author's Page on Facebook. Partake of the conversation and fun.

And finally, I love emails. No, I'm not that needy, I just love hearing from y'all. contact@craigarobertson.com.

A final favor: please post a review for this book, especially on Amazon. They are more precious to us authors than gold.

So, keep thinking only the good thoughts ... craig

TIME WARS LAST FOREVER (2019):

RYAN TIME, Book 1

LOST TIME, Book 2

FRAGMENTED TIME, Book 3

SHATTERED TIME, BOOK 4 (coming Summer 2020)

STAND-ALONE SERIES:

ROAD TRIPS IN SPACE SERIES (2019):

THE GALAXY ACCORDING TO GIDEON, Book 1

THE EATH ACCORDING TO GIDEON, Book 2

THE AFTERLIFE ACCORDING TO GIDEON, Book 3 (coming in Fall 2020)

OLDER INDEPENDENT NOVELS:

THE CORPORATE VIRUS (2016)

TIME DIVING (2013)

THE INNERgLOW EFFECT (2010)

WRITE NOW! THE PRISONER OF NANOWRIMO (2009)

ANON TIME (2009)